THE TWISTED STITCH SOCIETY

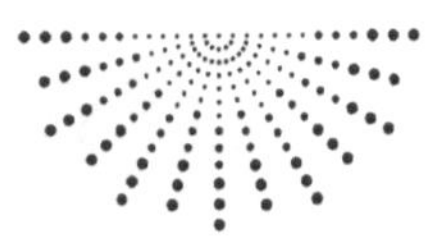

JOANN KEDER

No part of this book may be reproduced in any form or by any electronic or mechanical means, including information storage and retrieval systems, without written permission from the author, except for the use of brief quotations in a book review.

Publisher: Purpleflower Press

ISBN: 978-1-953270-05-4

First Edition December, 2021

Edited by: Benedict Brown

Cover Design by: Molly Burton with Cozy Cover Designs

ACKNOWLEDGMENTS

Thank you, as always, to my street team. That includes: my wonderful family, who all jump in whenever I need help with anything, beta readers, Dayle and Barbara, editor Ben Brown, always quick-with-a-name, Andy Gold and the Keder Readers. Without you, this product wouldn't reflect my vision. Each successful writer needs not just one but many people in their corner, helping at all stages of development. I'm especially fond of the team of people I've assembled; each an expert in their own way. I'm fortunate that you are willing to share your personal areas of expertise with me.

"In every conceivable manner, the family is link to our past, bridge to our future." - Alex Haley

For Ronda

CHARACTERS

<u>Lanie's Story</u>

November Bean–Lanie's best friend
Truman Coolidge–Cosmo's best friend
Gladys Petrie–octogenarian who runs Piney Falls
Public Records
Boysie Lumquest–Piney Falls police chief
Muriel–woman living in the cabin with her friend
Beverly Lumquist–Boysie's wife

<u>Piper's Story</u>

Doris–Cosmo's longest employee at the bakery
Boysie Lumquest–police chief of Piney Falls
Beverly Lumquest–Boysie's wife and Gladys's daughter
Elwood–Boysie's oldest son
Cornie Lumquest–Boysie's middle son
Obie Lumquest-Boysie's youngest son, the black sheep of the family
Ellie Fine–new employee at Cosmic Cakes and Antiquery
Scarlett Peters–Twisted Stitch Society President
Margarite Peters–Scarlett's daughter
Finnegan Lowery–owner of Cheese With Your Burger
Elaine Lowery–Finn's grandmother
Buster Lowery–Finn's grandfather

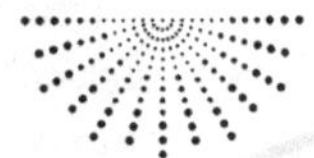

CHAPTER ONE

LANIE

"And then I cartwheeled down the hill. It only took about twelve to reach the bottom."

"November Bean, this is the tallest tale you've ever told." Cosmo Hill adjusts the backpack on his muscular back and shakes his head. "I don't think anybody at our age does cartwheels going down a hill, at least not on purpose. Even you have to realize that sounds ridiculous."

November puts her hands on her narrow hips and stops in the pathway. "I can do cartwheels, Cosmo Hill, I promise you. I would do one right now if I hadn't had a big lunch. You don't want to see cheesy sausage and kale wasted all over the gorgeous forest floor, do you?"

I stop as well, happy for a break from the strenuous hike. "November, Cos," I glance at one beloved face and then the other, "you two are the most important people in my life." Removing the water bottle from my backpack, I savor a gloriously long drink. "Actually, two of the THREE most important people in my life, including our daughter. Let's call it a draw. Vem, one day we'll watch you cartwheel down Flanagan Mountain while Cosmo documents the entire process, I promise. Just give me advance notice so I can ask the Piney Falls EMS team to wait at the bottom. Will that make you both happy?"

"So, let's say you can do a cartwheel." Cosmo continues, oblivious to my words. "Would this alleged cartwheel include any kind of moaning or barking, or, let's say, even howling? That I'd pay to see."

I sigh, loud and dramatically. "Remember why we came out here? We were planning to discuss our housewarming party. I had the idea that getting you both exercising while we discussed it might eliminate this kind of back-and-forth."

"Lanie, it was totally inappropriate for you to wait this long for a 'welcome to our new home 'home' party," November scolds. "This is more like a 'welcome to our broken-in home and who cares' party. Now that you've lived in your mountainside paradise for eight months, people will not be that excited. There is much more interesting gossip in town than the Anders-Hills-izuzz."

"Alright," I concede. "Call it whatever you want, Vem. My father's death hit me harder than I'd expected. The murderous sister I didn't know about was the cherry on top of the sorrow sundae." I take a deep breath. "Thanks to my wonderful Piney Falls family, I've put that darkness behind me and I'm ready to move forward. Let's make this party a really enjoyable evening. I even invited Gladys Petrie's entire extended family." My eyes dart to Cosmo. "Yes, I'm planning for large appetites."

"Did you remember to include all of Boysie's kids? Both boys and the daughter?" November asks, while pulling a ladybug from her frizzy head and encouraging it to fly away.

Our local police chief, my octogenarian friend Gladys' son-in-law, always wants his kids included in social engagements. It was strange to me after moving from Chicago, where neighbors barely knew each other's last name.

"On the list. Vem, your job is to make sure we've got enough tables. I rented twenty, but maybe we need more? I never know who's going to show up and who won't."

"Boysie actually has three sons," Vem replies. "His youngest is the black sheep. I remember seeing him around town when he was a kid. He stood out from the rest of the family because he was a little odd. Poor guy. He's probably hidden away in some cave."

Cosmo brushes tiny twigs that routinely fall out of the giant pine trees from his salt-and-pepper hair. He unbuttons the first button on his red-and-black shirt and scoops the rest of the offending bits onto the ground. His careful little gestures still make me warm inside.

When he notices my adoring gaze, he frowns. "What? Did I miss something?"

"Oh! I've got a great idea! I'll volunteer to be the shoe monitor." November puts her hand in the air with enthusiasm." Anyone who comes in the house with shoes on will face the Branch Blaster. Just finished carving it out of a nice elmwood. It can shoot goat dung up to forty feet!"

"I'm not sure I'm comfortable with your new weapon-making hobby. You could really hurt some-one." We start moving again, trudging up the steep path toward the top of the hill, where our cabin sits in a lovely meadow. The heat and my inability to keep up with my incredibly fit husband and best friend cause me to stop again after we've only gone one-quarter of a mile.

"I'm overheated today," I say, clasping my hands together on top of my blonde ponytail. There isn't a breeze in the forest and we're long past the actual Piney Falls, which provided a welcome spritz of moisture on our faces.

I can tell my companions are ready to move again, so I search my mind for some small talk to keep us in place a few minutes longer. "Cos, what about the new baker you hired? Will she be as good as Piper?"

"Nobody is going to be as perfect as our daughter." He beams. "With Piper organizing Cosmic Bakes at the farm location, she'll have to suffice. Ellie Fine comes with bakery experience, so I didn't ask any more questions. We scheduled orders next month and the remodel work isn't even finished yet. Poor Piper's up to her eyeballs in things to do, so Ellie will have to pick up the slack."

"What was it that brought her to town? There's usually a reason folks end up here."

"She came to see the coast earlier this year and she fell in love with the place.. That usually works out to our advantage." He winks at me, referring to my arrival in Piney Falls several years ago. I planned an extended vacation from Chicago but never left. "Seems nice enough, and Piper liked her as well. She starts tomorrow."

"I will need a sniff of her before offering my approval." One of November Beans many talents is the ability to smell a person's deceit. Much to my dismay, she's perfected this skill recently by practicing on customers at Cosmic Cakes and Antiquery. It hasn't done anything to improve her relationship with Cosmo.

My body has rested sufficiently and I'm ready to continue on, so I nod to Cos and November to follow.

When we reach the top of the mountain, the trees part to reveal a beautiful meadow. The sun dances on the raindrops from a midday shower, making for a dazzling display on multicolored wildflowers and greens in the field.

"I promised myself I'd never take this beauty for granted," I whisper.

"Do you remember our first hike together? To the top of Piney Falls?" Cosmo asks, grabbing my hand. "I proposed to you and you looked as if you were going to be sick."

"I wasn't used to you or this way of life and was afraid to let myself fall in love. But now, I'm so glad I did." I reach up and kiss the most handsome man in the world.

"The Anders-Hill-Hill couple will kindly remember we are in public. It's bad enough when the teenagers slobber all over each other, but you two are old enough to know better." Vem shadows her eyes with one hand. "One of my Moaning for Mondays students told me the wild animals have been active lately. I'd love to try my new howl and see if they respond."

"Who's going to protect us if these wild animals go crazy at the sound of your grunting?" Cosmo asks, motioning for us to keep walking.

"I shall stand right over there, in the most perfect spot in the middle of the wildflowers to practice my moan." November gestures to a spot only visible in her mind.

"Go for it," I encourage. "Cos and I will wait in our most perfect spot."

Cosmo finds the perfect spot where the long grass has been flattened. He drops his jacket and encourages me to sit on it. "We want a good view of the show. "How long do you think this will take?"

"I'm sure it won't be long. She only has six howls. She can't do them more than twice or it brings bad juju."

My husband looks at me, incredulous. "Are you hearing yourself?"

"Awooooo!" Vem's voice echoes through the meadow. "Awooo!" she says again. She turns around and looks at us for approval. Cos gives her the thumbs up and I clap my hands together.

"Arrrawww!" she begins her second howl.

There is a sharp cracking behind us and we both jump up. "What was that?" I ask, in my least panicked, panicky voice.

"I don't know," Cos replies calmly. "Hand me a stick and I'll go check."

I search around my feet and choose the most sturdy-looking piece of wood. "Here," I say, passing it to Cosmo. "Please be careful. If you're eaten by something wild, chances are I won't be able to help you, and Vem will most likely do some ritual and by that time you'll be dead."

"I don't plan on dying today." He blows me a kiss as he turns away.

I watch as my brave husband tromps confidently into the woods. A fearless woman would follow him. I am not that woman.

"Arrraww!" Vem continues her howling, oblivious to our concerns.

"Cos?" I call. There is no response. Many irrational thoughts swirl around in my head. What if Piper finally got the father she longed for and deserved, and he dies in the woods while I sit here? Doing nothing? There are two options: remain seated and reproduce every horror movie I've ever seen, or get up and investigate. Vem is still howling and probably won't miss me anyway.

I walk tentatively into the thick wooded area, looking for Cos or a carcass. I shudder as I think about the gruesome possibilities of the latter. There is a small branch at my feet that will serve as my own feeble weapon, should I need one. When I bend down to pick it up, I stand slowly, sure there is something lurking behind me. Turning my head sharply, the only thing visible is a rabbit chewing furiously on plump blades of grass.

The more I wander, the more I realize I may not know my way back. These trees all look the same and I have never been out in this part of the woods by myself. "Cos?" I call again. Nothing. Desperation is setting in when I feel something on my back. I turn around quickly, brandishing the stick wildly in front of me.

"Geez Lanie, you could really hurt someone with that." Vem grabs my weapon before it strikes her and breaks it in two. "I'm a little hurt that the two of you left me like that. You could have said something."

Her frizzy hair and bright red glasses are a sight for sore eyes.

"There was a loud noise that Cosmo went to check out. It sounded like an animal. Maybe your howls actually attracted a cougar or a bear."

"Not likely. I've only found wolves respond to my call."

Motioning for her to follow, we scour the endless pine trees, hoping he'll pop out from behind one. "He's been gone for a while and I don't see any sign of him. I'm getting really concerned."

Vem's demeanor changes from happy-go-lucky to focused. "This will require my extra senses." Before I can respond, she bends down close to the ground and begins sniffing, while moaning softly. "Only the most discriminating human nose can distinguish human from animal," she explains. "Moaning helps open my nasal cavity so I can smell better."

"I believe in you, Vem, but it will be dark soon. Can we just look for Cos?"

"Lanie, you can count on me. And if he's in a million pieces, I'll go back and get my new turquoise wheelbarrow. I've been dying to use it."

"That's all I am to you? Just pieces in a wheelbarrow?" We turn around and see Cosmo standing behind us, holding a brown shirt and a pair of jeans.

I run to him and throw my arms around him in a bear hug. "Cosmo Hill, you scared the daylights out of me. I thought maybe some wild animal had gotten you. You were just off shopping in the woods?"

"Whatever it was out here has left a trail. There are clothes all over. I also found signs of a hunt. Someone killed rabbits recently and left their cook-fire still smoldering."

"We've got a careless traveler living in the woods."

"You're right, Vem. We can try to contact them to offer our help."

"Great idea, Lanie." Cosmo brushes the debris from my pants. "As long as they aren't the crazy type who will look at us as a threat."

As we walk further, we see more signs of human life—broken branches, foot prints and matches. "Litterers!" Vem yells accusingly.

I bend over and pick them up, placing them in my pocket. "We don't know their circumstance, Vem," I remind her. Ever since The Great Depression, travelers have come through Piney Falls. Some stay for months, other are just passing through.

We are almost to another clearing when we hear

rustling and the crack of a branch. "That doesn't sound like an animal," I state, for my own benefit. If these are my last words, I want them to make sense.

"I know what that is!" Vem attempts to shove Cosmo out of the way as a large branch comes crashing down on all three of us.

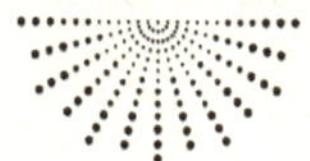

CHAPTER TWO

PIPER

"*A* little to the left!" Piper Moonlight Hill shaded her lavender eyes from the sun while the new corn-yellow sign, with the words "Cosmically Baked" written navy blue, hung above the old farmhouse. She knew she was lucky that her adopted parents trusted her to launch the second location of Cosmic Cakes and Antiquery, though it was an enormous stress. She stood back and took in the scene: the lavender farmhouse was ringed by multi-colored peonies and a long, shaded porch. Things were coming together.

"We're gonna need you inside, Miss Hill." Truman Coolidge, Cosmo's best friend, presidential expert and construction supervisor for the new bakery, stood beside her. He pulled off his red-and-blue-striped cap and wiped the sweat from his balding head with the crook of his arm.

She shaded her eyes again and looked up at him. Almost everyone towered over her. "You can call me Piper. You're practically family." She observed his serious demeanor and instantly felt a boulder in her stomach. "Oh, no. Last week when you had that look, it meant a back-ordered part for the commercial dishwasher."

Truman half-smiled, something Piper had come to recognize as a warning before shots were fired. "Well, Miss-Piper-our dear President Lincoln once said, 'people are as happy as they make their minds up to 'be.' I'd guess you're gonna have to work on that when I tell you what happened."

There were delays upon delays. The upstairs of the old country home was being remodeled into Piper's living space. It was almost completed when the workers found some rotted boards and they had to tear everything out and start over. Then the kitchen needed rewiring for commercial stoves. Her patience was almost at an end. "Rip the band aid off, Truman."

"Funny thing, when we were making a place for that fancy dishwasher that's missing a part, we forgot to plumb it. We're going to go back in and make it right. You wouldn't want a dishwasher that's just a decoration now, would you?"

Piper scratched her forehead and measured her words carefully. "I want a functioning dishwasher. Dad and I have orders from restaurants up and down the coast. They begin in less than a month." Her phone buzzed in her pocket.

She pushed her dark hair out of the way and put the phone up to her ear. "Hi, Dad. Things are going just fine. No more delays." Piper glanced at Truman, and they both shrugged. "I can come in this afternoon and train the new girl. I've got everything under control." She placed the phone back in her pocket and walked up three brand-new wooden steps to her porch.

"Don't you worry, Miss Hill. Everything's going to work out. Truman Coolidge never lets his troops down. When we finish, you'll be so impressed."

The same thing he told her last week and the week before.

Entering the construction zone, she heard saws buzzing and hammers banging. She worked her way through the maze of tools and workers, almost to the safety of the staircase, when she felt a tap on her shoulder. One worker, Geena, yelled over the sound of a buzz saw. "Forgot to tell you a box came for you yesterday." She pointed to the corner of the room that had been a large dining area in another life.

Piper hopped over tools and random pieces of wood to reach a big box marked, fragile. When she opened it, the contents were in many pieces. She dug through the pieces to find a piece of paper that read:

Thank you for your purchase of one commercial mixer. You'll find we package our products with just as much care as we put into making them. You can return anything that doesn't work, but be advised our turn-around time is 4-8 weeks.

If it took eight weeks, they would be in a real bind with their orders.

Her heart was racing and her head began to throb. Another worker tapped on her shoulder. "Miss? I need to ask you about–"

She slapped his hand away from her shoulder and spun around. "I need a break. You can ask later." Piper hopped over tools and people like a super hero until she reached the stairs leading up to her new apartment. She ran up, not even caring that the one step with the squeak still hadn't been fixed.

Her parents never questioned whether, at twenty-eight, she could manage a remodel and the running of a commercial bakery. They had confidence in her that she no longer felt in herself. In an act of childishness she rarely displayed, she ran into her bedroom and slammed the door, causing her mirror to shake.

Together, the new family decided that the farmhouse Lanie inherited from her deceased father should be a new beginning. For years, Cosmo had been approached by neighboring communities to provide baked goods for their restaurants.

The tiny space in downtown Piney Falls was barely big enough to accommodate their growing pastry and lunch needs. He never gave it a second thought before this property dropped in their laps unexpectedly.

With both Cosmo and Lanie's encouragement, Piper agreed to the massive undertaking, a complete remodel of the old farmhouse to transform it into their commercial space.

The almost-final result was much better than she expected: two spacious bedrooms, a full kitchen, two bathrooms, an airy living room and a lovely second floor deck.

She took in a long whiff of the new-carpet and paint smell as she shut the door behind her. Strangely, they were two scents that brought her calm. Pacing back and forth in her new living room, something else that brought her peace, she worked to center herself.

In the master bedroom was a large walk-in closet, inexplicably left unfinished during the remodel. "Gosh darn, Miss Hill," she mimicked in a low voice. "I don't know how we missed it. Now we're working on the main floor and it will be a few weeks before we can finish that for you."

She stepped inside the small space, inhaling the musty smell, and her anger rose once more. Piper bent down to the vent they used to communicate between floors. "Truman? Do you have a sledge-hammer I could borrow? Meet me on the steps."

Truman said this was the way his mother used to call him for dinner and always got a kick out of their communications.

The old man appeared at the agreed-upon loca-tion, hands resting on either side of his overalls. The hammer hung from one of the many loops on his pants.

"Now, Miss Hill, what would you need with a hammer up there? It's like a guest house on the White House grounds. If you start bustin' it up, there's no tellin' when we'll finish."

"I still need to make space for shelving in the closet. I'm going to knock out the wall, like we talked about. You already said there's no electricity in here so there's not much I can ruin."

Truman met her four steps up and handed her the heavy hammer. "I'll have one of the boys up there tomorrow to start framing it out again with your shelves. Does that sound good?"

He acted as if he was negotiating a hostage situa-tion. She wasn't sure if that made her want to laugh or cry. "Yes, thank you, Truman, that will be fine. I'm still going to need to release some frustration, though. Don't be alarmed if you hear pounding."

Truman studied her face. "You do what you have to. Don't worry, we're going to have this thing finished in time. Truman Coolidge never goes back on his promises."

Piper returned to the closet with resolve. Things had been building for a long time. There was her failed relationship with Finnegan Lowery, her first real boyfriend. He broke her trust and she couldn't find it in her heart to forgive him.

She pulled the hammer back and took the first swing.

Then there was the matter of her biological father, who contacted her only because he wanted money. She pulled the hammer back for the second time and heaved it at the wall. Pieces of wood fell to the ground, and she felt a tremendous release. She pulled it back again, this time ready to cause some actual damage. And then another. Sweat started pouring down her brow. There was another layer of wood beyond what she was destroying.

She didn't want to let her parents down by admitting this was too much. They'd just become a family and whatever she did wrong here might scare them away.

"I'm so MAD!" she yelled. "Who," she paused between blow "puts… extra wood… in their closet?"

On the next blow, her hammer hit something hard. Piper worried that she may have actually hit an unknown electrical box. "Big surprise!" She yelled sarcastically.

She carefully pulled the wood splinters away

until she could see inside the wall, where a black metal box sat, preserved from another lifetime. It had a clasp on it, similar to some of the items she'd seen on the antique side of Cosmic Cakes and Antiquery. The clasp had a lock on it, but that would be no match for her. Carefully, she tapped the hammer on the lock. Nothing happened.

She moved it to the floor and hit it again.

Someone was welding downstairs. She remembered one of the many workers was installing air conditioning and cautioned her to stay away while he was welding. Quickly, she skipped down the stairs and into the kitchen, where the electrician was on his knees.

"Excuse me? Sir?"

The man pushed his protective mask up on his forehead and stood up. "Ma'am, this isn't a safe area for you right now."

"Could you get this lock off? With your torch?"

He looked at her with curiosity and then at the box. "Sure. Please stand back."

She set the box on the old wooden table beside him and moved away.

He lowered the mask and fired up his torch, taking only a few minutes to cut through the old lock. When he finished, he grabbed the lock with his thick glove and yanked it out. "There you go!" He said, handing the box back to her.

"Thank you! And I appreciate all of your hard

work!" Piper practically ran up the stairs, moving quickly so she didn't run into Truman.

She felt like she was a little girl again, hiding evidence of a normal life from her then-mother. Piper made a habit of snooping through her neighbor's mail no matter where they lived. She was fascinated by the magazines depicting normal family living. She would push the magazine down the front of her pants and sneak up to her room, hiding under her bed until she'd devoured every article on Lemon tarts and sixteen ways to make your weekend festive.

Just like back then, she shut the door and slid her chair up against it.

Cautiously, she opened the lid of the foot-long box. After all of this time remodeling, she'd become an expert at estimating the size of things. She discovered several folded documents inside, along with some jewelry.

The first document was the deed of sale for the farmhouse. It was dated 1963. Finnegan's Lowery's grandparents, Elaine and Buzz, bought the home for $4000. *Cattle sold separately.* Piper chuckled. The next document she opened was their marriage license. They got married in 1965, two years after they bought the farmhouse.

"Piper? Everything okay?" Truman called through the vent.

"It's going fine. I'll be down in a bit!"

Not wanting to share her findings with anyone yet, she dumped the contents of the box on her bed.

More letters, a few more pieces of jewelry, and something brown and shriveled that she'd never seen before. She picked it up and brought it to her lamp, where she studied it carefully. When she was sure what it was, she screamed and dropped it.

Truman came clomping up the stairs. "What's wrong, Miss?"

She couldn't speak, but she pointed to the floor. Truman bent down and picked up the item. "Well, I'll be. That's a mummified human finger."

CHAPTER THREE

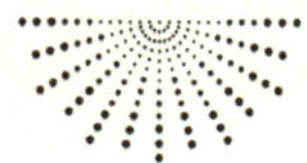

LANIE

I realize I've been holding my breath for several minutes and release it all in a gush. With my hot breath comes a moan, surprising me. My nails are pressed tightly into Cosmo's palm, and there are tiny spots of blood visible. I'm relieved he's sitting upright on the ground beside me, wiping bits of wood from his neck with his free hand.

"Anything broken?" he asks, his voice uncharacteristically shaky.

"I'm fine, babe," I say without checking to see if that's true. "And you?"

He nods. It is at that moment that I realize I've only been paying attention to the side of my body attached to Cosmo. When I look in the other direction, I see that my left arm is trapped under a heavy branch. The minute my mind and body connect, a searing pain shoots up the left side of my torso.

"I think I'm stuck," I say nonchalantly. "You may have to help me."

Cos stands to assess the situation. "Where's November? I don't think I can move that by myself." This formidable tree limb brought many others down with it and the ground is littered with twigs of all sizes.

"Vem? Where are you?" I can't hear her normal heavy breathing, which has me concerned. Cos circles around the branch and back to my side, inspecting as he walks. "Once I can roll this, you'll have to pull your arm out quickly. Keep that in mind."

I nod, trying to envision the horror-movie prop this limb might resemble when it's revealed.

Positioning his shoulder against the middle of the log, he nods solemnly in my direction. "Are you ready?"

I don't reply, but take my free hand and slide it underneath my opposite arm pit.

"One, two, three…" He pushes so hard I can see veins popping out of his forehead.

"Gahh!" He falls down to his knees and, more than freeing myself, I want to comfort him.

"That was just our first try," I say encouragingly.

My arm is now completely numb. Probably not a good sign.

"Maybe if I stand closer to you, we can both push at the same time. Do you think you can hold yourself up long enough to give it a good shove?" Cosmo stands and moves to within inches of me.

The idea of using up the last bit of my energy is not appealing. "You need someone with superhuman strength." We are quiet; both realizing this requires physicality I don't possess.

Smack. "Cosmo Hill, are we doing this?"

"Touch my rear again, and your howling won't be for fun and games!" Cosmo snarls.

"Vem? You're okay?" I catch a whiff of the comforting, earthy scent of my best friend.

She drops down beside me and gently pushes my bangs to the side so she can kiss my forehead. "I tried shoving you both out of the way. Guess I only managed to save the grumpy one before I fell."

"Are we chatting or are we saving Lanie?" Cosmo is at the opposite end, positioning himself to push. Vem braces her feet up against our end, clasping her hands around my upper torso and underneath the armpit of my pinned arm.

"On my count, November. One… two…"

"Heeeeyah! Vem lets out a primal sound and pulls hard on my body while she shoves the log with her feet, leaving Cosmo no other option than to follow her directions. I scream, whether out of fear or pain,

I can't say. The log rocks and then rolls away from us as Vem and I fall backward. She stands up and high fives Cos, both proud of their achievement.

I'm feeling lightheaded, and I swallow hard before glancing down at the damage. It's just as bad as I'd feared. "We need to get back down the mountain."

Vem bends down close to my injury, lifting her glasses to get a better look. "Criminitly, Lanie. There's a bone sticking out. I wish there was beetle dung nearby so I could make you a healing poultice."

Cosmo's face is an off-white shade I've never seen before. "Let's get her to a hospital and then you can cover yourself in whatever dung you see fit." I can hear the panic in his voice, something that rarely accompanies a conversation with November. He reaches for the red shirt he'd just shown us moments earlier and wraps it gently around my broken arm before tying it behind my head.

They maneuver beside me, trying to figure out the best way to get me off the ground. Cosmo grabs carefully underneath my armpits while November lifts me from the waist. Once I reach a full standing position, the forest rocks in front of my eyes. Both of them reach to steady me.

"She's not going to make it, Cosmo," November states, before turning her head to me. "I can always throw you over my back and fireman carry you. I've had lots of practice. Did I ever tell you about the fireman from Tellum I dated? He loved it when I carried him into restaurants."

I'm in too much pain to enjoy her stories right now. "If you'll both just stand on either side of me and help me walk, we can make it a few steps at a time. Isn't that how we do everything, anyway?"

"Lanie, you don't be a hero. I'll leave Vem here with you and I'll go back and get help. Cosmo's voice wavers and I want to take away his pain. "The town council tried convincing the cell phone company years ago to put a cell tower up here, and now we have an emergency and no service!"

"I can do this," I insist. We all take four steps together before my legs turn into noodles and my head is too fuzzy to continue. "Sorry. I thought I could make it work, but it's too much." My best friend and husband lower me to the ground carefully.

"Cosmo Hill, you look for branches. We need two sturdy ones of the same size." November places her hands on her hips and glances around. "Those clothes that we found over here?" She points to the pile of clothing. "We're going to tie those together to make a hammock and secure them to the wood. We're making a stretcher, Bean style."

"Lanie and I carried criminal mastermind, Zion out of here that way. You didn't invent the hammock, November Bean."

He's trying to be brave for me, but I can tell he's worried.

Cosmo removes his shirt and gently lowers me to the ground, before placing it, folded up, underneath my head. "I'm going to find the perfect hammock-making branches. Don't do anything crazy while I'm gone, okay?" I nod, now overcome by pain.

The next thing I hear is the familiar and reassuring sound of Cosmo and November bickering as my body sways back and forth on the hammock they made for me.

"Shows how much you know, Cosmo Hill. There are over 10,000 varieties of ants. You can cook up a whole pot full of ant chili and never use..."

When my eyes open this time, I'm in Piney Falls General Hospital.

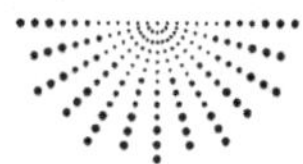

CHAPTER FOUR

PIPER

"Finnegan Lowery's grandparents, Elaine and Buzz Lowery, were the previous owners of this old place," she explained to Truman. "Finn was my first..."

"Your first boyfriend—I know. Not much gets by me." Truman thunked his head with his thumb. "He's also the owner of Cheese with Your Burger. Kinda young for that, if you ask me. Though, no one usually does."

After a recent revelation that Finn hid his involvement in a local scandal from her, their relationship never recovered. "Finn is very capable. At least in the business sense." Her therapist suggested she make a hard break so she could move forward in her life.

"You should call the authorities, Miss Hill. There's no telling what shenanigans took place in this old house. Boysie Lumquest will understand it." Truman held the box close to his face, examining the severed finger. "Yep. It's human. My dog, Grover's brought home some animal parts before and there's definitely a difference."

Boysie Lumquest was next-to-the-last person Piper wanted to call today, right before Finn. She had so much to do in preparation for their opening. "It's not really an emergency. Nothing in this box is dated past 1990."

Truman squinted. "Suppose that was your loved one who lost a piece. Wouldn't you want to know? Maybe they've been waiting all these years without an answer! Your parents wouldn't sit on information like that. They'd figure out what happened."

She already knew what her mother would say. "I trust your judgment, Piper, but…" She and Cosmo would both expect her to do the right thing. Like she didn't have enough on her plate already. "You're right. I'll get on that. You can go back to the remodel and I'll take care of it."

When Truman left the room, she took a comb from her dresser and gingerly maneuvered a letter out from underneath the shriveled appendage. She hesitated before picking it up, thinking about all the years it spent touching human flesh. In the end, her curiosity got the better of her.

The back of the pale peach stationery was covered with crudely drawn hearts. Giggling to herself, she remembered the time when she was sixteen and wanted so desperately to be in the drama club of one of the many high schools she'd attended. She wrote a letter with lots of hearts on it, convinced that would soften her mother's stance on public activities. It didn't work. It still stung that she missed so much. She cleared her throat and read out loud:

My Love,
I've put this off for too long. It's hard to know the right
thing to say, especially when you were forced to sacrifice
so much. I've wanted to share with you what was in my
heart, but the words always felt hollow.
This all began as a way to make our lives better. I thought
of the strong handsome man you were becoming, despite
your parents' negative words, and I wanted to give you the
world. You deserved success. Just like everyone else, I
became enamored with the power and forgot to listen to
the words. By the time I realized how destructive it was, it
was too late for both of us.
Please try to remember the good times too. There were
many. You know in your heart how much I loved you.
E.

Piper folded the letter up and reexamined the hearts. Now she realized they were there were drops of blood between each heart.

CHAPTER FIVE

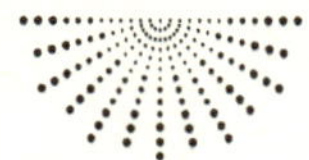

LANIE

"*L*anie? Can you hear me?"

There is a lot of noise around me, as well as a medical smell that makes my stomach queasy. "Why am I here?" The words stick in my throat and I try to motion for water, but my limbs won't move.

"It's okay, babe. You passed out halfway down the mountain. November was going to slather you in some kind of excrement, but I talked her out of it. You've had a complicated surgery, and they fixed your arm. No gymnastics for a few months." He kisses my cheek tenderly.

"It doesn't hurt. That's good, isn't it?" The voice

speaking doesn't sound like my own. It's disconnected and floating in the air.

"You're on so many drugs, you wouldn't know if a truck hit you. Get some rest now."

When I wake up the next time, there is sun peeking through the grey louvered window shades. I smell coffee and someone is clearing their throat.

"Lanie?" a deep voice asks. "You awake?" He clears his throat a second time because he needs to, and again to make sure that I hear him. Police Chief Boysie Lumquest is an unmistakable presence.

"Yes," I respond groggily. "I can hear you, Boysie. What day is it?"

"Thursday. My mother-in-law, Gladys, you'll remember, wanted me to come and check on you since you were out of it three days ago when she visited. I've got official business here, I can take care of two things at once."

As the room comes into focus, I watch Boysie straighten his grey-and-green-striped tie and force a smile.

"Mother wants to make sure you're going to survive, and to let you know that if you need anything, she's happy to bring it." Boysie's mother-in-law, Gladys, is the family matriarch and the only person working in public records for the city of Piney Falls.

"Thank you, Boysie. Tell Gladys I appreciate her concern, and that I do remember her." Has it really been three days? I can't believe that I've been knocked out that long. "The last thing I remember, Cosmo was here telling me I'd had surgery."

"Apparently, you had a bad reaction to the medication they gave you and you spent more time unconscious than they'd hoped. The doctor told me that. He said he's hopeful you'll go home tomorrow."

It always amuses me to think about the lack of privacy in this small town. Everybody knows almost everything about their neighbor. Almost.

I push myself up in the bed and a sharp pain shoots up my arm. "Aaaaa!"

Boysie moves quickly to my side, shoving pillows up against my back until I've reached the sitting position. He brings a cup of water to my lips. "Everything's fine. Pain is temporary. Just breathe in and out slow until you can control it."

When I'm done drinking, he moves away again and stands with his hands crossed in front of him, regaining his official demeanor.

"I'll tell her you're doing as well as can be expected. Now, on to the police business. I need to ask you a few questions about your accident. Routine, of course."

"I was in an accident?" It comes back slowly—the tree falling down, Vem and Cosmo performing heroic acts to save me. "Do you think someone did that on purpose? Trees fall down in the woods every day."

"I took a new officer up there with me to check it out. He's fresh from the academy, so he's got all sorts of new tricks to show me." Boysie chuckles as if remembering something humorous about the experience. "He pointed out that the limb had a straight break, like it'd been sawed almost clean through. We kept walking until we found a branch with a rope around it. Looks like there was some kind of trip wire attached."

"I can't think of anyone who would want to pull a tree down on top of me." It's all still a lot to process in my current state. "Did you find anything else in your investigation?"

Boysie pulls up his awkwardly fitting navy pants. Last year, when his wife went on an extended vacation to visit her sister, he lost forty pounds. During a monthlong ice cream challenge with his sons Cornie and Elwood, he gained most of it back. Without his wife to help him shop, he never bought anything new, so his once-tight, once-baggy-almost tight again pants still aren't the right size. "Obie says–"

"Why do I know that name? It sounds so familiar."

"My youngest son. Obie." His eyes dart around the room and I remember Obie is a sensitive topic with the Lumquest family. He left the family many years ago and, after that, they pretended like he didn't exist.

"Yes, it's my son," he repeats. "Called me six

months ago to say he'd come to his senses and joined the police academy. Asked if he could work here when he graduated." He scratches his cheek so hard it sounds like he's using sand paper. "We never told anyone because we weren't sure it was really going to happen. Maybe now his mother will come back from visiting her sister. She always said it was my fault Obie left."

"I'm so happy for you! I know how disappointed you were when your other boys decided not to go into law enforcement." Smiling causes an inexplicable pain in my head.

"Elwood started the auto parts store out on Steamer Way, and Cornie works in insurance. When Cornie told me he was choosing insurance instead of being a cop like I'd wanted, I thought it was okay. Just between us—Cornie's never been the bright one."

This is the first time Boysie has opened up to me about something so private. I don't want to do anything to dissuade him, so I nod, causing more pain in my temples.

"Obie's always been different," he continues. "Having OCD was his excuse for running off…" Boysie rubs his chin and looks down. "But me, I thought he didn't want to be a Lumquest." Boysie's eyes are misty as he drifts away to another time.

"Well, I'm glad he's back with you now. I'll look forward to meeting your youngest son."

"Where was I? Oh yeah, the tree. Obie says it

wasn't a trap for animals, but for people. Animals have much better hearing than people, you know. We're the dumber species."

"Someone wanted to trap us?" I ask, incredulous. "What if no one came out to that particular spot? It doesn't make any sense."

"Criminals have many ideas about why or how to hurt people. No use in trying to guess why until we find them."

"I haven't developed any new enemies recently, but since I've been out of it, a few more may have cropped up," I joke.

Boysie's expression is stoic.

"If you think of anything unusual in the days leading up to your accident, just call me. You've got my number. Get yourself settled at home and Mom will come with a hot dish soon, or she might have one of the grandkids bring it out. She wanted to make her famous tuna casserole. She's worried sick about you."

My stomach lurches thinking about Gladys' tuna casseroles. She loves to smother them in the most aromatic cheeses and tops them with a mystery ingredient that may or may not be a vegetable. Every time I've eaten some, it leaves me feeling like I swallowed lead.

Boysie stands sideways to move out of the door as Cosmo walks in. "Just a few questions. She's alert today," he says in passing.

Cosmo's face lights up when he sees me. "My sleeping queen has awoken!" He sits down on the bed and brings my good hand to his face, brushing it lightly against his unshaven cheek.

"Boysie thinks that tree came down on purpose. Someone was trying to kill us. Is that what you think too?"

"Is that any way to greet your favorite husband? I've been worried about you, Lanie." He bends over and kisses me on the lips as I take in his familiar scent, a comforting combination of woodsy musk and baked goods.

"Sorry. It really threw me."

"I'm not sure what I think. There is definitely something suspicious about clothing being scattered out in the forest like that, almost as if they were staging it to send us in the wrong direction."

"You and Vem are both all right? I never asked. And though I don't remember much of it, I appreciate that you carried me down the mountain."

"It was nothing." Cosmo grins. "In fact, after we had you loaded into the car, November wanted to run around a few minutes to burn off some extra energy. Clearly, you need it to be about fifty pounds heavier."

"Did they say how long it was going to be before I was functional again?" I motion towards my bad arm, which is covered from wrist to shoulder in plaster and positioned awkwardly in an outstretched bend.

"Just that it's going to be a several month rehabilitation. And, this is the tough part, you will have to take it easy. I know that's not in your vocabulary, but it's something we'll figure out together. I already spoke with your boss at the Resort and Spa at Fallen Branch. He said to take all the time you need. Their marketing can wait."

"Knock knock!" Vem walks into the room without actually knocking. She's carrying a basket of her homemade remedies. "Tomorrow when you're home I can show you how to use them, but it didn't seem right to visit without a gift. I'm planning to be over every day, at least four or five times."

Cosmo digs through the basket of unique products, pulling out a package that is marked, "not edible." "How did you get these things by the front desk?" He asks with disdain. "Don't they have rules about bringing toxic products inside the hospital?"

Vem ignores him and takes my hand. "Lanie, I'm going to keep a very close eye on you. Strange things are happening."

"In our little town, that's just another day," I remark. "What, in particular?"

She sits on the bed beside me, pushing against my body. "Well, yesterday when I was done with my Moaning for the More Aged class, I was taking the garbage out and noticed something."

"Like an old banana peel you could use for painkillers?" Cosmo asks.

"Like evidence that someone had been going through my garbage. They took every bit of my mail."

CHAPTER SIX

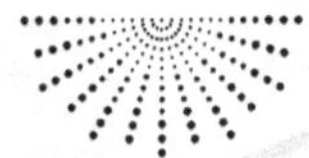

PIPER

She picked up the phone and put it back on her dresser seven times. Her last conversation with Finnegan took place four months ago and involved an unexpected meeting at Urica's Fine Art. Piper was there with her mother, Lanie, picking out paintings for Lanie and Cosmo's new home. They were trying to decide between the Oregon Coast landscape by local artist Von Schmeer, or the metal sculpture of a woman flexing her muscles that Urica constructed herself out of repurposed materials she'd found scattered on the beach.

"You know Dad will grumble every time he comes in the house." Piper lowered her voice.

"Thought that was an intruder, Lanie. Couldn't we get a nice waterfall instead?"

The two women giggled.

There was a tap on her shoulder and she noticed her mother's expression change from joyful to deeply concerned.

"Salutations, Piper!"

There was only one person who spoke like it was 1850.

She turned around slowly, hoping to give herself enough time to come up with something polite to say. It didn't work. "Finn! Are you out looking for someone else to scam? Or are you following me around now?"

Lanie poked her in the side and frowned.

His long frame curved forward, and he stared at her feet. "Um, neither, actually. I'm here picking up a painting Urica framed for my beloved twin. It's our birthday next week, and in celebration, I wanted to get her something exquisitely unique."

"Oh, I forgot." She felt stupid now. "How is Faythe? Does she like working at the beauty salon in Tellum?"

Finn's tense expression eased. "She loves it. I was hoping she'd come back and co-manage our eating establishment, but she wants to remain a silent partner in Cheese With Your Burger."

They stood in familiar silence. They never seemed to be able to get past this point now. He would apologize again, then she'd accept but feel resentment, rinse and repeat; it was one big circle.

"I've been meaning to communicate with you. If you'd be so inclined, I'd like to escort you to the new steakhouse outside of town for evening victuals. Rumor on the street is the food is delectable."

With the benefit of time, Piper's feelings for Finn, both positive and negative, waned. In fact, she rarely thought of him at all. She smiled politely. "Getting our second location open has taken most of my time. How about I call you when everything is up and running? I'll be ready for a big steak to celebrate."

She picked up the phone again, this time resolved to follow through. Finn answered on the second ring.

"Piper? I'm delighted to hear your voice! I think about you every–"

"Finn? I need to talk to you. Can we meet soon? Not for steak, but about something I found in your grandparents' farm house."

"Oh," his voice lowered. "Certainly. I have Friday off. Let me know what time and where and I'll gladly join you."

"Okay, good. Friday." She didn't want to hurt him, nor did she want to encourage him. "We could meet at the park down town? I haven't gotten much sunlight lately."

"I'd like to escort you to luncheon. If you'd come

by my establishment prior to our engagement, I'd eagerly prepare my special."

Between a rock and a hard place. That encapsulated her entire relationship with Finnegan Lowery, as well as the name of last month's burger special. "I'll see you at one on Friday at Cheese With Your Burger." She hung up quickly, wanting to avoid any more small talk. One of these days, when she had extra time, she'd sit down and figure out exactly where this was going.

That day would not be today.

She looked at her phone and realized she was supposed to be at work fifteen minutes ago. Piper dodged workers and jumped in her car without bothering to turn on her favorite music or check her hair.

"Sorry!" she called to anyone listening as she set her purse on the low shelf in her locker. "I haven't adjusted to the extra drive time in from the country yet. Twenty minutes is a long time when you're used to six." She touched her hair absently and shut the locker door, jumping when she realized someone was standing on the other side.

"You're Piper, aren't you? I've heard all about you. Everyone's descriptions don't do you justice. What a doll! I'm Ellie, by the way."

A woman in her mid-40s dressed in short jean shorts and a thin, blue tank top stuck a tanned hand out to greet her. Her long dark hair hung down her back and, from a certain angle, she could pass for someone Piper's age.

The scent of mint gum and Sweet Sassypants perfume assaulted Piper's nostrils. Ellie stood so close it was hard to escape either one.

"Nice to meet you, Ellie. Are these going to be your baking clothes?"

Ellie scanned her body and looked at Piper with confusion. "Usually, I wear what's the most comfy. Your dad never mentioned anything about a uniform."

"We wear pants when we bake. It's more of a safety issue." Piper's face turned bright red. She shouldn't have to explain this to someone almost her mother's age. "For future reference, think about what might protect your skin the best."

"Yeah, got it. The boss's daughter has to put on a good show." Ellie winked. "Your dad is sure nice-looking. What a lucky girl."

"Um…" Piper took a deep breath, both for clarity and to give herself a moment to keep from exploding. "I don't think of him as nice-looking, since we're more in the father-daughter type of relationship."

"I'm ready to learn all about your technique, Piper, though I'm sure I've been baking since you were in diapers."

If she could, she would go out the door and start over, forcefully telling this woman to take two steps back before they even met. "What brought you to

Piney Falls, Ellie? My dad mentioned you came for a getaway, but this morning he said you had some relatives here, too. I know just about everyone."

"Oh, no one who's here now. My parents lived here ages ago. It's a cute little town, though, isn't it? I can't wait to see what trouble I can stir up." She snapped her gum and blew a surprisingly large bubble.

CHAPTER SEVEN

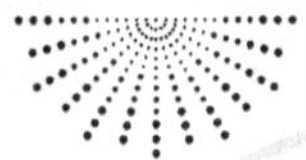

LANIE

"Mom? Where are you?" Piper walks in the front door of our new home and calls into the cavernous space. The maple wood cathedral ceilings make things echoey and dramatic, even when they aren't.

"I'm in the guest bedroom downstairs, hon!" I push myself up in bed and comb my hair with my good hand, trying to look like I haven't been lying here all afternoon. I'm in the same rose-print pajamas I wore yesterday and the day before.

My daughter breezes through the door, bringing with her a much-needed positive energy. She bends down to kiss me on the cheek, taking care not to touch the left side of my body. Piper is looking especially beautiful today—she's cut her dark hair short and is wearing a lavender outfit that matches her lavender contact lenses. I'm continually amazed by her poise and beauty.

"I got the pizza and I'll cut yours up if you like. Dad wanted me to come over and discuss the delays on our new location. There's also something else I wanted to ask you both."

I'm embarrassed that I'm not in tune with the stress she's experiencing. Instead, I spend my days feeling sorry for myself and watching reruns of old detective shows.

"How are you doing, Mom?" She takes in my disheveled appearance and knits her dark eyebrows together. "I'm sorry I haven't been here for a few days. There are lots of people down at the bakery who've asked if they could come help. You might want to wear some-day clothes for that experience," Piper suggests tactfully. "Urica Jollopy could come help you."

"I'm up to my eyeballs in assorted casseroles and crossword puzzles from people in town." I smile reassuringly. "Don't worry, I'm just fine. Tomorrow I'll put on new pajamas." I lay my good hand over my chest. "Promise. Tell me about the remodel."

Piper sits down on the bed beside me and pulls one of my feet out from under the blanket. She sandwiches it between her palms and begins massaging. "My apartment looks great. Other than change to the closet area, I think that part of the remodel is finished. I can't wait for you to see it!"

"And the downstairs?" I ask, pleased to have attention on another part of my body to distract from the constant throbbing in my arm.

"That's another story," she sighs. "Let's wait for Dad and I'll tell you both at the same time."

"He's over at Vem's place, borrowing some tools. He said if he's not back in twenty minutes to consider it a hostage situation and to call Boysie."

We share a knowing smile.

"You don't need to do that," I protest mildly, as she pulls out my other foot and continues her magic. "Though it does feel wonderful. Anything to take my mind off what's happening in the upper regions."

"Still in a lot of pain?"

"I'm afraid so. The doctor said it could be another month or so before I'm sleeping comfortably. What's going on at the bakery? How is the new pastry chef working out? Cos never tells me anything. I think he's worried that I can't handle any more stress."

"There's a learning curve with everyone." Piper's eyes dart away from me. "Her name is Ellie and she has ten years of baking experience."

"We'll invite her for dinner soon. I'm so curious about her!"

"I smell pizza, and I hear my two favorite girls! You should have left a bread crumb trail so I could find you!" Cos calls from the cavernous living room.

"I haven't moved all day! You know where to find me!"

Cosmo enters the room and grins when he sees the two of us. "I never get tired of that view. He leans over and kisses me on the cheek and then kisses the top of his daughter's head. "I'm starving. Having a conversation with that woman takes all of my energy."

His newly established mustache is covered in crumbs. It's odd he didn't notice, as Cosmo is always impeccably groomed. I brush the crumbs away and cup his chin in my hand. "You smell like something I'm not familiar with. Working on a new item at the bakery?"

"We're always trying to come up with the next cosmic scone. You know us, a couple of Einsteins in the kitchen." He winks at me and turns away quickly.

"Can I help you out of bed, Mom?" Piper asks.

"No, hon, that's okay. I can get up. It just takes me a couple of scootches. You guys go and get your plates filled and make one for me. Extra peppers, please."

"Can I get you a beer or a wine, Piper? Cosmo asks.

"I'll take an Over the Falls Stout."

In spite of my protest, she lifts me carefully under the arm and let's go when I'm in the standing position. She walks behind me as we make our way to the kitchen, like a mother following a wobbly toddler.

When our plates are full and we're all settled at the table, my heart swells with pride. "Will you look at us? The Anders Hill family eating pizza, like we're normal or something."

"We have been normal for…" Cosmo looks at his watch. "I'm gonna say at least today."

"About that," Piper wiggles in her seat.

"Have we run into a hitch somewhere that I didn't know about?" Cosmo shakes his head. "Truman was supposed to come in for a coffee three days ago, but he hasn't shown. I thought something was up."

"I know why. I made him promise to keep this to himself." Piper's cheeks are blotchy-red, a telltale sign something serious is about to take place.

"Before we get into the nitty-gritty of remodeling, I need to share something with you both."

Trying to find a comfortable way to sit with my very uncomfortable arm requires constant movement. Cos instinctively gets up from the table and brings a pillow, setting it in my lap for my cast to rest on. "Thanks, dear. I got a call today from the prosecutor's office," I continue. "Apparently, there was an attempted escape at the Oregon State Prison yesterday. My sister, Berit, made it as far as the corner of the property before she was caught."

Cosmo grabs another slice of pizza and returns

to his seat. "That crazy woman. I knew she'd try something like this. They'll lock her down for a while now."

"Oh, no! Are you scared, Mom? Your sister did try to kill you."

I smile and shake my head. "No, I refuse to spend my life living in fear. It does make me sad that because of her, my father left Piney Falls abruptly without seeing me. I wish we could've had one final conversation before his death."

"In a way, he's still here. He left you that farm house that will become our first joint venture as a family." Piper cuts a second piece of pepperoni pizza into small bites and hands me the fork. "What would you tell your father if he hadn't left town so quickly? My therapist says it's good to release those words so they don't haunt you."

"That's a very good question, hon." It only takes a second to find the words. "I'd ask if he understood he only chose broken women and his attempts at fixing them always failed. Knowing he learned from his mistakes would bring me some comfort."

The mood of the room has become so heavy that our happy family evening is in jeopardy of becoming something morose." Okay," I take a bite of the pizza and plaster a smile on my face. "Moving on, let's talk about the remodel."

Piper takes a long drink of her beer and wipes the foam from her mouth with the back of her hand.

"Every time I turn around, there's another problem. But the construction isn't the worst of it."

"I'm going to call Truman as soon as we're done eating and get to the bottom of this. He assured me everything would be ready to go, and I know the man is as good as his word." Cosmo says firmly.

"It's not about him. I found something in the upstairs closet and made him promise not to tell you."

She pulls a box out of her purse and sets it on the table in front of Cos.

"Are we exchanging gifts? I'm still not used to holiday celebrations," Cosmo muses.

"There is more to it. Unfortunately." Piper digs in her purse and retrieves a small plastic bag. She holds it up so that we can both see it.

"What is that?" I ask, trying to pretend like I don't need my reading glasses.

"Looks like an animal bone," Cosmo replies. "November Bean would love to dance around that while she howls at the moon."

"That's not what Truman said." She pushes the box closer to Cosmo, and he picks the item up to examine.

"Back when I lived with the cult, we had to go out and hunt for food when Zion felt like teaching us a lesson. Truman's right—that doesn't look like any animal I've ever seen." He glances at me, waiting for his words to sink in.

"If it isn't from an animal... oh, Cos! This is terrible! Should we call Boysie?"

"Where did you say you found this?" Cosmo asks Piper again.

"In a box that was in the wall of the closet. There are other documents in there, like the original sale document for the House in 1963. Oh, and this..."

She slides a folded paper covered in hearts over to Cos.

"I'm still new to this parenting thing, but shouldn't we just hang this on the refrigerator?" he asks.

"I didn't draw this, Dad. It was in the box as well."

CHAPTER EIGHT

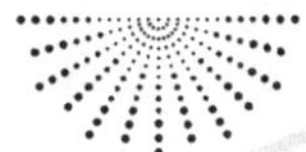

PIPER

"In my time as law enforcement–going on thirty-two years–I've seen a human bone twice. First time was when Dell Meters had his fishing accident. Second time was when city council poker night and too much alcohol collided."

"Someone cut off a council member's finger?" Lanie asked, moving her arm gingerly to a resting spot on the table in the interrogation room of the Piney Falls Police Department.

"Not exactly. One of the men promised his wife he'd never gamble again. She polished off a good twelve beers before she caught him and relieved him of his pointer finger."

Piper shuddered.

"I'm glad I didn't hear that story before I began working with them. What will you do with it now, Boysie?"

We'll send this to Portland to be analyzed, but I'm going to tell you right now, I'm pretty sure it's real."

"That still leaves many questions, Boysie. We don't want our daughter sitting out at the farmhouse alone without answers

"That's okay, Mom." Piper replied reassuringly. "I'll tell Finn about it and that will be the end. If I don't stir up trouble, no one will know. Isn't that right, Boysie?"

"It IS a police matter, though your family usually pretends otherwise." He picked up the finger, now safely contained in an evidence bag, and moved to the doorway. "Lanie, I can almost see your wheels turning. Finn's grandparents, Elaine and Buzz, were good people. I'm sure there's a rational explanation."

"For a severed finger?" she asked, incredulous. "What can you tell us about the Lowerys? What do you remember about them?"

"They moved away real sudden. Can't remember why, exactly. We thought it was strange they didn't leave the house to their children in the will." Boysie shrugged. "Either way, I'll need to speak with Finnegan. Just routine." He turned to face Piper. "Glad your mother persuaded you to come to me before you told Finnegan. It was the right call."

"It's my home and I have a right to know the history." Piper stood up.

"I'm going to have to agree with my daughter. Though, if something should happen, she always knows she has a room with us." She rubbed her daughter's back with her good hand. "And you will tell me, right?"

"Of course. Not much would get by you, anyway. Or anyone else in this town."

"I'll call him tomorrow about a formal interview. Won't be seeing Mother for pot roast tonight, she's got bridge." Boysie scratched his head. "She won't have a chance to grill me for information about my day, if that's what you were worried about."

"It was," Lanie and Piper said simultaneously. They glanced at each other and giggled.

Piper and Gladys Petrie had an acrimonious relationship. Gladys tried hard to insert herself into Piper's life as a surrogate grandmother, and Piper tried equally hard to keep her out.

"Oh, and Lanie, Mother wanted me to make sure you're well enough for company. She has a new casserole she needs to test out. That new salmon thingy." He shook his head in disgust. "Haven't tasted anything quite that awful since she tried making a sweet potato chocolate dessert."

"I learned my lesson when she made me the last tuna casserole and I didn't leave the bathroom for a week. November did a healing dance over it, but there was no hope. She fed it to her goats, sorry to say."

Boysie waved to the women and walked into the hallway.

"Boysie's given you a window to contact Finn," Lanie whispered. "If you wouldn't mind, I'd like to go with you to see him."

Piper shook her head. "No, Mom. I really want to go alone."

Lanie stood and adjusted the sling around her neck. "Are you still trying to punish him? He deceived you about the farmhouse and his role in our home burning down, but he was caught in a position where he didn't have any choice. At least not any that were good."

Piper's eyes widened. "Are you saying that you like Finnegan now? You always thought he wasn't good enough for me." She and Lanie never argued about anything, but the closest they came was during discussions about Finnegan Lowery. Piper was pleased she was so protective, so she never disagreed when Lanie made disparaging remarks about him.

"I was still new to this parenting thing. Now that I've had some time to reflect, I realize that being a good parent means giving you the space to make your own choices." She cast her eyes downward. "You may decide that you like him again, and I'm fine with that. We all grow and change; Finn included."

"Is this some kind of reverse psychology?" Piper giggled. "I'll keep that in mind. And thanks for getting up and dressed today. I know it was a big step."

* * *

"No thanks, I've been on a burger-free diet." Piper avoided Finn's gaze as she picked at the French fries slathered in Cheese with your Burger: Secretly Saucy Sauce.

"But I appreciate your meeting me today. I have something serious to discuss with you."

Finn took a fry from the Doozy Double Burger Basket he'd prepared especially for Piper and dipped it several times in the extra container of secret sauce before placing the entire gooey mess in his mouth.

"I've apologized a multitude of times for not telling you that Lanie's father bought the farmhouse. And I'm sorry she never got to meet him. He was a jolly soul. Had her eyes, I think." He wiped his mouth on a napkin he brought for her.

"This isn't about Lanie's dad. It's about the farmhouse. As you know, we're remodeling it for our commercial bakery. The other day I was helping with a closet demolition and I found something." She handed him the letter. "This is a woman's handwriting, so I'm guessing it's your grandmother?"

He picked up the heart-covered letter and

opened it carefully. "I haven't been out to the farm since the day I sold it. And, as far as my grandparents go–"

"Just read it," she insisted.

When he finished, he looked up in shock. "This sounds like someone decided to end their life. Is that what you're thinking too?"

"It was in a box of things, along with the original deed of sale for the house. I hadn't thought it was that serious."

He put the letter on the table and ran his fingers through his thick hair. "This will require some introspection. I loved my grandmother so much. She read me stories and made the most wonderful cookies. Faythe and I spent our summers there, along with our older cousin, Frankie. She was the perfect grandparent. Maybe it's someone else in the family? We must come from a sinister lineage."

"This is no reflection on you, Finn. I'm just looking for some answers." She grabbed his hand reflexively and then let it go. "There's one more thing." She took a deep breath and let it out slowly. "I also found a human finger in the box. Boysie's having it tested to make sure."

Finn laughed nervously. "Right. They stored skeletal remains in their walls so they'd have extra for experiments."

When Piper's expression didn't change, he put his hand up to his mouth. "You're serious?" He leaned back in the booth, his eyes wide. "No. I just can't believe it. This doesn't sound like them at all."

"Tell me what you remember about them. Maybe there's something you missed. You were just a little kid. Do you recall a farming accident?"

Finnegan looked like he might be sick. "They were planning on expanding and making it a big dairy farm, but my grandfather had a breakdown. It's something we all know but never discuss. It wasn't long after that they moved away. We never saw them or our cousin, Frankie, again."

CHAPTER NINE

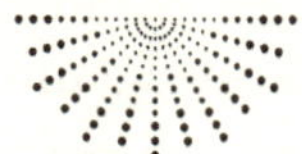

LANIE

"I've decided I need to do something productive," I announce, as November consumes her third cinnamon roll at my kitchen counter. "We're having that housewarming party we've been putting off. It's time to move forward."

November licks each finger and shakes her head. "Do you think that's wise, Lanie? There's someone out there who wants you dead. Well, all three of us. And then there's the matter of whomever has been digging through my trash. Not a good time for cele-bration."

I'm skeptical that humans, and not raccoons are responsible for her trash problems. "Those things are all the more reason to put on a party. To show whoever it is that we aren't scared of them. That life goes on." When she still doesn't seem convinced, I add, "just like we discussed before, you'll help organize it."

She grins and I can see the bits of cinnamon roll still working their way through her large teeth. "I've already planned it all out in my head. I was thinking, maybe we could do a barbecue. I'm happy to dig a barbecue pit in your backyard. You don't have any lawn or landscaping to speak of, so it won't take long."

"That's it? You don't have any other 'creative' ideas?" It's so unusual for Vem not to throw in something really off the wall.

"What were you expecting?"

I can hear the hurt in her voice.

"I thought we would barbecue some meat and then ask people to bring side dishes. Honestly, Lanie. What kind of weirdo do you think I am?"

"I'm sorry, Vem. I didn't mean to–"

"Of course, I'll need to assign just the right dishes. Something healing for our shared traumatic experience. For my dish, I'll grind up some tree bark-cedar, and mixing with some Parmesan cheese to top a nice tater tot casserole. It will bring your home good luck."

"There we go. That's the Vem I know." I retrieve a pad with the words, *Fall into Luxury at Fallen Branch* written across the top. "Could you take notes? Even though it's not my right hand that's out of commission, it's still awkward to write."

Vem obediently takes both the pen and pad and looks up at me expectantly.

"About fifty people. The frequent customers of Cosmic Cakes and Antiquery. Then, there's a group at The Inn and Spa at Fallen Branch. Probably ten there." I pace back and forth, excited there is a use for my brain again. "A few friends that don't fall into either group. You'll know most of them."

Vem clucks her tongue in disapproval. "That's not sufficient. "Your wedding was the event of the decade here. The natural progression of things is to invite all the same people to your house warming party. What is someone like Fred from Fred's Fine Floral Fixins going to think if he isn't in any of your categories? He's going to be hurt. That's what."

"We haven't seen Fred since the wedding. While I appreciated the garden fertilizer, I'm not sure he qualifies as a good friend. Let's just keep this fairly intimate, shall we? Piper will want to make some sort of delectable dessert and I don't want her baking for a huge crowd."

"Has Boysie said anything more about the 'event in the woods?'" She makes giant air quotes with her hands.

"He's got another more pressing project." I don't dare share the severed finger information with Vem until it's a story that can be spread all over town. "I think he's decided that it was an accident. It's ludi-crous to think someone would sit out in the woods for hours, waiting for people to show up and drop a tree on them."

Gonna close the books on this one, Lanie. Can't find any more evidence of wrongdoing, so I'm assuming it was kids who thought it would be funny to catch an animal in their homemade trap.

"But Lanie thinks something different?" Vem asks, adjusting her blue-framed glasses on her face.

"Lanie does think something different. I've had a lot of time to ponder and while I don't believe someone was waiting in the woods for us, they were out there doing something suspicious. All of that clothing lying around was weird. Don't you feel a little odd about it? What does your nose tell you?"

"My nose was a little bent out of shape that day. Got a big snort of tree bits and it plugged up the system." Vem touches her large proboscis uncon-sciously. "We could always head back up there and see what we come up with now that we're not in such a scary situation."

The thought of going back to that place makes me physically ill. "Someday soon," I say noncommit-tally. "Back to the party. I was thinking next Saturday?"

"Oh no, Lanie. That will not do. The full moon is the Wednesday before and people will not be on their best behavior. We may end up with a front yard fracas or someone stripping off all their clothes. We're having it this Saturday."

My mouth drops open. "Vem? Are you serious? How are we going to pull this all together so quickly?"

"Easy-peasy, that's how." Vem smiles wide. The food has disappeared, thankfully. "You have absolutely nothing else going on right now, so you can immerse yourself in the details and I'm at your service for the rest."

There isn't much use in arguing with her, right or wrong. Once Vem sets her mind to something, it's better to move with her flow. She is my strongest ally and she will do everything in her power to make sure the party is success. At least, her kind of success.

"The invitations will have to be purely verbal. You can help with those calls, Vem?"

"Right after I dig the pit in your back yard. That should only take me an hour or so. I've already stretched."

"What pit? We're cooking burgers on the grill. I've already talked to the butcher about the meat."

"No, we're roasting a hog in the ground, the way they do at a luau. If we don't put our all into this production, we'll never live down the bad vibes sent our way."

"Okay, fine," I concede. "You get everything ordered and I'll take care of the sides."

Vem's superhuman strength never ceases to amaze me. I watch from the window, drinking my coffee as she digs. She pauses only twice to wipe the sweat from her brow. The second time she sees me and makes a drinking motion with her hands. I give her the thumbs up and find a glass to fill with water.

As I'm about to deliver her well-deserved drink, my toe catches on something on the garage floor and both the glass and I go flying. Vem moves swiftly, grabbing me before I hit the ground. The glass is not so lucky, shattering into a million pieces as it slides across the cement floor.

"Are you sure you're okay, Lanie?" Vem asks, setting me carefully on the ground. She walks to the garage wall where she removes the broom from its hook and begins sweeping up the glass.

My cast is still intact and nothing else seems out of place. "I think so." I glance around the garage from my new vantage point. "What in the world?" There are tools missing from the pegs on the wall where Cosmo proudly displays them. A quick scan of the room offers even more disturbing information. "His tools are all over the place, and it looks like they're dirty." His favorite wrench set, the one Truman bought him as a thank-you gift for letting him stay with us, is underneath his work bench. "Cos would be sick to see this. "I stand and pick up one of the wrenches that has stars and stripes on the handle.

"He won't even let me touch these unless he's in the room."

Vem makes a tidy pile of broken glass before picking up the tools for her own examination. "Ew," she says, wiping her hand on her pants. "This one has blood on it." She holds it up to the light in dramatic fashion and then brings it to her nose. "Human, to be exact."

Horrified, I stare at the smudges all over the handle. "This is bizarre. Why would someone bleed all over our garage?" Vem and I walk to every corner, trying to find more evidence of the invader. There isn't any visible to the naked eye. "I guess we need to call Boysie. I should be paying that man a retainer fee."

Vem places each of the six wrenches on the bench and stands back to view them. "I'll tell you what needs to happen here. First, we need to do a cleansing. Get rid of the bad juju that's floating around from the tool assailant. Second, we need to set up a booby trap. Actually, I hate that word. It's so sexist. We need to set up a trap to catch these villains. Razor wire and maybe some poison-dipped arrows will do." She studies my face with concern. "It's all going to be fine, Lanie. You've got a neighbor with super human strength and superior sniffing skills. I won't let anything happen to you."

"This just makes me want to host the party all the more. We are not going to let something like this stop us." I hope she only hears my words and not the doubt behind them.

"No, we aren't going to let this stop us. The fire pit is almost finished. Let's go inside and knock out those phone calls," she says with determination.

While we're making the last of the invitation calls, Boysie arrives, carrying plastic evidence bags in his gloved hands. "Should I put a car out here permanently? Folks will bellyache if their taxes go up because of your problems."

"I know you're joking, but for a moment, I thought that might be a good idea."

When he finishes, he returns to the garage and pulls a lined pad of paper out of his pocket. "All right. You ladies know the drill. Any strangers around? Have you seen other things out of place?"

"I've been home in bed every day. If there was a funny noise, I would have heard it."

"You know there are cameras all over my place." Vem uses her irritated voice, the one she brings out when she's ready to scold someone. "This isn't a case of two women being irresponsible."

Boysie turns away purposely from Vem. "What about your husband, Lanie? Has he mentioned anything?"

I didn't stop to think about Cos. His prized tools have been raided. He'll be devastated. "No, he hasn't seen anything or he would have told me."

"Well, I'll be in touch. Or more likely, you'll be in

touch because you can't seem to go more'n a couple of days without a problem lately."

I stare at the ground, feeling the weight of his words. *Life could always be worse,* I tell myself.

After he's gone, Vem and I decide we'll continue preparing for the party to keep our minds off this worrisome development. While Vem is writing down our menu, my mind wanders. "The fact that his prized tools were covered in blood will upset him more than knowing someone dug through them, you know."

She stops writing and looks up at me. "I know. I can stay if you want? We could tell him together?"

"That's okay. You go on home and we can talk later."

Cosmo walks in the door an hour later with a somber look on his face.

"Good day?" I ask, giving him a kiss on the cheek. I can see his face is drawn, and he looks more tired than usual. His breath smells strange again, like something I can't quite place, but now isn't the time to ask about it.

"The new chef is struggling. She and Piper are at each other's throats all day long and I'm not sure why." He takes off his shoes and tries to pass me, but I stand firmly in his path.

He sniffs the air twice and squints. "I smell my favorite dinner and you look like you're ready to drop a bomb. Should I look for a helmet first?"

"No, it's not that." I begin slowly. "Something happened today, and I didn't want to upset you."

He takes me in his arms, carefully avoiding my injury. "You could never upset me." His body tightens suddenly, and he pulls back, his eyes scanning my body for trouble. "Did something happen to you?"

I can see bits of food in his mustache again and it makes me angry. "I'm fine. Everything is fine. There's no reason to be upset. Just a little mix up in the garage is all." For some inexplicable reason, I begin to cry. I'm not that upset, but the thought of hurting the man I love with my words is enough to get the waterworks flowing.

"Mix up?" he asks suspiciously.

Cosmo hands me a tissue and I wipe my eyes. "It appears someone has been messing with your tools. The nice ones that Truman gave you."

"What?" Cosmo rushes past me, throwing the door open so hard it bangs against the wall.

"I've already given them to Boysie!" I call after him in vain. "You'll get them back soon, I promise."

Reluctantly, I follow him outside. "He just wanted to see if he could get any prints from the blood on there."

He whips around as I approach the empty tool wall. "Blood? There was blood on my tools? What happened in our garage?" His face is ashen. "Was someone injured, and I didn't even know about it?"

"I'm not really sure. It could have been a random

robbery. Maybe they fell in the woods as they approached our place. There are a lot of tripping hazards out there." I point to my arm, trying feebly to make a joke.

He doesn't seem to catch on.

"At least all the tools are still there. None are missing." I have no idea how many were there to begin with.

"Also, Vem and I have made plans for our house warming party. We're having it this Saturday night. It has something to do with the moon."

Cos walks to the outdoor refrigerator and helps himself to a can of Over the Falls Stout. He opens it and takes a long drink of his beer. "That's quite a lot to drop on a guy ten minutes after he gets home from work. This tool thing really bothers me."

CHAPTER TEN

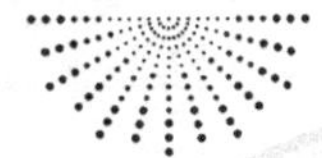

PIPER

"There's something off with Ellie, the new person we hired. She's nice enough, but she follows my dad around like a puppy. She's practically his age. Don't people grow out of that behavior?" Piper took a sip of her soda. The paper cup, labeled Cheese With Your Burger Medium Drink for clarity, had condensation on the side; sweating, just like she was. "I'm sorry. I've been talking nonstop about my life and we need to get back to the business of your grandparents."

Finn folded his hands together in front of him. "This is what I can share with you about my paternal grandparents: They never took a vacation, concentrating all of their energy on the farm. They raised three offspring there and planned to retire on that property. If it weren't for Grandpa's dreadful malady, they would have realized their dream."

The corners of Piper's mouth twitched. She covered it with her hand until her emotions passed. "Your unique language always catches me off guard," she remarked. "What is it that caused them to leave?"

"It's never been fully explained. One year at the end of May, Faythe and I got our suitcases out and started packing for our usual summer trip. Our mother came in and advised us this summer would be different because Grandpa was afflicted and they had to leave the farm." Finn let out a big puff of air. "They sent us cards for our birthdays, signed perfunctorily, Grandma and Grandpa. Each card included a crisp, twenty-dollar bill. But we never saw them again. Our cousin, Frankie, who lived with them from age four on, left with them. He was always kind when we visited, but aloof."

"How sad. Why didn't he live with his parents?"

"As children, we learned very little of his circumstances. We pretended he was a prince from a faraway land. It's one of those things that seems completely normal in the context of childhood."

That makes this even more important. You need to know what went on in that farmhouse."

"What does that mean, exactly?" Finn raised his eyebrows.

"I wish I knew."

"My grandmother, Elaine, was an enthusiastic seamstress. She'd drop Faythe and me off at the community pool before going to her meetings. Usually, she was cheery when she picked us up."

He took a long sip of his drink, making a loud slurping sound. "Though, I do remember one occasion when she asked us to sit in the car while she visited an old friend. We were wet and cold and it seemed like she took forever. Faythe said I should go looking for her, but by the time she'd convinced me, Grandmother returned. Her eyes were red and puffy and she said we both deserved a big ice cream cone for being so patient."

"Did she say anything else about her experience?"

Finn leaned his head back and closed his eyes. "We were standing at the window of the Dairy Dream and her hands shook as she paid them. 'Help me, Finnie,' she said. We ate our ice cream, pistachio for me and rocky road for Faythe, and didn't speak." He bit his upper lip before continuing. "As we were driving back out to the farm, I could tell she wasn't feeling right. I asked her if she needed a hug, and she pulled the car over and took me in her arms. She squeezed until I started sweating. No air conditioning in that old beast. She made me promise not to tell anyone, and that she was doing what she thought was right. I did, even though I had no idea what secret we were keeping."

"That's scary for a kid," Piper commented. "Is that everything?"

"When we got home, it was like a switch flipped. She pretended everything was normal and so did I. Frankie helped with dinner, Faythe went upstairs to play with her dolls and I watched it unfold with awe. It was peculiar for its normality. Does that make sense?"

"It actually does."

"Did your grandparents ever have guests over? Someone you might have felt uncomfortable being around? I'm just wondering if this happened right under your nose and you were a kid and didn't notice."

Finnegan opened his eyes and shook his head. "Though we spent our entire summers on the farm, the only socializing we did outside of our family was pool time. I don't remember any company, nor do I remember my grandparents speaking of friends. They never came for holidays. And now that I'm thinking about it, I'm wondering if maybe my parents and grandparents never liked each other. They did a very good job of hiding it, but whenever they dropped us off at the farm, they never came in. It was just, 'get your things out of the back and go inside. We'll wait here until we see you go through the door.' They came back a month later and sat in the drive-way, honking till we came out. Every single year."

"Your grandmother must've enjoyed sewing, and it sounds like that was her only socialization. I wonder if I could locate some of those women?" Piper slid away from Finn when his hand touched her leg. "Maybe there's still somebody around who remembers her."

He was staring at her now. She could feel it, though she didn't want to give him the wrong impression, so she didn't return his gaze. Piper moved toward the edge of the booth and grabbed her purse.

"It's really disturbing to think that one of my grandparents could have hurt someone. They were good, hardworking people. You don't begrudge me their failures, do you, Piper?"

She grappled with her feelings. One thing she'd learned from her parents was that compassion should be shown to everyone. Even those who were starting to creep her out. "I didn't mean to stir things up for you, Finn. But I do need to find out what happened in that–my–house."

Finn stood inches from her, towering over Piper. "What if I helped you? Would you mind? It would be like old times–except that we would just be friends." He looked at her pleadingly.

She scratched her head and her eyes shifted back and forth. "Well… our schedules are so demanding these days. I've got the new bakery, I'm training a challenging new hire, and you're doing manager things, and I–"

"Please? What if I get on my knees and beg profusely? Would that help?" Finn immediately dropped to his knees, knocking the remains of the burger he made for Piper on the floor and scattering French fries underneath several tables.

Piper's face was crimson as other customers turned in their seats to stare. "Finnegan, you're making a scene!" she hissed.

There was a tap on her shoulder. She turned around, grateful for the diversion. A slim, dark-haired police officer grinned as he crossed his hands in front of himself and patted his shoulders. His face seemed familiar, and yet she was certain she'd never met him before.

"I'd like some salt for my fries. Do you have those little packets?"

Finn, as if removed from a trance, stood and wiped the crumbs from the front of his pants. "I'll get you some, sir."

Piper mouthed "thank you" and ran for the door.

CHAPTER ELEVEN

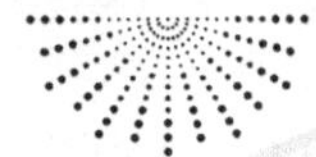

LANIE

The bell over the door of Piney Falls Public Records plays the theme to "The Perry Mason Show" when I enter. Gladys is sitting behind the heavy wooden desk reading one of her sordid novels. Ever since her daughter lent her a copy of *Red Hawt Hal,* Gladys has been hooked on cheesy books that, in my mind, border on pornography. She's wearing very thick, black-framed glasses magnifying her eyes to three times their normal size. It's a startling new development I wasn't prepared for.

"Oh! Gladys! You've added a new accessory to your look!"

I shouldn't stare, but her eyes remind me of a marketing campaign I once did for Work Ahead Office Supplies-The Most Profitable Office Supply Chain in the World. We sold books about building your home office by using a picture of an owl with glasses on. I demanded we make his eyes so big they filled half the page.

"Well, I'll be a turkey's giblet!" She slams the book on her desk and pulls off her glasses. "What are you doing out of bed, Lanie Andershill? Shouldn't you still be convalescing in the strong and sturdy arms of your beloved?"

"I have to rejoin real life someday, Gladys. And it's Anders-Hill. There's a hyphen separating the two." I pull a folding chair up to her desk with my good arm and lower myself slowly. For some reason, all of my body needs extra care. "You're quoting one of your smut novels again? I don't want someone coming in and being offended by your reading mate-rials.. This is a public space, after all."

"Humph," she snorts. "Don't care for hyphens or anyone who comes in and judges my choice of readin' material." She turns her attention to the crip-pled talk of the-town in front of her. "Anything I can get you, toots? You need some water? I've got some rum in my drawer. It was a gift from old Ned Parker that I keep for special occasions, or sometimes just when somebody really irritates me." Without waiting for my response, she pulls a half-empty bottle from her desk drawer. "That's what happened yesterday, so no questions about how much is left."

It's better just to smile and nod.

"Can I get you some water?"

"Yes, please."

"I'll be right back." Gladys shuffles to the water cooler in the backroom and returns a few minutes later with a glass that's too full. "Drink it down a bit, dearie," she commands.

When I finish and set it on the desk, she stares hard at me. "What got you out of bed today in your sorry state? Urica heard you don't move unless your husband is there to carry you. Is there another mystery needs to be solved?"

It's always best to give as little information as possible when dealing with Gladys, unless she's working on a case with me. Anything I tell her will be twisted into a completely different story within a few hours, when word gets back to me.

"Urica has some faulty gossip sources." I sniff. "I'm getting out quite a bit. Cosmo or Vem still drive me, but I'm doing just fine. The reason I'm here is that Piper has some questions about the farmhouse she's remodeling. Historical questions. She wanted me to ask what you might remember about the Lowerys? Did you go to the sewing club on Thursdays with Finn's grandma?"

Gladys leans back in her chair, eyeing me up and down. "Well, that's a rather specific question, isn't it, toots? Still fluffs my feathers, thinking about the way your girl treated me at Urica's."

I swallow hard. "I've been meaning to talk to you about that. She's very sorry. She and Finn had an awkward encounter and then you made a comment about her size that pushed her over the edge."

"Puffy as a marshmallow is what I said. Girl needs some sunlight and heavy lifting." Gladys squints. "Did she send you here in your time of misery to tell me? The girl could've brought me a scone and told me herself."

"No, I offered to come." I squirm in my chair uncomfortably.

Gladys can sniff out a liar as easily as some people breathe. Piper tells me repeatedly how much Gladys "creeps her out" and that she'll never speak to her again.

"She told me about a project she was working on and I offered to bring her apologies when I came to see you. You are the local expert, you know." I hold my breath, hoping this is convincing.

"Makes sense." Her shoulders drop into a natural posture. "What can I help you with, toots?"

"The Lowerys. Finn's grandparents. What can you tell me about them?"

Gladys clasps her hands behind her head. "Well,

they were nice enough folks. The husband was quiet, and them types are the ones you can't trust. I wasn't a bit surprised when he lost his noodle." She taps her head. "The kids were embarrassed by them, I think. They never came back to Piney Falls once the older Mister and Missus moved."

"And what about the sewing group she was involved in?"

She shrugs.

"Stumped the great Gladys? This is something that has never happened before!"

"Don't tease me. A sewing group would have been a normal thing here, I suppose. Especially at that time, we didn't have any clothing stores around. We did our best to make do. I'm surprised, frankly, that I don't remember anything about it." She gets up and shuffles into another room without any expla-nation. When Gladys has an idea, it's best to let her run with it.

After a few minutes, she returns with a large book with a worn blue cover. "We used to have these made every year." She plops it on the desk in front of me, forcing a puff of dust into my nostrils.

"Achoo!"

Gladys offers me the tissue she's been storing in her shirt all day and I shake my head.

"Piney Falls City Directory, 1992. I never knew about these!" I open the cover and marvel at the detailed pages, complete with pictures of local organizations. "This isn't your average directory. There are stories about people in the community!"

"Thought it was silly then and I still do now. City directories should contain the names and addresses of all who live within. Nothing more. We had to send it to a printer in Connecticut, so the people and places were a year old once we got the finished product."

I thumb through the book until I find a page that says, "The Twisted Stitch Society, making one of their famous quilts." There are ten women sitting around a long table, each posed with a quilted square of fabric. They are all smiling broadly, all except the attractive curly-haired woman at the head of the table. Her face is stoic and instead of a quilt square, her hands are clasped in front of her.

"Who is this?"

"Hm? Let me see." Gladys slides the book over to her side of the desk. "Oh, that's Scarlett-something-or-other. Never got to know her, but people sure talked like she was the Queen of Sheba. When she wanted something she got it."

"How do you know that?"

"I still had two kids in school. They came home complaining about the special treatment her daughter got. Name was Margarite, I think. I went up to complain and the office staff told me there was nothing they could do. Scarlett had the principal scared as a hen on butcher day."

My phone buzzes and I pull it out of my pocket. "Cos? What's going on?"

"Tell him I need a scone and a coffee. Since you can't carry anything, it's up to him." Gladys yells.

I nod, turning my head away for a moment so we can talk. "Yes, for sure. I'll be right there, love." I rise to leave, forgetting we were in the middle of a serious conversation. "Cos is still driving me until I get this clunky thing off." I motion to my cast, wincing as I always do when I look at the evidence of my injury. "He needs to go home and get some paperwork for the contractor, so I can't miss my ride. Can I take this book with me and look it over?" I ask, sliding it off the counter clumsily with my good arm.

"You can take it for a coupla days. But I'll need it back. Never know when someone might have use for it."

Gladys is just as protective of the items stored in her building as she is of her own family.

"Promise. See you soon!"

The bakery is only two blocks from public records, but I find myself struggling to keep the large, awkward book under my arm. It's a relief when I reach the door, but I soon realize I don't have a free hand to open it.

I lean my head against the glass, hoping someone

will take pity and let me in. It's a busy day, as usual, and customers fill the tables, each group lost in their own conversation. "Hello?" I call helplessly. My phone is safely tucked away in my purse, leaving me with no options. *If I stare at one table in particular, someone is bound to notice me.*

As my eyes focus on the table closest to the door, I can see a familiar salt-and-pepper head. It still gives me butterflies when I see him. He is sitting sideways in the chair with his arm draped over the back. Standing next to him is an attractive, brown-eyed woman wearing a tank top and short shorts. She is running her hand up and down my husband's arm.

Adrenalin pumps through my body as I reach up with my good hand and pull the door open with one finger. Marching past the offending table and up to the counter, I slam the book down and the volume in the room instantly drops.

The woman, who is giggling as she tells Cosmo a story, looks up with surprise. "I'm in the middle of something, ma'am. I'll be with you in just a minute. She moves slightly closer to him, her body language suggesting she's interested in more than a story.

"Cos? I thought we were leaving?" My voice carries through the dead air. I turn around and snap, "You can all go back to your conversations. Nothing to see here!" It's embarrassing to meet the sympathetic gazes, so instead, I turn toward the counter.

Almost immediately, I feel a tap on my shoulder. I'm in an impossible situation: I want him worried that I'm upset, but I know tongues will wag if I make a scene. Reluctantly, I turn to him, my face pinched in a scowl.

"Ellie, this is my wife, Lanie. You'll be seeing more of her around here once her arm is healed." He winks at me and I turn my head away. He is oblivious to my suffering.

"Lanie! Your husband and daughter have told me so much about you!" She walks up and plants herself inches from my face. The half-bottle of cheap perfume she's wearing assaults my nostrils, causing my sensitive stomach to lurch.

"You and I will become close friends, I can tell!" She leans in even closer, the way she did with my husband and her long, dark pony tail slaps my face.

I take a step backward.

"If you're doing any baking today, you'll need to wear a hair net. Long hair and bakeries don't go together. Nobody wants to find that surprise in their scone," I snap.

She pulls on her pony tail unconsciously. "You're so right. That's exactly what I need. In fact, I've got a shower cap with donkeys on it that I'll wear tomorrow. Nothing like an ass making your muffins, am I right?" she slaps Cosmo's arm and they both giggle.

"Where are you from, Ellie?" I ask, trying to

remove the tension from this situation. "Piper tells me you've been baking for several years."

"Idaho. My mom and her sister were estranged, but when my aunt wanted to be a part of my life, I jumped at the chance. She invited me to live with her and we worked together for almost a decade." Her eyes dart back and forth as though she's going over something important in her head.

"Nobody at that bakery was as charming as your Cosmo."

She tilts her chin down and bats her eyes. I can't tell if this is aimed at me or Cosmo. Only one of us will respond in a positive way.

"I heard you were here to do some genealogical research? Word travels fast in a small town. I know someone who could help you."

"Something like that." She takes a wash cloth and begins wiping down the counter in front of me. "Give the information to your handsome hubby." Ellie glances up at the clock and abruptly drops the wash cloth on the counter and walks to the alley door. "I'm gonna take my break now."

As we watch her sashay outside, it takes every ounce of self-control to keep from picking up the rag and whapping Cosmo on the head.

"You can't seriously think this is a good idea."

Cosmo looks perplexed. "Why not? She's the only person who applied with baking experience. She may be a little odd, but we attract those types, don't we, Lanie?"

He forgets and squeezes my bad shoulder and I jump in pain. "Ouch! Most of the odd types we attract aren't that aesthetically pleasing. Or touchy-feely."

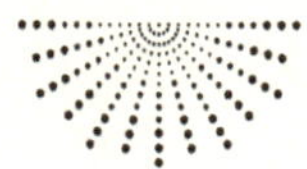

PIPER

Urica Jollopy, known around Piney Falls for her unique stories about her years spent living in the Fallen Branch cult and her multi-colored tunics, ran a successful art gallery. Besides winning the title of Best Local Artist three years in a row, she was Gladys's best friend.

Piper hadn't been inside Urica's Fine Art Gallery for six months, and the previous time she encountered Finnegan and Gladys, the two most uncomfortable conversations had to take place in the span of ten minutes. As she opened the door, the doorbell began playing a long, complicated piece of classical music. Beethoven's Fifth, if she remembered correctly.

She wandered through the maze of colorful paintings hanging on corrugated panels, listening as the music continued. "Urica? Are you here?"

"Just a minute! I'm in the back. I'm trying to reattach these toilet paper rolls to this mixed media piece. I told Backus it wasn't going to work." She finally emerged, unusually harried. Her long, grey hair, neatly braided into two plaits and connected by hand-painted butterfly clasps, hung down her back, touching her waist. Urica was a burst of sunshine in her signature, bright-flowered tunic and black stretch pants.

"Piper Hill! Aren't you a sight for sore eyes! I've been wondering when you'd be back. You and I haven't chatted since–"

"I've been meaning to apologize. Gladys just rubs me the wrong way and you got caught in the middle. I'm really sorry I snapped at you. It's not your fault."

"Everything is a-okay. Gladys can be a pistol and she's really been taken with you. Old Urica here doesn't hold a grudge." She wiped her hands on a cloth she found under the counter and motioned toward the back of the gallery. "Come look at Backus's work. He takes household items and makes them into things that he thinks would look good hanging on people's walls. This is his masterpiece-a collage made of hangars and green paint he calls, 'Hanging in Chaos.'"

Piper tilted her head to the side, trying to decide

if she was missing the point. It looked like a paint accident that someone dropped their hangars on. "Nice."

Urica bit her bottom lip and looked away, putting her hands on her hips.

Piper sensed all was not forgiven. "The last time I was here, I'd just come to the conclusion my relationship with Finn was over and at the same time, we were finding it impossible to find a contractor for the farmhouse. Gladys made some comment about my weight and that was the last straw." She smiled hopefully at Urica. "I took out all of my frustrations on you and Gladys, and I'm sorry. Your art is beautiful and nothing in here looks like rainbow vomit. That was me lashing out."

Urica fiddled with a nametag below a painting.

"Every stage of this remodel has brought new challenges," she continued, "and I've never done anything like it before." Her voice wavered. "I just don't want to disappoint my parents. But that's not why I'm here today. I needed to ask you about some Piney Falls history."

Urica moved in close and the strong scent her homemade shampoo, local greens mixed with patchouli filled Piper's nostrils.

"What is it? I know just about everything that goes on in town, you know."

"I wanted to ask you about a sewing group that

existed in the 90s. Finn's grandmother, Elaine, was a member."

The perpetually nervous woman took her middle finger in her mouth and began chewing on her nail furiously, like a rabbit with a carrot. When she'd accomplished her task, she stared hard at Piper. "Yes, I know all about the sewing group. They did more than just sew. Who told you about them?"

"Finnegan Lowery. He said that his grandmother went every Thursday in the summer after she dropped him off at the pool."

Urica nodded. "Sewing and drinking. What a combination! Lucky none of those women lost a finger!"

Piper gulped. "They drank during their sewing club? Weren't they there to create?"

Urica fingered one of her braids before flipping it behind her back. "So much more than sewing happened in that room. I went once. You know, we weren't supposed to leave the cult compound unless we were going to town with specific orders." She sat down on a bench painted with wands and potions over a purple background. The title card read, "Sit for a spell. $5,000." She patted the space beside her, motioning for Piper to join her..

"I couldn't help myself. I'd heard whispers that a group of women was becoming more powerful than our leader, Zion. They were committing crimes and found a way to get whatever they wanted."

"What kind of crimes?" Piper edged closer. "Were they violent?"

"That was the rumor. But in my time there, the women acted as if they had nothing to discuss but the price of apples."

"Oh," Piper replied, not attempting to hide her disappointment.

"They were piecing together a quilt for the Piney Falls Historical Society's 60th anniversary, so they thought the cult sent me to help. One woman started talking about her employer and how he'd fired her unjustly. The leader of the group–her name was Scarlett–the shut her up pretty fast. When I left, I paused on the steps and put my ear to the door. I heard something about the woods. I'd already been gone from the cult too long so I had to hurry back."

Piper shook her head. "I wonder what other secrets they left in the woods?"

Urica was never one to mince words. "One of the few things of value I learned from the cult was never seek out pain. If there is no reason to go looking, why would you?"

They sat in silence for a moment while Piper tried putting this picture together in her head: Finn's grandmother, who baked him cookies and treated him like her own child spent her Thursdays with a secretive group who may have harmed others.

" Those ladies scared me more than Zion," Urica continued, "and I forgot about them for a time. One day, toward the end of our time in the cult, someone brought up the Twisted Stitchers in our group sharing time. Before I could sensor myself, I burst out, 'whatever happened to them?' The person who brought them up didn't even blink. Had to wonder if she'd visited the sewing circle too. She said 'oh, they disbanded. Their leader disappeared.' I admitted I'd gone to a meeting, and Zion sent me to the Thinking Shed for a night. That was the end of that."

"Thank you for telling me." Piper stood. "I'm going to have to research this a little more."

" You're gonna want to be careful about who you ask. There are still some hard feelings around town and I'd imagine there are some ladies who don't want their secrets coming out."

"Thanks, Urica. Your next coffee and scone are on me. I promise, I'll be the friendliest person you meet all day."

Piper turned to leave, but stopped and came back. "Urica, you didn't mention Finn's grandmother specifically. Did you know her?"

"Heard her name mentioned, but I wouldn't recognize her if I saw her. If she was a part of this group, though, she was dangerous. Your best bet would be to head to the Piney Falls Historical Society and ask to see all the quilts those women made. It might give you more insight."

Piper walked to the door and noticed a police car sitting in front of Urica's store. Inside sat the same officer she'd seen at Cheese With Your Burger. Her history of running from authority with the people who raised her filled her head with doubt. "Urica, do you have a back door?"

CHAPTER THIRTEEN

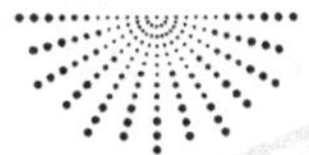

LANIE

"Cos, you know I'm not the jealous type," I begin, as he unloads groceries from the trunk of the car for our big party. "But that woman is up to no good." I walk in front of him and hold the door while he carries four bags on each arm.

Cosmo heaves them to the floor and turns to me. "It was painfully obvious. You didn't talk to me until this morning. When I rolled over to kiss you, all I got in return was, 'don't forget the charcoal. We need lots of charcoal.'"

My cheeks burn. "It took some time to process. Are you sure you did a background check on this woman?"

He returns to the trunk and I follow, unable to let this drop. "Maybe she's got ulterior motives?"

"Not everyone is out to get us, Lanie. You have to trust that I know what I'm doing. He reaches deep into the trunk and removes the last three bags. "Your sister is locked away in prison. The bad guys are gone from our lives and now it's time to celebrate new beginnings, not fret over someone who hasn't done anything wrong."

He smiles and gives me a peck on the cheek as he walks up the path to our front door. "Are you coming? I need a sexy door opener. I'd hate to let the ice cream melt waiting for one."

I move around him and open the door with my good arm. "But what about the branch falling on us? Don't you think that was suspicious?"

He sets the last of the groceries on the counter and turns to me. "Honey, what I think is that there are kids in this town who need more supervision. We were just unlucky enough to be there at the wrong time. That has nothing at all to do with Ellie."

I purse my lips. "I hate it when you're logical."

"If you're still not convinced, take Vem out there once you're healed and you can look around for evidence that proves me wrong, while she's smearing some kind of excrement all over her body."

My mind is more at ease knowing he isn't shutting me down entirely. "I think we should go to our cabin. It's not far from where the branch fell and would be the most logical spot for squatters. I'm feeling pretty good-we could do that any afternoon, or today."

He sighs. "That's what this is about? You're wanting to take an adventure when we're in the middle of planning this party?"

"Yes? It's been bothering me, Cos. A lot. I want to know that I'm not ignoring a real danger to all of us just because I want to lie in bed all day reading magazines."

"I really don't think you're ready for that kind of physical workout. It's harder to get to the cabin than you remember."

I'm determined to prove to Cos that I'm fit enough for this expedition. "What about November's four-wheeler? I could ride behind you and if you go slow, I'll be fine."

His face clouds over with worry. "I don't like this, Lanie. You can't hold on to me very well with one arm."

"I've got that strap we used for hauling the kitchen table that Truman made for us. I may have put on a few post-surgery pounds, but I'm still smaller than the kitchen table. I'll put it around my waist and you can clasp it to your chest."

He gives me the, "I'm exasperated with you but being patient," look that usually makes me back down. Today, there is something in my gut telling me we need to pursue this.

"All right," he says with exasperation. "Go tell November you've got a crazy idea."

I skip out the door like a child on my way to get a lollipop.

"But we're not staying long!" He calls after me.

I find the keys to the four-wheeler hanging on the hook in her garage, beside the wooden painted sign that reads, "The keys are only the first step." I should go inside and tell her I'm taking them, but I'd rather not. She'd want to come with us, and I'd like to make this journey without her.

"I'll bring it back in an hour!" I yell at her security camera, though I know she's doing a meditation for her indoor plants and won't have any idea I've taken it.

It takes a true professional gymnastic-level set of contortions, but finally we're strapped together. I'm twisted at the waist so my cast isn't pressing into his back – not the most comfortable position.

I kiss his neck lightly as he starts the engine. "If I wasn't riding side saddle, this might be a real turn on."

He shakes his head and we start with a jolt, almost knocking us both off. "Sorry," he yells over the sound of the engine. "I haven't been on this since last winter when November asked me to check on the chipmunks during that big snow storm."

There is a road that people use for recreational purposes to get up the mountain. The dirt road isn't quite as steep as the hiking trail but the ground is strewn with horse droppings, empty cans and car parts. The trip requires agility and concentration.

Cos does his best to dodge all the obstacles, but by the time we reach the top, my sideways stomach feels upside down. I've been taking pain medication that already makes my insides delicate without the added challenge of travel. He stops the four-wheeler at the edge of the meadow, where the cabin is within walking distance.

As he works to disconnect us, my head begins to spin. "Quicker, Cos," I say breathlessly.

"I'm going as fast as I can!" he insists, as I attempt to turn myself as far away from him as possible. When it happens, I realize just how much I had for lunch. The doctor warned the pain meds would make my stomach sensitive. Vomit splatters all over the freshly washed four-wheeler and on his shoes.

"Got it!" he says, undoing the strap, oblivious to the chaos happening behind him. He steps off the four-wheeler and right into what's left of my lunch. When he looks up at me, his face is twisted in disgust. "Is this when I say I told you so?"

I shake my head, trying to regain my composure, and he brings a water bottle to my lips. "You don't want to get dehydrated." He pushes my hair out of my face and wipes the cold sweat from my brown.

When I finish, he helps me carefully off the four-wheeler, mindfully avoiding the mess I created. I stand still for a moment, trying to regain a sense of calm and my center of gravity.

There is a peacefulness here, with only the sounds of birds tweeting and the occasional breeze rustling through the tall trees. This kind of medicine calms my stomach quicker than anything from a bottle. "I'm sorry. You were right. I'm not ready for something like this. But we're here. Let's take a stroll out to the cabin and see if anyone has been there. I promise this will be the end of it."

Cosmo takes my good elbow and guides me through the tall grass. "I'm fine, really," I protest.

"Oh no. I'm not riding home with anything else on my shoes."

We walk closer to the cabin, where clothes hang over the wooden railing and a pile of fast food containers lay haphazardly on the porch. "I wish they would have asked before they made themselves at home." I pick up a Cheese With Your Burger wrapper under my foot and put it on the pile with the others.

"I'm going to check around back. You stay here and yell if you see something."

I nod. *Poor Cos.* He got more than he bargained for today and there are still groceries sitting on our counter. I hate being this impulsive. "It's not spying when it's our cabin," I announce.

To my surprise, there are dishes on the table. One is covered in egg yolk and the flies are feasting on a half-eaten slice of toast. I can see another plate with an untouched sandwich and two dirty glasses.

Forgetting that two seconds ago, I cursed my impulsiveness, I knock on the door. "Hello? We don't want to intrude. We're just checking to see if you need help."

There is no answer. I reach under the door mat, searching for the key, but it is gone. "Cos? Could you come here?"

He races around to the front of the building. "Are you okay? Feeling sick again?"

"No," I reply calmly. "I'm fine. Someone is living here. I saw breakfast dishes inside. We can clean up this trash and take it with us. I wish I'd brought something to write with. I'd like them to know we come in peace and they can stay here for as long as they want."

I bend down to pick up another wrapper and Cosmo beats me, picking up two and placing them in the pile. "Just how do you propose we take this trash? On your lap?"

"You've got a point. Is there room in the shed out back? We could store it there until we can come back with a trailer." Together, we carry trash to the shed, only to find it full of garbage bags already. It's clear these people, whoever they are, have been here for some time.

"I'll come back up with Truman and a trailer. Let's get home for today. "As Cosmo places the belt around my waist and prepares to strap us together, he looks at me with concern.

"What?" I ask. "Are you worried this time I'll get your entire body? I think I've rid myself of every-thing in my system."

"No, it's not that. When I was around the back of the cabin, I found this." He pulls a crumpled receipt from his pocket and hands it to me.

"It's for a hotel in Spokane. They must be moving from place to place. I feel sorry for–"

"No, look at the signature at the bottom."

My stomach lurches once more. This time it's not from the bumpy ride. "What kind of a game are they playing?"

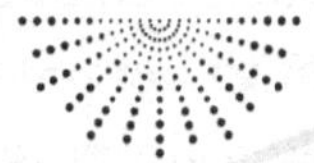

CHAPTER FOURTEEN

PIPER

"What are you doing?" Piper asked with irritation. "You can't put the scones in until the oven is at temperature or they won't be crisp."

Ellie stood up and tucked a wisp of hair behind her ear. "I've been making scones for longer than you've been out of diapers," she retorted. "Where I worked before, we put them in a cold oven and everything turned out just fine." She placed her hands on her hips defiantly and widened her stance in front of the oven door.

"Where you work NOW, my family's business, we let the oven preheat. If you're going to be here long term, you're going to have to learn how to do things our way." She shoved Ellie to the side and pulled the tray from the oven, slamming it on the counter before exiting the kitchen.

Piper had experience with teenage employees and they were never this much trouble. Doris, the elderly woman who had been at the bakery since Cosmo opened it, kept to herself and didn't make a fuss, always obediently following directions. Piper sat down on Cosmo's chair in the office and put her head in her hands. She didn't want to call him and make it sound like she couldn't handle things.

Her self-doubt, something she had recently named "Booger" in a therapy session, came creeping in. She picked up the picture of her family - Lanie and Cos - and smiled apologetically.

"I don't know if I can live up to your expectations of me. From the beginning, you gave me credit for being stronger than I am. And on top of that, I'm incapable of handling relationships of any kind. I push Finn away And Ellie…"…"

There was a knock on the door and she looked up to see Ellie in her tight-fitting blue shirt and equally tight jeans with her head cocked to the side.

"I thought about what you said. I'll preheat the oven from now on. It is what most recipes call for anyway. I didn't mean to upset you. I know you have a lot going on and I don't want to be responsible for adding wrinkles to that cute face." Ellie grinned so wide her cute face actually changed shape.

"I shouldn't have snapped at you." Piper sat up straight in her chair. "I've only trained part-time help up until now. You and I are both learning." She stood and offered her hand. "Should we start over?"

Ellie moved around the desk quickly and pulled Piper in for an unexpected hug. Piper could smell her strong perfume, a new kind that was a pungent mixture of roses and cedarwood. She gulped, trying not to make it obvious she couldn't breathe.

"I like more contact than a simple handshake. You can learn a lot about a person by the way they hug," Ellie whispered in Piper's ear.

When Ellie loosened her grip, Piper pulled away quickly, smoothing the front of her shirt. "I'm not a big hugger at work." She drew her diminutive body up tall, reaching Ellie's shoulder.

"I'll try and remember that. At my last job, people lined up for my hugs." She tilted her head to the side and smiled. "I'm hard to resist."

"Did you put the scones in the oven?" Piper felt the irritation building in her again. "After it preheated?"

"Huh? Oh, yeah. They're already baking. I was thinking I would make a few loaves of my signature bread. It's got raisins, and—"

"We have specific menus for each day of the week." She'd already explained this to Ellie three times. "Today, you've got six types of scones and cinnamon rolls and there is plenty of pita bread for the lunch special. I don't think my dad would appreciate your using up time and ingredients to make something that isn't already on the menu."

Ellie leaned against the doorway, adjusting her shirt. "Well, I spoke with him yesterday and he was fine with it. Enthusiastic, you might say. 'Go for it, Ellie. We can always use a new menu item.' Then he grinned at me, like he does. That man has a smile that would melt a hundred hearts."

Piper's face burned bright red. "Just make sure you don't run behind with our regular things. We have people who come in precisely at 8:00 AM and expect their usuals." The door jingled and Doris walked in, carrying a heavy bag.

"Doris? Could I speak with you in the office for a minute?" Piper called, relieved for a way out of the sticky situation. Doris moved to the doorway and gestured for Ellie to stay out of her way. When Ellie stepped into the hallway to let her by, Piper quickly shut the door behind Doris. "Have fun experimenting!" she called.

"You're wanting to talk about the new hire," Doris said matter-of-factly, setting down her red lunch bag with the words *Hot Doesn't Stop at 60* written in bold letters across the side..

"Have you seen it, too? She seems to know exactly how to push my buttons. And I don't think she's dressing appropriately for bakery work. Even with the teenagers, I've never had to have a serious talk about wearing more clothing."

Doris blinked rapidly. Her half-hooded eyes traveled over Piper's shoulder, staring at an empty space on the wall. "I'll keep watch over her. She's the type who causes a stir so you don't see what's underneath."

Piper smiled. *Good old Doris.* She kept her life outside of work private, but there was never any question of her allegiance to Cosmo and the bakery.

"Oh, while you're here, do you know anything about a sewing group called 'The Twisted Stitch Society? They were a big deal back in the 90s."

It was as if a jolt of electricity went through Doris's body. "Why would you care about that? Way before your time."

"I was told they were very active in the community. Maybe in ways they shouldn't have been."

There was a knock on the door and the women said in unison, "We're busy!"

"There's someone here to see Piper. He's good-looking, but he keeps patting his shoulders. I don't know if they drug test police officers, or–"

Piper swung the door open. "It must be the cop I saw at Cheese With Your Burger. He's been lurking around wherever I go. I'll deal with him."

As she walked to the front of the bakery, she went over the speech in her head. "I'm not going to be intimidated by you. If you want to throw your weight around, do it somewhere else."

The same handsome green-eyed police officer she'd seen twice before tapped his fingers one at a time on the counter impatiently.

She put on her best customer service smile. "Can I help you, officer?"

He fiddled nervously with his badge and then tapped his shoulders. "There's no way to do this without it being awkward. I overheard your conversation the other day while I was eating lunch, two-fifteen to two-forty-five."

She tilted her head to the side. "Okay. Yes, I was there." Unlike earlier this morning, when Ellie's perfume made her gag, the air was filled with a clean, musky smell.

"My family has a history with The Twisted Stitch Society. I believe I can be of some help."

"Oh really? Who is your family?" Piper noticed that when she leaned forward, he took a step back. Her pride was hurt a little.

"Lumquest. I'm Obie, the youngest in the family by six years and thirty-five days." A smile flickered across his face. "My sister hates that I count in days." He brought a bright, orange handkerchief to his face and wiped his brow. Piper couldn't see that he was sweaty.

"You're Boysie's son? I didn't know he had a son my age."

He hugged both of his shoulders again and looked at the ground. "I'm the black sheep of the family. Because I left for almost a decade, they have a hard time explaining me. Dad still hasn't accepted that his youngest kid can be fully functional and still have OCD."

"I didn't–"

"Yes, you did. Everybody notices. These are called tics, these things I have to do in order to function. My roommate used to say, 'Obie, everybody's got their weird stuff. Yours are just always on display. The people who have it locked inside are the ones you have to worry about.'"

"Your roommate was very wise." Piper relaxed, forgetting for a moment how unnerved she had been by his presence. "Would you like a coffee? On the house? I'd like to hear more about this Twisted Stitch Society."

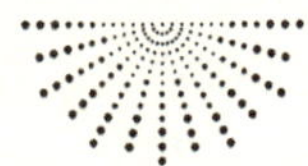

CHAPTER FIFTEEN

The air is thick with hickory smoke from the barbecue pit. I can hear Truman's voice as he relays another Civil War story his great-great grandparents kept in his journal. The other guests will be arriving shortly. Since I'm stuck with only one good hand, everyone has stepped up to fill the void, bringing colorful salads, steaming casseroles and thickly frosted desserts to set on a long picnic table in the garage.

We placed locks on all four bedroom doors, not because we don't trust our friends, but because I'm still unsure about the intruder who bloodied Cosmo's tools. I'm jiggling the knob on the door of the final bedroom when I feel hot breath on my neck and jump, even though I know exactly who it is.

"Lanie? Are you coming? We have to make sure everything is perfect before my guests arrive. I'm going home to give myself a twenty-minute friendship moan before hosting this party."

It's not worth mentioning for the hundredth time that this is not her party to host. "Yes, Vem. I'll be out in a second. I wanted to make sure everything was secure. I touch the door one more time, just to reassure myself it's locked.

Vem's face tightens. "No new developments, right? I'm sure whoever broke into your garage was some bored kid. He probably cut himself while hiking out here drunk. You know how crazy people are at that age."

I nod, even though I don't agree. There have been too many "crazy kids" stories lately for it to be a coincidence. I hate keeping things from her, and what we found in the cabin would bring out the bloodhound in my friend before it's needed. "You can never be too safe. I've recently started feeling like someone is watching us. I'm probably being paranoid. Too much time to sit and think."

"Let's join the party." She rubs my back before we walk together to the kitchen, where Vem pauses to open the refrigerator and sticks her head inside. "Wish you'd let me contribute more than my organizational skills. Hopefully someone is coming with the peanut butter, marshmallow and apple salad that I requested. The healthy one."

"Yes, I did make sure that someone is bringing that just for you." I straighten my lime green blouse with my good hand and touch my hair to make sure there are no surprising developments since I styled it with my non-dominant hand. "If I would have known about what was happening at the cabin, I never would have agreed to this party."

"Lanie, are you coming?" Cos sticks his head in through the back door. "I think the meat has rested long enough. Roasting a hog in the ground is a new one for me." He turns to my best friend and frowns. "You were supposed to help, November Bean. 'It's easy, I'll show you, Cosmo.' Ring any bells?"

"You refused to let me do my ceremonial roasted hog dance before you began. I couldn't possibly participate after that," Vem retorts.

Cos ignores her motions to me. "Can I help you out?"

"I think I'm good to walk outside, babe. My legs still work fine."

Walking through the garage, I kick a large cooler of beer and lose my balance. Both Cos and Vem reach for me and hold on tight until I'm standing tall again. "Crisis averted, thanks to my crack team," I say, trying to lighten the mood.

"I'll move that right now." Cos reaches down and shoves the cooler until it's safely tucked under the long table set with food and condiments. There is a wonderful, rich, smokey smell mixed with the scent of pine trees and the ocean that fills me with gratitude.

I wander to the other side of the garage, where the second table is set with desserts artfully designed and covered in swirls of thick frosting. They are impressive enough Piper must've made them. "I told her to skip this. I know how busy her life is at the moment."

"Piper didn't make them. Ellie did." Cosmo, who acquired a beer during the move of the cooler, takes a long sip and stares at the fire pit. "She insisted when I told her we were having a party. Didn't even ask me to pay her. Really nice of her, wasn't it?"

I turn my head so he can't see my eyes rolling.

The folding chairs are set up along the driveway as well as in the dirt area where green grass should be growing. I see several cars coming up the winding road to our house, almost at the top of the hill and my chest tightens.

"Don't worry, friend. I've got eyes like a hawk. No one is getting by November Bean." She pats me reassuringly.

I'm sure everything is going to be fine," I say to Cos as I watch her march-back up her driveway for her pre-game moan.

"That's my girl." He kisses me on the cheek and I notice, once again, there are crumbs in his mustache. It's happened enough that we need to discuss it, but not today.

Urica and Gladys walk up the driveway, both wearing makeup and matching chunky turquoise necklaces. Gladys has forgone her usual skirt and button-up blouse for jeans that come up almost to her armpits. I giggle to myself at the sight.

"Gladys? You are a vision. I've never seen you in pants before."

Gladys scowls at me. "Women my age don't care to be looked up and down like a half-naked teen. I look like I always do, and you don't need to tell me about it."

"Can I get you something to drink?" As soon as I say it, I realize my ability to pour anything is limited.

"Gladys made you a casserole. Cod and cheddar cheese with brussel sprouts. Is it okay if I pop it in the microwave for a few minutes?" Urica asks.

"Sure. Help yourself." As if heat will cure whatever peculiar flavor it will have.

"You have some Sassy Lasses wine?" Gladys asks after we've watched Urica and the casserole safely enter our home. She gestures toward my casted arm. "Can you carry it with that contraption on your arm?"

"I'll get her some wine," Cosmo says, passing by us. "White or red, Gladys?" He hollers over his shoulder.

"Red, please. That white is just glorified soda."

"We haven't heard anything more about the robbery in our garage. Has Boysie said anything to you?"

Cosmo returns with a glass of wine in a plastic cup and hands it to Gladys.

She holds it up to eye level and twists her face in disapproval. "What's this, for toddlers and the incapacitated? You don't think you can trust me with glass?"

"It's just easier for everyone tonight. We don't want to spend our evening in at the sink washing glasses," I soothe. About the robbery? Do you know anything?"

"They didn't have anything conclusive with the blood. That's all he told me. He's getting secretive, with his mother-in-law." She takes a large drink of the wine and I fight the urge to remind her that just because she's drinking from a kid's cup, it's not a sugary drink she's consuming.

"They probably had some kind of foolish ritual out here - painted their chests and howled at the moon. You never know what gets into somebody's head when they're under twenty. No common sense."

"Well, I'll feel a lot better when we have more information. We've had too many things going on here lately with no explanation."

"Tell you what, toots. I'm going to ask around. I'm going to find out everything I can for you. And we'll get this solved. Can't do a dark web search unless I know who I'm looking for." Gladys pats my good arm and walks towards the fire pit, where a crowd has gathered.

I hear laughter and voices and they comfort me. Our musician friends, who played for our wedding, are setting up their instruments. As dusk begins to settle in, everyone helps themselves to the food tables.

Truman, dressed in his best white overalls with a blue handkerchief in the pocket, pulls up a chair and sits down beside me while he eats. "I think we did pretty good for ourselves. A feast fit for presidential gathering, don't you think?"

"I do, Truman. Each dish is better than the last." I put another bite of potato salad into my mouth and make a mental note to figure out who brought it and what their secret is. "Have you heard about the attempted robbery here? And Cosmo's tools being covered in blood?"

He sets his plate on his lap and wipes barbecue sauce from his lips. "He hasn't mentioned a thing to me. Maybe he didn't want to upset an old man. What happened?"

"Someone broke into our garage and tried to steal Cosmo's tools. Something must have scared them away because they only took a wrench. Not one you gave him, an old tool Cos has had for years." Truman's face is pinched and I regret saying anything. He gets so upset when anything happens to us.

"Blood on them too? That don't sound good. I'm worried about you two. Should you come stay at my place for a while?"

"Thank you for the offer, but we're fine. I was hoping you'd heard murmurs around town, is all. No need to worry." I pat his back, hoping this will be the end of it.

"Have you filled in the police?" He takes a big bite of his sandwich and barbecue sauce oozes from the side. "Mmm. Gets better with every bite."

"Yes. In fact, Boysie is here tonight, and I'm going to ask him for an update."

Being a new parent, I can't waste an opportunity to brag about my child. "She's not here tonight because she's working late on a project. Our daughter has an amazing work ethic. We couldn't be prouder. I should check on the rest of our friends." I stand and Truman attempts to stand as well, but I put my hand on his shoulder. "No, you sit and enjoy. I'm going to mingle with our guests."

Before I realize it, three hours pass. I haven't seen Boysie, though I've heard his voice and we need to talk. The mass of people and the darkness of the hour make it nearly impossible to search him out. The lanterns Vem installed only provide minimal visibility. Finally, I see him talking to Urica, gesturing wildly as he tells a story.

"That was the biggest fish I ever caught and lost." He chuckles, turning to me as I join them. "Great party, Lanie. Just wonderful. I don't remember the last time I had such a nice evening. I haven't laughed much since my wife left."

"Thank you, Boysie." He rarely mentions his wife since they've told everyone she's visiting her sister. "I'm so happy you felt good. We're always here if you need friends."

"Nice of you, Lanie."

"I do have some things I'd like to ask you about. Could we go somewhere a little more private to talk?"

He follows me as we walk behind the garage, making our way on a dark path lit only by our yard light several hundred feet away. He pulls out his police flashlight and lights the ground the last few steps. "The food is superb, Lanie. Hope you two do this again. I've already had three desserts, and darned if I'm not going back for a fourth. Even though it's feeling mighty uncomfortable in there." He pats his large stomach with his free hand.

"I'm so glad, Boysie. We wanted everyone to forget their troubles for an evening. The reason I wanted to talk to you is that Cosmo and I were out at the cabin in the meadow recently. There is evidence that someone is living there." I take a deep breath. "I don't have a problem with helping those in need, though Cos has grumbled about it. What is concerning is that we found a receipt from a motel in Spokane they signed using my dead father's name. Gavin Anders."

"Well, now. That brings a new level of intrigue, doesn't it?" He pauses for a moment. "I still think it's kids up to no good. They sawed that branch off and tried stealing Cosmo's tools. Could be they came across something with Gavin's name on it and had themselves a party in that motel."

"Did you find anything with the bloody fingerprints?"

"I haven't. There is no match to the blood and I don't have any leads. Usually there's someone who wants to brag about a crime they've committed, but right now it's pretty quiet."

I hear a noise over Boysie's shoulder and see a family of raccoons, their eyes glowing as they fight over an open bag of trash "Would you excuse me for a moment?" Luckily, they scamper off as soon as I reach them and the bag is light and easy to maneuver with one arm.

"I'll handle that for you!" Boysie offers.

"No, thanks," I call over my shoulder, walking quickly to the other side of the yard. "Everyone has been doing everything for me for so long that it's time I contribute. Vem's trash intruders appear to be the furry variety. She'll get a kick out of it."

As I heave the bag back into the barrel, I hear a rustling sound and footsteps running off. Squinting,

I can barely make out the shape of a body, a woman's body.

"Wait! I'm not going to hurt you!" I call. "Just tell me who you are!"

I watch in frustration as they continue running until they are out of sight. I don't want to send anyone else after them in the dark on uneven terrain, so I stand, trying to figure out what to do next.

"Lanie? Were you hollering back here?" Boysie asks, breathing hard from rushing to find me. "You injured?"

"There was someone digging through our trash again. Vem was right."

"I'll call it in."

"It's dark out there, Boysie. I don't want anyone getting hurt. But thank you. Tomorrow, we'll look and see if we can determine what they took." I turn around and begin walking toward the party, but Boysie remains.

"Maybe I'm wrong about it being kids," he says between gasps. . "Could be professionals looking for new identities and your dead dad was an easy one. They might be thinking… they might be thinking… you'll have more information in your trash. That's my thought." He leans over abruptly and puts his hands on his knees. "I'm not feeling right, Lanie." He looks faint for about five seconds, barely able to make a sound, and then drops to the ground with an almighty thud.

Though I have a hard and fast rule against it, I run. "Cos! Someone! Boysie needs help!"

As if he's been waiting for my call, Cosmo appears. He has a beer in each hand and several bottles of wine under his arms. "I was replenishing the drinks. What's wrong? Did you fall? Are you hurt?"

"It's not me," I say between quick breaths. "It's Boysie. Around the back, by the trash. Please hurry!"

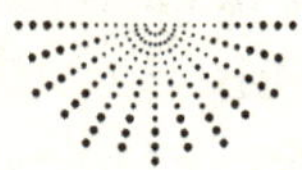

CHAPTER SIXTEEN

"I was going to re-organize the new kitchen tonight." Piper leaned back on the blanket and clasped her hands under her head as she stared up at the stars. "That was my excuse for skipping my parents' big party. You're a bad influence, Obie Lumquest."

Obie patted his shoulders before taking a bite of the impromptu cheese-and-cracker picnic he'd put together. "I've heard that before. OCD really stands for Obie's Cautiously Demonic. I cause problems, but I clean them up."

Piper tried, unsuccessfully, to suppress a giggle. "No offense, but I didn't know you could have a sense of humor and be a police officer."

"Well, if you're referring to my dad, it's a family trait. Grandma Gladys told the story of his first date with my mom. He came to the door with an apology card. He'd heard of Grandma's reputation and wanted to beat her to the punch by apologizing for not being good enough for Mom. She didn't find it humorous."

Piper sat up abruptly. "Oh, god. Gladys."

"What? Is something wrong with Grandma?"

"No, I just… well, she and I don't exactly click. Us being friends will make her head explode."

"Grandma doesn't have a 'like' switch in her. She tolerates about ten people, one of them being your mom. Don't worry about it."

She laid back down, deciding for now to enjoy the stars and worry about Gladys's judgement later. "You lured me out here to tell me about the sewing club, yet we've only talked about my sordid past and your favorite foods."

Obie took another bite of cheese, separated on the plate from the crackers by three finger lengths. "To be fair, it was you who asked me to come back when the bakery closed. I just suggested we find a scenic place to talk."

Piper rolled on her side and propped herself on her elbow. This is all new for me.. When Finn and I began dating–"

"You and Finnegan Lowery are together? I don't mean to intrude."

"No, we parted ways. I like him. He's a great guy. He's just not as easy to talk to as you."

Obie grinned. "I'll take that as a compliment." He

wiped his brow with his orange handkerchief.

"Can I ask you something?"

"Why I'm carrying around this ridiculous orange cloth? It comforts me. I've got two, both made from a blanket my mom made for me. It's one of those things I have to do a certain number of times every day, touching it to my face. I can't explain it. I come with a lot of baggage. And handkerchiefs."

Piper giggled. "We all have baggage. Someday, I'll tell you about mine. But not tonight. I want to enjoy this."

Obie put a cracker in his mouth, chewing each bite exactly six times. "Fair enough."

"You've never mentioned what came between you and your dad, exactly. You said it had to do with your disorder, but you've had that your whole life, right?"

"Mmhm. It got worse as I grew up. Puberty and that kind of stuff. I couldn't cope, or they couldn't cope and I acted out in very bad ways. My family likes to pretend we don't have secrets. We're supposed to be perfect. The Lumquests have been a part of Piney Falls history since the 1940s, blah blah blah. Things with my dad are too complicated for an easy night like tonight."

Piper nodded. "I know all about secrets. I spent my childhood thinking my parents loved me. I don't think either one of them was capable of that, for their own reasons. It's better to know."

"The Hills? Everyone talks like they're the shining stars of the town."

"No, not them. They adopted me recently. I grew up with some really disturbed people."

Obie nodded. "Fair enough. We need to talk about The Twisted Stitch Society. Dad's sister, Aunt Trixie, used to take me to the pool every Thursday. It made me feel special that she wanted to take me there, even though we weren't spending time together. She said she was going to a women's group and that I should be ready to leave promptly at four. In the beginning, she was in a good mood when she came to pick me up. The next summer, something changed. She walked around like she had a dark cloud over her head."

"Did you ever ask her about it?"

Obie stared at Piper. "It's hard to concentrate. Not to be syrupy like a squeeze bottle on a Sunday morning, but you are beautiful in the moonlight. You have the most exquisite–"

"Eyes? They're contacts. I wanted to set myself apart from my family. Not Lanie and Cos, the first one." She looked away.

"I was going to say face. The shape of your face is a perfect circle. In the police academy we called those faces,'fleek.' Almost too beautiful to be real."

She grabbed his hand impulsively and squeezed. "It's just easier if we get this out of the way while we're thinking of something else. If you need to let go and pat yourself, I won't be offended. Let's continue. The Twisted Stitchers…"

Obie smiled contentedly. "When the group started, Aunt Trixie would take our clothes and mend them, but later on, she made quilt squares with all kinds of fancy designs. She said they each meant something, but we kids didn't really care. Nobody asked her about them. I regret that now."

"Could we talk to your aunt? Maybe now that some time has passed, she'll be happy to talk about it."

Obie cleared his throat. He let go of Piper's hand momentarily and crossed his arms, hugging his shoulders. "Trixie's living in Montana. My mom is staying with her now and neither one will answer our calls. " He grabbed Piper's hand again, squeezing it reassuringly.

"Oh. I'm sorry. I'm sure it wasn't your fault, though. Parents' issues are between them, not their kids."

"I would agree with you, Piper Moonlight Hill, but I was a troubled teen. I knew my OCD embarrassed my family, but we never talked about it. Very bad, indeed."

Piper looked at his handsome face, trying to decide if this was the step before he told her he was a serial killer. For some reason, she didn't care. "I did a lot of acting out, too. You don't need to apologize to me." She took a deep breath and slapped a mosquito on her face. "The next thing I need to do is go to the Piney Falls Historical Society and ask to see the quilts. Urica told me the woman who works there has lots of information."

"I'd like to go with you, if you wouldn't mind," Obie said shyly. "You've piqued my interest in more way than one."

Piper's heart began thumping wildly. "I have so much more to tell you…"

"Not tonight, though." Obie said, leaning in close to Piper's face.

Obie's phone buzzed and he moved away from her, pulling his phone out of his pocket and glancing at the screen. "My brother. He never calls with good news." He slid the phone back into the pocket of his jacket and a few seconds later, it buzzed again. "Where were we?" He closed his eyes and moved toward Piper once more, ignoring the persistent buzzing.

This time, Piper didn't allow her mind to wander. "You should answer. It could be important."

Once more, he removed the phone from his pocket and put it up to his ear. "Elwood, this isn't a good time. Can I call you back tomorrow?"

He let go of Piper's hand and push himself up to standing. "When?" he asked with concern. "I'll be there as soon as I can."

"What's wrong?" Piper asked.

"It's my dad. They think he's had a heart attack."

CHAPTER SEVENTEEN

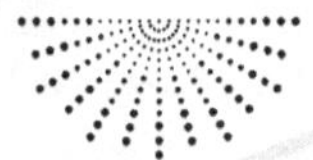

LANIE

Although our emergency crews are all volunteer and only meet at the ambulance garage after a group texts, Tom Tucker, who was on call, drove the ambulance to our party just in case there was a problem. Luckily, he knew exactly what to do to stabilize Boysie until he could get him safely to the hospital.

We all jumped in our cars, leaving the food out for any opportunistic animals, and made a caravan to Piney Falls General Hospital.

Boysie's entire family is sitting in the waiting room, playing cards and talking in whispers while they wait for word. The Lumquest side, the Petrie side and everyone in between comes out to thirty-five bodies crowded into the tiny hospital waiting for word. That leaves no room for the rest of our party guests, some of whom managed to avoid marrying into the largest family in town.

It's a deceptively beautiful night. The stars are out, something rare in our cloudy existence, and a gentle breeze carries the salty sea air to our nostrils. We all stand on the lawn of the hospital, trying to cheer each other up with funny stories about Boysie.

"Do you remember when his car caught on fire?" A faceless voice in the dark asks. "All he had was the two-liter bottle of soda. He shook that thing up and sprayed it under the hood." There is a smattering of laughs and then we are all silent, each thinking about what we don't want to say out loud.

Boysie's oldest son, Elwood, walks out to the cement pad in front of the hospital, where two blue tube lights barely illuminate his face. He's the tallest of the Lumquest family at a height of six foot five inches and he inherited his father's long, droopy face. "Dad made it through heart surgery. They think he'll be okay."

We all applaud, not knowing what else would be appropriate. I hug whoever is next to me. In the dark I know it's a woman, but I'm not sure exactly who. It doesn't matter.

Next to Elwood is a stockier figure with a thick

neck and light hair. He could be any one of the Petrie relatives.

"I'm Cornie." There is a snickering from the faceless crowd. "It's a family name, for those of you who don't know. Anyway, our family appreciates any and all help right now, especially dinner." He chuckles as if he's the only one in on his joke.

"Who's going to run the police department?" someone asks. "We barely have enough police the way it is. Without Boysie, things'll fall apart."

"They know what they're doing," I hear Cosmo's deep, soothing voice.

"My brother recently joined the force," Cornie continues. "I'm sure he's willing to step up and help. We can all do our part by watching for crime and reporting it right away. There won't be time for extras."

A shorter and thinner young man moves to Elwood's side. He's wearing a dark blue Henley shirt with one button undone. He has his mother's full lips (Gladys has a picture of all of her children sitting on her desk) and his father's large, expressive eyes. In the dim light, he looks like a teen heartthrob from a boy band. "Some of you may remember me from childhood-I'm Obie Lumquest." Curiously, he crosses his arms and pats himself on the shoulders.

"How's the city gonna afford another employee?" somebody grumbles.

I wonder what will happen with our investigation–the broken branch, bloody tools and theft of my father's identity. This boy looks to be barely out of high school. *Shame on me.*

Cosmo squeezes his thumb and forefinger against my neck. "I know exactly what you're thinking." He leans forward and whispers in my ear, "we're going to catch the bastards who broke in, I promise. And if junior, here, can't take it on, then it will be you and me."

Vem appears out of nowhere. "Cosmo Hill, you're leaving me out of this again. Really! I've been on so many adventures with the two of you!"

I remember that we left the fire burning in the pit. "Vem, did you happen to–"

"Put the fire out? Cover all the food and take it inside? November Bean is always on the job." She salutes me and I want to hug her.

"Is there anyone left at the house? There was someone digging through our trash when Boysie collapsed. I don't want them coming back and finding another token in the garage."

"Truman stayed behind. Nothing to worry about as far as intruders go, but salvaging any leftover desserts may be another matter."

"There's nothing more to do here, Lanie." Cosmo pats my shoulder expectantly. "We might as well go home and join Truman in a truffle cake deep-dive."

As we drive back to the scene of tonight's tragedy, I watch the silhouette of giant trees passing by as the memory of Boysie's collapse runs through my head on constant replay.

It's no better after we get into bed. I was completely unaware that he was in pain. Just going on about my issues. I toss and turn for hours until pure exhaustion allows me to shut off my brain.

The next morning, as I'm sipping my coffee on my second-story balcony, I watch, amused, as Vem dances in her garden, singing a song familiar only to her. In between hip twists and arm raises, she pulls what looks like weeds. I have no doubt that she'll take them inside and slather them with cheese for lunch. It's a lift I needed this morning.

The noise of a car driving up our steep street is an unwelcome distraction. As it gets closer, I can make out the vehicle–it's Boysie's Piney Falls police car. For a moment, I wonder if Boysie has new information about the intruders, and then I remember that he's in the hospital and my heart sinks.

The car stops in the driveway and the door opens. A thin, dark-haired man dressed in police uniform gets out, straightens his tie and tucks in his shirt. I remember him from last night, but he looks much better in the daylight. His face bears the unmistakable oblong shape and wedge-shaped nose of the Petrie family, though he is much more hand-some than the rest.

I set my coffee on the small glass table and close my robe. "I'll be down in just a minute."

There is no dressing quickly when I'm doing it one-handed, so I throw a multi-colored muumuu over my head, the one Vem gave me for my last birthday. "Plenty of space for your parts to breathe, Lanie."

My hair is still mussed from the restless night, so I pull a comb through it quickly and put on a dab of lipstick. At least I won't look like someone's crazy aunt who's been locked in the attic for ten years.

I open the front door while catching my breath. "Come on in, Obie. Would you like some coffee?" I gesture toward the living room, but he shakes his head.

"I like to stand. It makes me think better. You're Lanie, right?"

"Yes, Lanie Anders-Hill. My husband, Cosmo, already left for work. And how is your father?"

His head falls back as he gazes at the massive open ceiling and its intricate wooden pattern. It is breathtaking. I've spent many hours myself watching clouds float by through the two picture-window-sized skylights.

"This is spectacular. My dad told me this place was a showpiece, but you really have to see it for yourself. You guys could sell tickets for this view."

I blush, even though I feel the same way. "My husband and I put in many hours with an architect and our friend, Truman, to get the details just perfect. It's our dream home."

The lovely picture of the morning Cosmo picked me up and carried me into our first home together flickers through my head and I feel warm inside.

Obie clears his throat and pats his shoulders. "Dad is groggy from his surgery. Four stents! But he filled me in on your case and I'd like to get to work on it."

I look at him skeptically. "That's very nice of you, Obie, but you have a lot on your plate right now with your dad being ill and you starting a new job."

"I know you probably think that I don't know what I'm doing. You may be right, but didn't you, in your life, have to start somewhere?" He blinks rapidly. "Wasn't there someone who gave you a chance the first time?"

My first job out of college was doing the marketing for Tools, Tacos and Tanning. It was an odd combination of businesses, but it seemed to work. They didn't have much money, so they hired a first-time marketer to try and get their business on the map. If they hadn't taken a chance on me, I wouldn't be where I am today. "You are absolutely right, Obie. You need to start somewhere. What can I help you with?"

"Well, ma'am, I was going over the file this morning. Dad made some notes, and he thinks there may be a connection between the tools and a tree that was sawed down in the woods? He didn't provide any details on that, but I was hoping you could fill me in."

I look up with surprise. "Last I knew, he thought the broken branch was a bunch of unruly kids. I'm surprised it would be in the file. He thought it was kids responsible for both incidents until I told him they were using my dead father's identity, too. We were talking about that, when… I'm so sorry." I choke back a sob and then realize he is standing, without emotion, waiting for me to finish.

"Your dad doesn't keep secrets from me, Obie. We've worked too many cases together, he knows it just wastes valuable time."

"Are you in law enforcement, too? He never mentioned that."

"No, you might say I'm an amateur sleuth." Now that I say it out loud, it sounds childish. "Somehow these things always find me and I usually put the pieces together."

"Oh?" Obie reaches into his back pocket and pulls out a slim pad and pen. The pen is one that I passed around town for our big celebration last summer, Piney Falls Proud Days. When the pens were made, they messed up some of the lettering so the pens read, Piney Falls Plowed. It was too late to send them back and everyone thought it was a funny statement, given how many residents were inebriated for the entirety of the celebration.

"Tell me everything you know about this tree falling. I want to check it against what Dad has in his file and make sure we haven't overlooked anything."

I set my judgement aside and start from the beginning. "We were out in the forest and a rather large branch came down on us. Your father investigated and decided that kids shimmied up the tree and started sawing. They got bored with it and left, not knowing it would come down and hurt us."

"When you say, 'we'…"

"Myself, my husband and my best friend, November Bean. She lives next door." I glance at the clock on the wall. "You've got about fifteen minutes until her Moaning Nudes class if you want to speak with her. I'd suggest going over now because some of those folks are eager to disrobe the minute they get out of the car."

He appears shocked.

"I thought you grew up here? Aren't you used to odd people?" I walk over to the coffee maker and pour myself a cup. "Would you like some?" I'm proud of all the one-handed kitchen duties I've mastered.

"No ma'am. I'd rather keep my head clear while I'm on the job." He clears his throat and scribbles on his pad for a minute. "I'll wait to talk to Ms. Bean another day. Would you say that tree branch was big or medium sized?"

"It came from a tall pine, so it was impressive in

girth. I don't think that's really relevant, do you?" I take a long sip of my coffee.

"You never know. They taught us at the Academy that there is nothing such as an irrelevant clue early in the investigation. Now ma'am, what else do you remember about that day?"

The overwhelming feeling that something was wrong with my body and then darkness. "Cos and November probably have better recall than I do. We found some clothing scattered around, like someone had been living there."

Obie raises his eyebrows. "What kind of clothing, exactly?"

"Oh, I remember a red shirt, some dark blue jean shorts and a pair of pants with a ripped pocket and a flower on the back…."

"Excuse me for a moment ma'am." Obie scurries out the front door to his car. He returns a few seconds later with a pair of pants with a daisy embroidered on the pocket.

"Do these look familiar?"

"Those are exactly the pants. Where did you find them?"

"In the alley behind the house of…." He brings the notebook close to his face. "Fester P. Rubottom of 99 Blossom Road. He called yesterday and said his trash was all over the alley." Obie thumbs through several pages. "Here it is. He said his private trash was scattered like lawn clippings, and he didn't like the neighbors seeing it."

"Does he have any idea what was taken?" I take another sip of my coffee. "It might have been animals rummaging around. I know it may be difficult to tell, but–"

"Lots of half empty food containers. The offenders were hungry. Can't blame them." Obie puts the pad back into his pocket. "Oh, he also mentioned finding a photo. Said it had some scribbling on the back and all he could make out was 'Gavin Anders.'"

CHAPTER EIGHTEEN

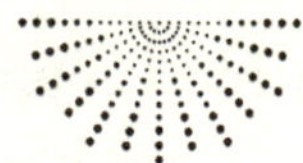

PIPER

The Piney Falls Historical Society Museum sat on Main Street, in between the failed Juicy Tunes Records location and Grannie Sue's Pizza. The two-story brick building occupied the former location of Piney Falls Bank of Prosperity in the 1940s.

"Of all the subjects I missed in school, history was the one I wished I could have experienced first-hand." Piper lamented.

Obie cocked his head to the side. "You weren't allowed into museums?"

"Maybe you can come into the shop for coffee one afternoon and I'll tell you everything. I'm surprised your dad or grandmother haven't made a big deal of my story."

"I'd like that," Obie said eagerly. "I mean, hearing about you, not that your life is full of drama. Everyone has some kind of story to tell. We're all books. Just have to find the right person to read them."

Piper blushed. "In any case, thank you for setting this up."

"There are advantages to being law enforcement." Obie nodded toward the door. "I can't open it. I haven't been here in the last thirty days, and who knows what kind of germs are on the handle. Usually, I bring gloves with me, but I'm off the clock."

"No problem." Piper opened the heavy wooden door and stepped inside. A soothing voice spoke over elevator music:

"Return to the time when merchants bore mail upon oxen-pulled wagons from the city. The men and their wives, merchants and bonders, a century's worth of people. It's not a small town, but it isn't a bustling metropolis either. You're in early Piney Falls, then known as Flanagan, Oregon."

The height of the beams and rafters reminded Piper of her parent's home, with tall polished-wood ceilings. Fake flowers that hadn't been dusted recently lined the old window sills. The air carried the musty scent of history.

"Hello and welcome!" A woman with straight, grey bangs and a twinkle in her eye smiled, exhibiting three gold teeth. "It warmed my heart that you called about the quilts. We don't get much traffic in that room." The elderly woman adjusted her name tag, which read, *Mrs. Williams, Volunteer. Ask me about our Pine-tastic Postcards!*

"I take it you've not been here before? We have a wonderful collection of historical artifacts." She motioned to the first room, where an exhibit displaying mannequins dressed in stylish 1920s garb as the centerpiece. "Meet the Flanagan women upon their arrival in the strange new land," the speaker blared.

The sound of saws in a paper mill startled all three of them.

"Imagine how frightening it was to experience the hustle and bustle of an American city after spending most of their lives in the quiet Scottish farm country..."

They passed by an elaborate stage, portraying the fire that destroyed the Scheddy Salmon Cannery. The next room showed the official renaming ceremony, where city officials and the governor were in attendance.

"The City of Flanagan became Piney Falls in the coast's grandest celebration…"

Finally, they reached the quilt exhibit.

The newest room in the museum was a large, open space. Bright, uniquely patterned quilts were draped over free-standing racks throughout the room. Staggered between them, large quilts hung from the ceiling. It was a dizzying amount of history contained in intricate designs.. "Where do we start?" Piper scanned the room.

"Normally, you would listen to the pre-recorded explanation by pushing the button in front of each exhibit." Mrs. Williams pushed her palms together. "But I'm not busy today, so I'll be happy to give you the history. She motioned for them to join her in front of a large quilt with purple-flowered squares slanting left to right and bright yellow squares slanting in the opposite direction.

"The Piney Falls Stitching Society began in 1978. The women wanted to create a place where they could come together and talk about their troubles. It was a safe space in a tumultuous time." The floor creaked as she walked to a bright orange quilt with a sunburst in the middle.

Piper giggled. "When is it calm here?"

"I suppose you're right." Mrs. Williams laughed nervously.

"Were you in the Twisted Stitch Society, Mrs. Williams?" Obie asked.

"No, of course not," she answered quickly. "I went, only briefly. But I don't want you to think anyone in my family had anything to do with the wild events attributed to the group."

"Of course not. We're just here looking for some history," Obie reassured her. "No one wants to stir up trouble."

She studied him with curiosity. "Your face looks very familiar. Do I know you?" Mrs. Williams leaned in close to Obie, causing him to jump back and pat his shoulders furiously.

"He's Boysie's son and Gladys's grandson." Piper stepped in between them protectively. "You know those Petries, they all have the same face."

Mrs. Williams relaxed her stance. "Oh, yes. How's your father doing?"

"He's feeling much better. He sat up in bed and had green gelatin last night."

The conversation stalled momentarily.

"The women started meeting to support each other. That's positive, right?" Piper asked.

"It's beginnings were innocent. As I mentioned, the women needed social time, and at that point, we didn't associate with the people from other small towns up and down the coast. They thought we were strange, and we thought the same of them. It was a social hour, and everybody had some kind of mending to do, so we didn't feel guilty for sitting together for hours."

Piper nodded and folded her arms.

"We talked about this one's husband and that one's sister. Before long, we all knew each other's business." Mrs. Williams sat down on a bench with a golden plaque attached that read, "In memory of Ethel Watts, World's Record Holder for Belching 1967," attached to the back rest.

"The mission of the group changed when Scarlett Peters moved to town."

Piper walked between the hanging masterpieces and touched a quilt with a blue theme and many small circles. The stitches were so tiny she could barely see them. "What was Scarlett's deal?"

"She blew in like a winter storm, all the way from New York State. I remember her most for her hair out to here." Mrs. Williams made a large circle over her head with her arms. "She bragged she'd modeled for a clothing catalog and I'm sure I wasn't the only who didn't believe her." Mrs. Williams chuckled to herself. "Scarlett, her husband and oldest daughter, Margarite, moved to town. She'd sent her younger daughter to some fancy boarding school. I later learned it was as a punishment for defying Scarlett and having a boyfriend." She shook her head in disbelief. "Anyway, Scarlett struggled to make friends, so someone from the PTA invited her to join our group. It wasn't long before she took over and made her own rules."

"What do you mean, 'took over?'" Obie asked.

"She said we should begin a project together that would unite us and make us more powerful. We thought, okay, that's fine. Scarlett brought a quilting pattern and assigned us each a square. She told us later on those would have significance. We were excited to try something new." Mrs. Williams smiled guardedly. "After we'd put together our first quilt, she came in with another pattern. One Thursday, she showed up enraged by the events going on at the school. Her daughter was being bullied, or at least that was her story. Kids at the school said SHE was the bully."

Mrs. Williams rolled her eyes.

"Scarlett said that every day when her daughter walked home from school, she was harassed by the same boy."

"It's so hard moving to a new town. I've been there many times. Poor kid." Piper remarked.

"All the women were sympathetic," Mrs. Williams continued. "Despite the fact that Scarlett's daughter was no angel, this boy had a reputation for being cruel. He'd beaten up or harassed just about every kid in school. Each woman told of her own experience with the bully and his equally rude parents. They sympathized with Scarlett, but there wasn't much that could be done."

Obie patted his shoulders and walked to the wall where a quilt with pink and green tiny triangles hung.

"That's when Scarlett said, 'we've been making these quilts together and have developed a strong bond. If you'll notice, even though the patterns of each square are different, they connect. That's us, ladies. We're connected. Together, we can do anything.' Every woman sat a little taller after that."

"Wait," Piper put one hand on her forehead. "She created the quilt squares to join them all together, like a gang of quilters?" She giggled and immediately covered her mouth with her hand. "Sorry, I didn't mean to–"

"Yes, that's the way it started. She assigned two quilters to follow this boy home from school. They picked up their own children and drove slowly behind him as he walked. Mind you, his father was the president of the hospital board and that made him very powerful in our small community. It was a risky thing to do. Each woman took turns, so that every day after school, a different car followed him home. He caught on soon enough."

"And did that work?"

If one of the women had a problem with, say, the grocery store manager, three members of her club would sit in their cars outside of his home, watching. They did that for weeks until he made the peas sixty-nine cents, or whatever it was that was demanded of him."

Piper suppressed a giggle. "Are you telling me that they were a gang of seamstresses?"

"That depends on whose perspective, I guess. From the victim's standpoint, I think they were criminals. But they all thought they helped the community."

Piper took a moment to digest this information. "What happened when you visited undercover? Did they try to recruit you?"

"For a time it scared him, but then he realized he could tell his parents he was being followed by two women." Mrs. Williams sniffed. "They threatened to go to the police if the women didn't leave him alone."

Piper glanced at Obie, whose head was tilted to the side as he studied a hanging quilt with black and red squares. He tapped his foot furiously. "So they went to the police, and that was the end of it? That doesn't seem so bad."

"Scarlett was used to having her way. In Texas she'd run a similar group, so she had experience. She reminded all the women that if they stuck together, no one could defeat them." Mrs. Williams stared at Obie. "Is he all right?" She whispered.

"He has his routines, just like all of us. He recently lost something important to him and it's got him out of sorts today."

When Obie called to tell her about Boysie's

surgery, he mentioned that he must've dropped his orange handkerchief while they were sitting together the evening before. She promised to go look for it, but she came up empty-handed.

"Well, I like that idea. In theory, it sounds like something we all should do. Band together and be powerful," Piper said.

"It wasn't. They all decided each one should take turns following the boy home and sitting in their mini vans in front of his home. And that's just what they did, only they ramped it up and soon they drove by honking at all hours, throwing rotten fruit at the house or whatever they had in their kitchens. They were relentless. I don't know that it was about the bully at that point. They were releasing all of their pent-up emotions from every corner of their lives and it felt good." Mrs. William's eyes moved back and forth quickly. "But not me, you understand."

"The police were okay with this?"

"The police chief's wife was one of the members, so yes, the police were absolutely fine with it. The family finally gave up. One day a for sale sign was placed in the yard. Not long after, they left town, never to return."

"That's pretty rough." Piper couldn't see how this would lead to somebody's finger being cut off, but she didn't want to divulge that part of the story to Mrs. Williams just yet.

"Scarlett showed them they could accomplish anything they wanted. So, from that day forward, one Twister each week presented a problem. As a group, they solved her issue in one way or another. It was supposed to be empowering, but soon things took an even darker turn."

CHAPTER NINETEEN

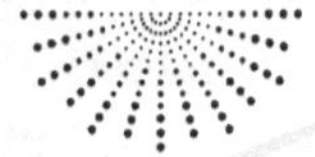

LANIE

"I've developed a new weapon I'm calling The Veminator. I added small nails to a simple compact hair brush that women can keep it in their purses." She pauses, obviously pleased with herself. "It's one of my most brilliant ideas. I'm going to use it for my class on moaning for self-defense. Do you think it would be a good idea if I included a disclaimer?"

She waves her modified hair brush around like a wand and I duck just in time. "I was wondering why you've been so quiet in the evenings lately. No new howls or barks when I open my windows and, frankly, I miss them." I can't believe what I'm saying, but it's true. It comforts me when she is so vocal: I know she is right there if I need her.

She drops the brush on my leather chair, and I quickly retrieve it and place it at a safe distance from my furniture.

"You're getting your cast off today, right? We have to celebrate. If you save the remnants, we can make a fire in your fire pit and I'll do a ceremonial dance of release over it." She shrugs. "Could be fun. You can bring the wine and cheese."

"I would love to come, Vem. But I'm going to head out with Obie Lumquest soon."

Vem raises one eyebrow. "Is this some sort of May-December thing? Not that I'm against them, in general. It's just that you and Cos are still newly-weds. You might want to wait awhile before spicing things up."

"No, I would never cheat on Cos. Obie has taken over his father's job temporarily. He's going to go out into the woods with me so that I can show him where we were when the tree fell. Obie thinks that if we start from the beginning, we may come up with some new clues. His idea is that the bloody tools are related to our accident in the woods." There is no point in hiding my triumph. "I'm glad someone is finally thinking like me."

I promise you, Mrs. Hill, we're going to sort this out. I'm going to prove to both you and my dad that I can do this job.

"Oh. That's all." Vem sounds disappointed. "I'm not sure I would trust Obie. He's very green and doesn't have the skills that his father does. I heard this story the other day that, when he was a kid, he set the police station on fire. He was shooting paper airplanes into the trash can and someone lit a cigarette and threw that match in the trash can. Obie didn't tell a soul until the office had filled up with smoke. Then he just walked out and pretended like nothing had happened."

"Those things happen when we're kids." I say dismissively. "He's an adult now and a very nice young man. I think he genuinely wants to solve this."

"I bet that's why he became a police officer. He wanted to make amends for what he did as a kid. And then there was the time that he was in high school and was racing someone out on the highway. It was a six-car pileup, and they were all hospitalized for months."

"I think you should have led with that one." I sit down in the leather chair, protecting it just in case she gets another burst of energy. "I'm sure he feels bad about that, too. It still doesn't change my mind about working with him."

The doorbell rings and I rise to answer it.

"Don't worry, Lanie. I'll get it for you. You're still somewhat disabled."

"Not my legs," I grumble.

There are mumbled sounds at the door, and then I hear, "Please don't sniff my–"

His voice resembles Boysie's. Without seeing his face, I could easily mix them up.

"Come on in, Obie!" I call, hoping to distract Vem.

"I sure hear lots of good stories about your moaning classes." Obie smiles and pats his shoulders as he joins me in the living room with Vem not far behind.

"People talk about my classes?" Vem smiles and turns to me. "My reputation is growing, Lanie. The best moaner on the West coast."

I nod enthusiastically.

"Are you ready to go, Mrs. Hill?"

"I feel I should accompany you both. Lanie is still an invalid, and I can give you more details. You know she was unconscious for much of this experience."

I begin to protest and then realize it's useless. "Vem should come with us," I agree halfheartedly.

The community of Piney Falls has recently purchased a very large vehicle, requiring tires the same size as those on the city snow plow. Boysie was excited to try it out on the last drug bust. He drove cross country instead of via the highway, just so he could try his new toy. It is convenient today, however, because I am not up for a big hike in the woods yet. I've been using my convalescence as an excuse not to do much and my first actual hike will be a chore.

When we arrive at the sight of my accident, Vem bursts out of the truck and begins sniffing vigorously. "Somebody's been out here recently, Lanie. I can tell."

"Do you have some kind of bloodhound skills?" Obie asks with a chuckle.

"She does, in fact," I say proudly. "Vem has been underestimated her entire life. Who is it, Vem? Can you tell?"

She shakes her head and picks up a clod of dirt, bringing it to her nostrils. "No, it's a mixture of smells. All I can tell you is it's not an animal. It's definitely people. And look at this," she points to the ground where someone has been cutting apart the large branch that fell. We could so easily have been killed. I shiver at the thought.

November places her hands on her tiny hips and swivels them in a circle with her head following her hip motion. This act would constitute a stretch for others, but Vem is taking in the sights around her. "Anything could be a clue, Obie. A leaf, a dead bug, or an unusual mark on a tree. Lanie and me have had lots of experience in this area, so it might be wise to watch us first."

"Thank you, Ms. Bean. I'll take that all into consideration." Obie turns away from us both, but I'm almost positive he's cursing.

"I'm going to walk toward the meadow," I announce.

I leave them, relieved to remove myself from those dark memories. When the cabin is in view, I look up at the beautiful tall pine trees and notice there is a camera attached to one of them. "Obie? Vem?"

They both come running.

I point up at the tree. "Look, someone is watching us."

"I am going to have to get a ladder and come back to get that one down. Do you both want to stay here, or ride back with me?" Obie asks.

"I'm not staying here alone. That's when bad things happen," I mutter.

"I'd have stayed out here and fended off anyone if you would have let me bring the Veminator," Vem says, irritated.

"What weapon are we talking about here?" Obie pats his shoulders and bends down to assess just what the camera is trying to record.

"Don't ask," I say quickly.

"It appears they trained the camera on a trip wire." He points to a thin wire that runs between two large trees.

I look up and see a branch hanging down, as though they have sawed it half off. "I wonder if that's what happened to us? Vem, are you seeing this?"

She shades her eyes and looks up. "Like they're trying to capture an animal!"

"I'm willing to bet that if I come back with a ladder, I'll find the wire is attached to the branch, so it comes down on another unsuspecting person. This is very suspicious." Obie walks toward his vehicle. "Ladies, I'm going to get the proper tools and come back for a thorough investigation."

"Wait! There's something you both should know." I look at Vem apologetically. " I never told you this, but Cos and I found evidence someone is using my father's identity. Obie, my father died some time ago. He was on the run from my evil sister."

"I know who she is." He nodded. "My brother told me this story. We were trying to find a conversation that didn't involve our family, so he brought up yours. Kept us talking for two hours."

"Lanie Anders-Hill! How could you!" November wraps her arms around her waist, causing her pale pink jumpsuit to wrinkle. "You never keep things from me." She pushes her pink-framed glasses up her nose and sniffs. "I'm hurt."

"Vem, we've had so much going on. I didn't want to worry you. I've got the receipt back at home."

We ride down the hill in silence. Cos will be upset. He's been acting strangely lately anyway, hurrying into the bathroom every day when he gets home.

November and I hop down from the impossibly

tall vehicle and Obie leans toward the steering wheel. "I'll let you know what I find."

"Thank you, Obie!"

Vem is already on my porch, where a package has been delivered. "You weren't expecting anything, Lanie. Not till next Tuesday."

"Sometimes I wonder if we are a little too close." I comment, unlocking the door. We walk inside and Vem places the package on the counter.

"Are you sure you don't want me to go back up there with him? Make sure he doesn't fall off the ladder or something?"

"Let's give Obie some credit. I'm sure he knows how to climb up a ladder."

Vem goes into the kitchen and begins digging through drawers. "Where is it?" I just cleaned them out last week and I didn't see one."

"What are you looking for?"

"Something sharp to open this package. We could see if the Veminator can double as a package opener, if you like," she says helpfully.

"No, I have scissors under the microwave. And why were you digging in my drawers again?"

"I have to keep things fresh in my mind so that when something happens to you and Cosmo, I know right where things are. Piper will be distraught and she won't be able to concentrate. One of us has to have a clear head."

"I suppose you're right." I agree grudgingly.

Vem takes the scissor and stabs the package in serial killer fashion. Whatever is inside there should be good and dead.

"Do you want to try cutting it open now?" I ask.

She frowns at me. "There is no return address on this, and I don't want to have something pop out to surprise us. You go sit in the chair over by the picture window." She gestures to the furthest point from the kitchen. "I'm going to open it carefully and, if it explodes, I want you to take all the squirrel dung from the shelf in my garage and make a nice body mask for Cosmo. There's ruggedly handsome and then there's just a leathery old man."

"Promise," I say. I move to the living room and sit in the far chair, as instructed. Being stuck at home has given me lots of time and headspace to order things that I don't really need. Yesterday, I received a box that was full of blue and yellow scarves that I'll never wear. I'm sure it's another embarrassing purchase.

Vem opens the box slowly and closes one eye as she peers inside. "Phew!" she exclaims. "Nothing explosive."

"Well, what is it?" I ask impatiently.

"Pictures, I think. Yes, lots of pictures." She makes no move to do anything more.

"Vem, you're trying my patience. Take them out and show me."

November picks up the box and brings it to me.

There are six postcard-sized framed photos inside. She takes one out and holds it up to my face, apparently forgetting my eyes haven't suffered any damage.

"Who is this?" she asks.

I push her hand away from my face so my eyes can focus. When they do, my heart drops. "It's my father. And that's me, when I was a little girl. It was shortly before he left, I think." The first one is a black-and-white photo. He is sitting at a desk in a nice suit, his hair parted on one side. I'm standing in silhouette, my hair pulled back in a long pony tail. I'm gazing at him with admiration. "I have no memory of this picture. He was so handsome and Idolized him. He was my world before he left us."

Vem takes the picture and examines it carefully. "You're both happy. Wouldn't expect this seemingly nice guy to run out on his kid."

My eyes fill with tears. "I never get to the point where I'm past all of that. But he's gone now and I need to concentrate on my wonderful family here. You, Cos and Piper."

Vem pulls a monogrammed handkerchief from her pocket and places it over my nose. "Blow!" she commands.

I obey, trying not to think about where that piece of cloth has been today. "I'm not going to dwell on this anymore."

Vem bends down and kisses the top of my head.

"Do you want some ice cream? Or maybe a hot fudge and cheesy potato chip sundae?"

"No thanks. But I appreciate the offer." I pat her arm. "If the box hasn't been completely pulverized, could you look at the postmark and see where it was mailed from? Who would have any of his photos? My sister is in prison. I guess I do have some other relatives, but I haven't had much contact with them."

She inspects the package closely. "It didn't come from any of them." She stands up and puts her hands on her hips. "It came from right here in Piney Falls."

CHAPTER TWENTY

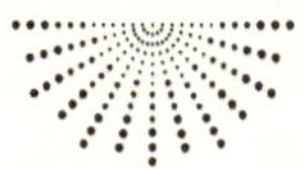

PIPER

"The school board got its first female member, the first in the state, as a matter of fact," Mrs. Williams continued her explanation of the Twisted Stitch Society sewing group.. "That wouldn't have happened if those women hadn't gotten together. They ruled the community. Some might say they ruled through fear, but I like to think it was strength." She smiled at Piper. "Some of those women were probably about your age too."

"How did they come up with the name 'The Twisted Stitch Society?'" Obie asked from across the room, where he was examining a quilt patterned with blue-and-white stars, alternating with red-striped squares.

"It was Scarlett's idea, just like everything else. Before she joined, they were just the Thursday women's sewing circle."

"Why not Thursday Stitchers? It sounds less ominous."

Mrs. Williams folded her arms across her chest. "You kids are just lovely. I wish my grandkids were as nice. They always have their noses in electronics. Can't be bothered to visit with their elders."

They sat quietly for a few minutes. The only sound was Obie's foot tapping on the concrete floor.

"I suppose it's all right to tell you." She studied Piper's face with concern. "You're not going to go spreading this to other people, are you?"

"Even after all these decades, you're still concerned?" Piper asked, incredulous.

Mrs. Williams nodded vigorously. "You don't understand how complete Scarlett's control was. Her minions terrorized children who they felt were slighting theirs. And then they moved on to adults. A man who was cheating on his wife disappeared. Never to be seen again. Each woman got to take her turn. She stood up in front of the group and announced what was holding her back in life. It could be a lack of money or her husband or anything. Whatever it was, the women of the group would meet after she left and figure out how to fix it."

Mrs. Williams laughed softly and wrapped her

hands around one knee, leaning back against the bench. "They all came up with suggestions, but the decision to proceed was Scarlett's, make no mistake. The Stitcher in question would never know how things were going to be resolved. That way, if it were a law enforcement matter, she could be questioned and not have any idea what had happened."

"That's pretty devious," Obie remarked. "I thought they had the police under their control."

"The *local* police. We never knew when they might get tired of women telling them what to do and bring in the state. Scarlett was smart that way: she covered all the angles."

"How many crimes were committed?" Piper asked, still unable to process all that she'd heard.

"Oh, I don't want to speculate."

"Did you know Elaine Lowery? They owned a farm outside of town. She was a part of the group, from what I'm told."

Mrs. Williams ran her hand up the inside of her shirt collar. "Maybe. That family moved away from the area a long time ago."

"She took her grandkids to the pool on Thursdays and went to the meetings. That's what Finn remembers, anyway."

Mrs. Williams stared across the large room, where Obie was studying the largest hanging quilt, at least nine feet wide. It comprised all the colors of the rainbow in zigzagging patterns. "It's a stunning sight to behold, isn't it?" She called out to him. "That's the last creation of the actual Twisted Stitch Society."

"What does that mean, exactly? I don't know anything about quilting. What is a twisted stitch?"

Mrs. Williams motioned for Piper to follow her. When they reached Obie, she pushed a button on the wall that lowered the quilt to eye level.

Piper examined the tiny, delicate stitches. "How long did it take for them to make this? I can't imagine sewing something of this magnitude."

"A few months. By this time, there was a real energy that came from their time together. They created beautiful quilts and solved each other's problems. At least they tried. Scarlett's sewing skills were superior to everyone's. She would go home and create three blocks and then come back the next week, and no one knew how she did it so quickly. It would have been fine had she not expected the same level of devotion from everyone."

"It sounds like a cult." Piper tapped her knee, trying to push away bad thoughts about her past. "This town already had one of those."

"More like an organized crime family. I could tell you stories about these women and their power over others. But they would only be stories. I don't know anything for a fact. Wait here for a moment, please." She disappeared into a room with the sign, "Staff Only," over the door.

"Obie, what are you thinking about all of this? What does your police training tell you?" Piper whispered.

Obie patted himself three times on the shoulders. "That this story goes much deeper."

Mrs. Williams returned with a large magnifying glass. "I know your eyes are younger than mine, but you won't fully understand unless you can examine this carefully." She pulled a section of the large quilt up to eye level and maneuvered the magnifying glass to her liking. "There. You see that? The 3-d-looking stitches along this row? That's yarn intertwined with the thread. It was a badge of honor and also a way to mark the twist in their fate."

Piper ran her finger over the raised sections of blue yarn. "That's really cool! It must be so difficult."

"This method is called couching. You stitch a yarn on top of the thread in whatever pattern you like, and in the end, it looks kind of twisted together, thus making a twisted stitch."

"The twisted stitchers!" Piper remarked. "How cool!"

"Not cool." Mrs. Williams shook her head emphatically. "Every time you see that yarn inter-twined, a woman created that row to show how her fate had been twisted by the Society. Some thought for better, others thought for the worse. Either way, Scarlett made everyone create their twisted stitch rows as a rite of passage."

Piper moved closer, trying to examine the work of art hanging high above her head. There were some rows combing brightly colored yarn with white thread and others using only dark colors. "What you're telling us is that each 'twist' could be a crime. The finger I found in my wall, whose twist was that?" She hadn't meant to let that slip out.

"Finger?" Mrs. Williams' jaw dropped. "Could be any number of–"

"Piper likes to kid," Obie interrupted. "She told me a joke yesterday about unattached fingers walking around by themselves."

"Yes, that's what I meant." Piper nodded absently. "What was Elaine Lowery's twist? Do you know?"

Mrs. Williams put her hand on her chin and smiled. "Elaine was a lovely lady. Made us jam in the summer from their mulberries and apple cider in the fall."

"What was her twist?" Piper asked again. "Did Elaine do something she later regretted?"

"Elaine and Scarlett had words more than once. Elaine didn't want to do her dirty work and by then, Scarlett was in complete control."

Piper walked to the next closest hanging quilt, trying to quell her growing frustration.

Mrs. Williams took her cue and moved to Obie's side, taking care not to come too close again. "If you look at this one," she pointed to a quilt with brown and gold squares, each exhibiting a unique pattern, "you can see the twisted stitches. They stand taller than the rest."

Piper joined them and peered closely at the clover design. The ten raised stitches were visible when she knew to look for them. "Whose twisted stitch was this one?" She looked up at the date, March 1988.

"I think that was Marge Duncan." Mrs. Williams bit her bottom lip. "I can't remember for sure what caused her twist. She moved away shortly thereafter."

"You mentioned things got dark. Do you remember what happened?" Obie continued to the next quilt, a rainbow themed creation named "Rebirth of Woman."

"Scarlett was going to do whatever it took to keep these women under her thumb. This is going to be shocking, but I'll show you what I mean." She moved to the furthest corner of the room, where a lone quilt hung in relative darkness. It was labeled, "Prints that Connect Us." The quilt was done in red and white squares with one finger print flower on each of the white squares.

"That's cute!" Piper remarked.

"Those finger prints are not paint. She had the women take a blood oath, each sharing blood until they could all dip their fingers in it and make a print. That's the point in time when I-couldn't take it anymore. It was much too gruesome."

Piper and Obie exchanged horrified glances. This could be the connection to the severed finger they were looking for.

"How did this all end? Does Scarlett still live around here?" Obie asked.

"That was Belle's doing." Mrs. Williams sighed. "Poor Belle. She tried to do the right thing."

"Belle Watkins? Are you referring to Old Ma?" Obie looked surprised.

"Who is Old Ma? I've never heard that name."

"You've seen the fluorescent yellow house, the last building before you leave town? That's where Belle-Old Ma-lives. I'm ashamed to say as a child I taunted her and threw rocks at her house, just like everyone else. She'd come out and yell something crazy and we'd all run off, excited and scared at the same time." Obie patted himself and turned around in a circle twice.

"Everyone does stupid things when they're young, Obie." Piper reminded him.

"She wasn't Old Ma then, and she wasn't considered crazy. There were windows knocked out and threatening letters sent. The whole town was living in fear. It came time for Belle's twisted stitch and she boldly told Scarlett she wanted no part of it. No one stood up to Scarlett like that."

"Why didn't she just quit? It seems like it would have been easy to just stop going to the group?" Piper asked.

"Because she told them she couldn't. Even though she wasn't about to have a crime committed on her behalf, she'd already committed several in the name of the group. She came to our home and had a late night tea session with my aunt. She told her Scarlett whispered to her in private that Belle had to follow the rules, or she'd be the next target of the women."

"That explains it. She was between a rock and a hard place." Piper started wondering if Obie had a stronger connection to all of this than just his aunt dropping him off at the pool. He was exhibiting more ticks than he had before.

"The next week, Belle's husband reported he'd been followed home from work. She knew it was only going to get worse, and it did. They harassed him mercilessly until Belle agreed to do their bidding. Soon after, her husband divorced her, took the kids and moved. She was never right in the head after that."

"Do you know what she had to do to get her twist?" Piper asked.

"Yes," Mrs. Williams replied quietly. "She was told to steal something from the jewelry store and make it look like Elaine Lowery took it."

"How did that benefit someone? It doesn't even make sense." Obie tapped his foot and patted his shoulders.

"Elaine didn't want her twist and tried to leave. That was her punishment."

"Did Mrs. Lowery—lose a finger?" Piper sputtered.

"Goodness no! This is the second time you've mentioned that!"

"Well—"

"Piper has a good imagination." Obie walked over to Piper and touched her back with one finger. "We won't take up any more of your time today, Mrs. Williams. Thank you so much for the tour."

As they walked outside, Piper could barely contain her anger. "Obie Lumquest, that was incredibly rude. I'm an intelligent woman and if I think she needs to know about my findings, I will most certainly tell her."

"I didn't mean to upset you." Obie hugged himself and paced in a circle again. "We can tell her the next time we go. While you ladies were talking, I memorized every single woman's name on the quilts. We can go talk to them and see who's missing a finger."

"I didn't see you write anything down." Piper looked at him skeptically. "How can you be sure?"

"I've got lots of quirks. One of the best is that I have a photographic memory. The names are the same on all but the most recent. Belle Watkins is missing from that one."

"Then we visit her first. Should we go now?" Piper opened up the passenger door of Obie's car.

"No, she's going to require a delicate touch. She's been harassed by every kid in town and I'm sure doesn't trust any of us. I'm going to need to think of the right approach."

The door to the historical society squeaked as it opened. Mrs. Williams appeared at the top of the steps and waved to them as they both stood.

"Wait, please!" She maneuvered sideways down the steps, one at a time. When she reached them, she was out of breath.

"I wasn't honest with you kids," she said, grasping her chest.

"It's all right." Piper patted her back reassuringly. "Take your time."

"That wasn't Marge Duncan's twist. It was… mine."

They both attempted to look surprised that she would admit to being a part of the Twisted Stitch Society. "What did she do to get her twist?"

She kicked the tiny gravel around her and looked at the ground. "She was tasked with getting someone to sleep with Butch Lowery, Elaine's husband."

"What?" Piper asked, in shock. "Who?"

"Belle Watkins."

CHAPTER TWENTY-ONE

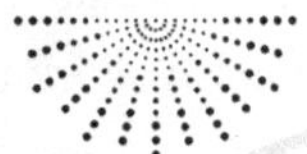

LANIE

"No offense, Mrs. Anders-Hill, but sending family pictures isn't a crime." Obie pats his shoulders. "I'm afraid you're on your own with the mystery of the family photos for now. At least until I clear up this backlog of paperwork Dad left me."

Whenever someone says, "no offense," they are preparing to offend me and Obie Lumquest has succeeded.

November pushes her rust-colored glasses up her nose and moves close to Obie, examining his appearance in a way that causes him to take a giant step back. This is the second time these two have done this dance.

"What Lanie is trying to tell you, young man, is that her father is dead. Her sister is in the pokey and there is no one, absolutely no one on planet earth who would send her these pictures. Especially from right here in Piney Falls. If you think about it, it's most likely the person who has been in her garage getting their bloodiness all over her tools." She takes another step forward and pokes him in the chest, causing him to jump high in the air like a cat.

"I don't like to be touched, Mrs. Bean. It's also not wise to put your hands on an officer of the law."

I am visualizing Vem placed in handcuffs over a misunderstanding with a young policeman trying to prove himself. "I think November is trying to tell you we might be able to solve two mysteries at once. We know your plate is full. Filling in for your father and combining these issues could lighten the load, so to speak."

He shrugs. "From my perspective, it seems like a friendly thing to send pictures, Mrs. Anders-Hill. I don't see a connection to the bloody tools, or anything else."

It is becoming painfully obvious that we aren't going to get anywhere with Obie. "I never heard what you found when you took your ladder out into the woods. Was it the same situation that caused the branch to fall on us?"

Obie cleared his throat twice. "I can't tell you

details of my investigation. It did appear suspicious. All of them were suspicious."

"All?" Vem asks. "There were more? Who is setting up their own war zone in our beautiful wilderness?"

"I didn't mean to say that." Obie pats his shoulders three times and turns in a circle. "It's an ongoing investigation, and I'll contact you when I have definitive proof."

Vem displays an, "I want to put him in a defensive hold," demeanor.

"When Dad comes back, we're going to have to have a serious chat about how to be organized," Obie continues, oblivious to the potential dangers in my living room on a random Monday. "This is not the way things are supposed to work in a police station." He shakes his head and touches his forehead four times. "I think as far as the tools go, we're dealing with some juveniles who maybe cut themselves while trying to steal your tools and that was that."

"Young man, I'll have you know Lanie has solved many mysteries. She's got more mystery solving skills in her broken bone than you do in your entire body," Vem says sternly.

"It's okay, Vem. We've taken up enough of Officer Lumquest's time." I move to the door and open it. "Thank you for coming today."

Obie's phone squawks. Instead of leaving, he

walks to the corner of my living room and puts the phone up to his ear. Vem follows.

"Mm-hmm," he says. He looks back at Vem and frowns. "Okay, I'll be there in fifteen minutes." He puts his phone in his pocket and turns around, a hint of a smile on his face.

"What is it" I ask. "Sorry, I'm snoopy by nature."

"A theft. Someone on Driftwood Drive had items stolen from their garage this morning."

The hairs on the back of my neck stand up. "More tools? It sounds like a theft ring, not a bunch of kids."

"I've got to take a statement." Obie walks toward my front door. "I'll be in touch, Mrs. Hill. For now, enjoy your family photos. Someone must really care about you."

"Well, if that doesn't just beat all!" Vem slaps her hand on my counter after we hear his car driving down the gravel road. "That kid needs to be taken over someone's knee. And I don't mean to make him giggle. He has no idea of your crime solving skills."

"Nor yours," I add. "But what if he's right? What if we're just being paranoid and it has no connection to our accident?"

"Then, in true Lanie fashion, we're going to get to the bottom of this."

I smile slyly. "What do you suggest, Vem?"

"That we go back out to the cabin. Whether they're trying to get under your skin or they're using your father's identity to create a fake persona, they're up to no good. Whoever is living in the cabin sent those pictures."

While I'm intrigued, going back to the cabin without Cosmo and Truman makes me a little nervous. "All right. I will go with you, but I have two conditions. First, that you don't get carried away. We don't know who these people are, or if they're dangerous."

"I'm offended by that, Lanie!" November brings her hand to her chest in mock horror. "I'm always even-tempered, especially when we are investigating things. "Well? What's the second thing?"

"That you put your Veminator in your back pocket. You never know when that might come in handy."

She grins and gives me two thumbs up before heading out to warm up the four-wheeler.

I look down at my frail arm. Instead of taking me out of a cast entirely, the doctor exchanged my plaster cast for one made of sturdy nylon and Velcro straps. It's going to take months before it's fully functional. I've started physical therapy and I'm no longer in a sling. It's almost worse to have it out and vulnerable than when it was safely tucked next to my body.

When she has the four-wheeler warmed up, Vem beeps the horn. She throws her leg over the seat and motions for me to do the same.

There are still signs of life in the cabin when we arrive. More trash is sitting on the porch and an old bicycle rests against an empty window box.

"You're the only one I know who would possess enough strength to ride a bicycle up here." I turn to Vem, but she has already proceeded to the cabin. "Vem!" I hiss. "November Bean, come back here! We need to do this cautiously!"

When it becomes obvious she is ignoring me, I follow her. As we reach the edge of the property, she puts her arm out in front of me.

November turns her head to the right and then to the left, sniffing the air. "You stay here, Lanie. I'm going to sniff ahead. If you see anything, just howl."

"Will do." I'm relieved to wait for her signal. She's much more physically capable of handling whatever may arise than me. I find a spot in the tall grass and sit, feeling my body relax the moment I'm settled.

Hopefully, the only visitors to my spot don't slither. I've learned stillness brings the forest to life. The more you think you're alone in the woods, the more you really aren't.

I've just closed my eyes, ready to meditate, when I hear her heavy breathing again. November is displaying her 'I'm not messing around' face. "I'm going to search in the woods-there's a strange scent that I can't place. Do you want to stay here?"

"Sure," I say, grateful for a few more minutes listening to the sounds of nature. Meditation in nature makes things clearer. What is coming through today is the conversation I had with Piper last night. She mentioned Obie Lumquest three times and I'm starting to suspect there is more to their relationship than she will admit. The sound of footsteps jolts me back to the present.

"Nothing. I thought for sure I'd at least find an animal carcass." Vem doesn't hide the disappointment in her voice.

"What about the cabin? Shouldn't we focus on that? Unless you're getting tired."

"It's barely past noon and I haven't even done my mid-afternoon moans. I won't be tired for another ten hours. But are you?"

I nod. "Yes. I'll be fine. Just help me up. I want to see for myself what's going on in the cabin. Vem gently lifts my good arm until I'm on my feet.

"What are we looking for?"

I brush off my pants as best I can. "I wish I knew. We're going to keep searching around here and something is going to pop out at us. Something that's going to blow this entire case wide open."

She shrugs and follows me. When we reach the front door, I see there is a gun propped underneath the bike. I turn to her and put my finger to my lips, hoping she'll realize we need to be quiet and not disturb whoever is in there for fear that there are more weapons inside. She nods.

"Go around to the back window," I whisper. "See

if you can find anything inside that will tell us who is living here."

Vem makes the "okay" sign with her fingers, followed by the thumbs up sign, followed by a deliberate nod before disappearing.

I press my head against the window, finding two half-empty plates of eggs on the table. There are more clothes than the last time we visited. Given the lack of clothing store options in Piney Falls, I'm curious where these came from.

Vem taps on my shoulder, smiling like the cat who ate the canary as I jump back.

"Do you recognize this, Lanie?" She hands me a bright orange cloth.

"That's Obie Lumquest's. He carries it around with him all the time and must've dropped it when he came up to inspect the trip wires. Where did you find it?"

"By the back door." She clucks her tongue. "That's not anywhere close to the sawed off branches."

"Let's not get carried away. We already know he was up here."

Vem brings the cloth to her nostrils and sniffs. "I don't know, Lanie. This is an old scent."

I'm usually a skeptic, but with Vem, I've learned she's right more times than she is wrong. "We'll take these back and just pretend like we never saw them. I'm sure Obie has a good explanation for things." Vem does not move. She continues sniffing for a moment and then lets out a loud howl. As long as I've heard these, I'm still never prepared for their randomness.

"There's more here." She scoops up some dirt and leaves and brings them to my side.

"Are we making a mud pie today? I ask. "Because if we are, we're going to need something to stir with and maybe a pot of some kind?"

"Don't be silly," Vem scoffs. "It's human. Somewhat familiar but I can't place it."

"Shhh!"

"Sorry!" she whispers. "But I also saw two mugs, two plates and two spoons sitting on the table. And something else." She bites the inside of her mouth and stares at me.

"What is it?" I ask, irritated. "We don't have time for games."

"I recognized some of the candy wrappers from your trash can. I've got something to tell you and it's not going to be easy to hear."

Even after all my years of knowing her, there is quite a lot Vem could tell me that would shock me. I brace for whatever comes next. "Okay, go ahead."

"Well, Cosmo has been doing things behind your back. I decided I wasn't going to say anything because-you know me-I'm not one to gossip or get into anyone's business."

"Everyone's business is your business, Vem,"," I retort.

"Lanie, this is going to be so hard for me to tell you."

"Please, just get this over with, these people could show up at any minute."

"Cosmo Anders-Hill has been cheating on you." She pauses, evidently expecting me to fall apart. When I don't, because I know how ridiculous this accusation is, she continues. "He's been eating behind your back, Lanie. I've caught him more than once and it isn't pretty. Last time, it was Fudge Frosties. I know you've forbidden him from partaking in the world of boxed cereal, but there it is."

"That's not–"

"It's not just the Fudge Frosties. He's been bringing home things from the bakery. I see him disappear into the woods with big boxes. Big, Lanie."

I release all the air I was holding in anticipation of something bad. "Oh. Well, as far as bad things go, there could be much worse."

"Oh, it gets worse, Lanie." Vem puts her hands on her hips. "There was one day, I was out in my yard getting ready for my midday moan when I caught him red-handed. He was walking down the hidden pathway behind my house, lumbering like an elderly Bigfoot. When he saw me, he glared at me like he was going to explode, more than usual. There he was, double fisting berry-filled donuts." She leans in close. "One in each paw, Lanie."

I want to burst out laughing because this is the very last thing I thought she would tell me today. But I don't dare. It crosses my mind that we don't currently have anything like that on the menu at the bakery.

"I will definitely address this with him. We're trying to eat healthy because I want him to stay around for a good long time. Junk food isn't allowed."

"When I caught him red-handed, he made me promise not to say anything." She leans in close to me for dramatic effect, breathing her most recent snack of sardines and peanut butter on my face. "He practically BEGGED. I agreed, knowing the poor man would sleep outside for six months if you caught him."

I have to admit; it bothers me that either of them would so willingly keep a secret from me. "He wouldn't, Vem. That's not an outside sleeping offense."

"Well, he put the Fudge Frosties in the trash can and they were still mostly uneaten." She says encouragingly. "That's what is sitting on the table inside the cabin right now. These are the people who are stealing from you. They took your trash and they've been eating it."

I glance through the window at the table, still full of breakfast dishes. Something catches my eye. "If they need a place to stay and food to eat, I'm not opposed to them taking our trash. But there is another orange cloth sitting on the table inside. If Obie has been inside, then maybe he's–"

"Get lost! I'm not messing around!" A voice yells from the woods. And then, the shooting begins.

CHAPTER TWENTY-TWO

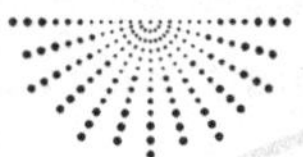

PIPER

"On the surface, I agree with what these women were trying to achieve. Making each life a little better. Maybe that is what your grandmother intended, and it just got out of hand?" Piper put the straw to her lips and sucked it slowly. She glanced at her watch, aware that she had exactly one hour before Ellie would be on her daily break. She took it at two p.m.; whether Piper was there or not.

"I can't imagine my grandmother doing something that horrible. She baked cookies for us every week. My sister and I used to lie on her bed while she told us stories of her childhood. She was the kindest, sweetest woman. She cried when we had to butcher the chickens." Finnegan Lowery took a sip of his own Triple Chocolate Marshmallow Shake Down.

"Even the sweetest people can get caught up in something they don't know how to handle. And what about your grandfather?"

You kids should know, I was tasked with getting someone to sleep with Butch Lowery, Elaine's husband.

"Maybe it isn't about the Twisted Stitch Society at all. The finger could be the result of dirty business dealings."

Finn shook his head firmly. "No. Grandma was in charge. Grandpa just did what she told him to do. They were good people, Piper." He said emphatically. "I would have known if they were anything but law-abiding citizens. It was probably those stitching women, and my grandmother agreed to keep their secrets."

He sat back against the vinyl booth. "Now that I think about it, I'm sure that's what happened. She probably didn't know how to help them, so she hid their secrets in the box in her wall, hoping no one would ever find them. Do you have any ideas about where we should go next?"

Piper put her elbow on the table and placed her head in her hands. She wasn't inviting Finn into the little investigative team of Piper and Obie. "I'm not sure. We've-I've-kind of hit a dead end. There isn't really anything else to do."

I'll go with you to visit Old Ma," Finn insisted. " She's dangerous and you shouldn't go unaccompanied. Especially if she was the person who cut off this finger."

He wasn't making this easy. Piper grimaced.

Finn scrunched up his face, as he always did when he was thinking hard. "We should scour the farmhouse for any other clues."

"It's a disaster, Finn." Her insides twisted just thinking about it. "They're trying to get everything completed on schedule and if I mess that up, my dad will never forgive me."

"Well, what ideas do you have then?" Finn snapped.

"Mr. Lowery?" A new employee appeared beside their booth with a phone in his hand. "There's a supplier on the phone. Sounds like our buns are going to be late again." He thrust the phone forward, his eyes darting back and forth between Piper and Finn. "Sorry to interrupt your conversation."

Finn took the phone and smiled at Piper. "An owner's work is never done. Sorry, I need to take this." He stood and put it to his ear. "What is it now?" Finn walked away from the table, barking angrily at the person on the other end while customers glared at him. When he made it to his office and shut the door, the energy in the room went back to its normal buzz.

"Piper Moonlight Hill?"

Piper turned around to see a welcome face. "Obie? What are you doing here?"

"I stopped by the bakery. Ellie told me you were here. She said I should remind you of her break."

"At exactly two. I know that." Piper rolled her eyes.

"I was concerned about how Finn might react when you told him. I wanted to make sure you were okay."

She was at once flattered and insulted. "You didn't think I could handle Finnegan Lowery?"

He patted himself on his shoulders and reached into his pocket. "I keep forgetting that one is missing; I used it on Tuesdays. Nothing I can do now." He looked up. "Of course you're capable of handling Finn. I wanted to be here to support you, is all. I'm an officer of the law, and we are trained to take the emotion out of every situation."

Finn returned to the table, eyeing Obie suspiciously. "I need to pause our conversation for today. For some reason, these obstacles appear when I'm the least prepared to deal with them."

Obie stuck his hand in front of Finn before he could sit down. "Obie Lumquest. I think we've met before. You came here in the summers to see your grandparents? I would see you at the pool sometimes."

Finn thought for a moment, and then a look of recognition crossed his face. "Oh! You're Boysie

Lumquest's kid. I remember you now. You were always nice to us outsiders when other kids weren't. We were just here for part of the summer and small town children don't take kindly to that."

"You could do a bomb off the high dive like nobody else." Obie chuckled. "That was a sign of stature within the swimming pool crowd. I envied you."

Finn crossed his arms over his chest and widened his stance. "What brings you here now? Haven't seen you around before."

"I left town for a few years. You might say I was trying to find myself." Obie scratched his nose three times. "Cut off contact with my family because I didn't think they understood me. I ended up in criminal justice classes and really liked them. As much as I tried to run away from the family profession, it found me. My dad and I made up, and I asked if I could come back and work for the force. Graduated from the academy three months ago and here I am."

A large, noisy group of mothers and children entered and stood at the counter, overwhelming the one employee working at the cash register. "I'm afraid I need to attend to my business. It's been nice to catch up with you, Obie. Or should I call you Officer?"

"My dad is Officer Lumquest. Until I can fill his very large shadow, I'm Obie–at least to friends. Oh, by the way, how's your sister doing? Faythe Isabelle

Lowery. She didn't dive, but she could swim faster than anyone else in that pool."

"Faythe is laboring away in a hair shop in Tellum. She seems contented. I keep asking her to come back and help me out here, but she's not interested."

Faythe and Piper spoke on the phone quite often. She was pleased to have her own identity away from her brother.

"Piper, I'll connect with you another day and we'll go on our field trip." Finn winked and touched her arm.

She smiled feebly. "Yes, soon!"

Finn walked away, and Piper and Obie avoided each other's gaze. "What about…" "Would you want to…" They both tried speaking at the same time and then stopped and laughed.

"You go first." Obie gestured toward Piper.

"I'm going to visit Old Ma tomorrow. I'll stay late to clean and Dad said he would handle Ellie's break."

"I'll be there. I'm trying to catch up on all the paperwork my dad left and I've got it organized into piles, so I can step away easily. You're a determined woman, Piper."

She held her head up proudly. "Of course I am. Now what did you want to say?"

He looked down at the French fries on the floor. "Grandma has been pressuring me for information. She said she can tell I've got a special someone in my life and she won't stop until she figures out who it is."

"Gladys!" Piper said in an exasperated manner. "I keep forgetting you're her grandson. Did you say 'special someone?' I didn't consider eating cheese together the definition of a serious relationship.."

Showing interest in her grandson would attract Gladys like angry bees to a toddler. This blissful quiet would be over. "I don't want her to know that we even speak to each other. She'll be in our business and if you want our relationship – or whatever it is - to continue, I'll have to insist you keep it from her."

"I'll need you to keep something between us as well. I haven't mentioned the reason my mom left to anyone. I'd appreciate it if we keep that quiet."

"Deal."

CHAPTER TWENTY-THREE

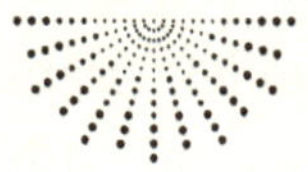

LANIE

We were lucky that the four-wheeler was close by when the shots were fired. I didn't worry about further injuring my arm. In our haste to get out of there, I flopped myself side-saddle across the four-wheeler and yelled, "Go!"

Vem hurled her Veminator before jumping on and, to my surprise, I heard someone yell, "ouch!"

Vem and I came to the same conclusion: Obie Lumquest was behind all of this. The identity of the other person was still a mystery. I don't know how I'm going to break this to my daughter.

It takes two days before the four of us can return to the cabin in the meadow. Even though I insist he tread lightly, Cosmo has brought along his machete.

Truman brought a weapon as well: his family heirloom musket from the Revolutionary War that he swears was carried by James Monroe.

Cosmo has also insisted on bringing a first aid kit and radio so that he can get help if needed. Piper has the other one down at the bakery. There is no cell service out in the meadow, so this is his assurance that I will be okay. It all seems a little silly.

"Lanie, do you need to stop again?" Cosmo asks me for the 15th or 16th time.

"I'm fine, hon. Thanks for asking though." We stopped several times after climbing the pathway at a turtle's pace. I'm grateful for the special care.

"We're here," Truman announces. "We didn't really come up with a plan, though. Am I going to take my weapon and go around back? So they can't escape?"

"This isn't about capturing anyone, Truman," I remind him. "We're going to go to the front door like civilized people and knock. If nothing happens from there, we'll figure out the next step."

"Are you sure about this, Lanie? These people shot at you last time you were here. I'm still not comfortable with this whole set up. Truman and I could have come by ourselves."

Vem huffs. "Cosmo Hill, are you suggesting that I am not woman enough to take on any kind of criminal? I got us out of here in one piece last time, didn't

I? Through a hail of bullets, too. I could put you on your back right now if I wanted."

It wasn't exactly a hail of bullets. We heard exactly three shots and someone yelling. We got on the four-wheeler and left immediately. "We're going to be fine. We're all capable of taking care of ourselves."

Cosmo runs his hand through his hair. "I'm sure you could put me on my back right now. That's not the issue. I just wanted to make sure that nobody got hurt. And you do tend to rattle off at the mouth at the most inopportune times."

"How dare you…"

"Shh!" I warn as we approach the cabin. "I can see people walking around inside. We're all going to approach quietly and calmly and knock on the door. Got it?" I look at the three faces, each with a different idea of the heroic measures they might take. They all nod solemnly.

The smell of bacon frying and coffee percolating drift to my nostrils as I step onto the porch. It smells just like a package I threw out yesterday because I suspected it was past its date.

I knock on the door, trying to exhibit a calm I don't feel, but I want our group to assume. There is loud arguing inside, a man and a woman. Finally, the door opens a crack. A woman with long stringy brown hair and a rather pretty face peeks through.

"What?" she snaps, not bothering to open the door any further.

I clear my throat. "We're your neighbors from down the trail. I'm Lanie Anders-Hill and that's my husband, Cosmo, along with our friends, November Bean and Truman Coolidge. We just wanted to check on you and see if you needed anything. We brought you some groceries and a few blankets." I motion to Truman and Cos, who both have backpacks full of items. They hand them forward and Vem sets them down in front of the door.

The door opens wider, and the woman slides the backpacks inside. Her bare legs are visible, tan and muscular. She stares at me as if she expects more.

"Is that it?" she asks with no emotion.

"I–"

Vem steps forward. "What my good friend Lanie is trying to say is we are wondering what happened here. Why did you need tools and why would you be using Lanie's dead father to get to us? It's all very upsetting."

For once, I am grateful for her awkward forthrightness.

"We're just passing through. Will be gone in a month or so." The woman looks over her shoulder at something in the room. "if it's in your trash can, it's fair game, ain't it?"

"I've got all sorts of day-olds from the bakery that I

can bring to you. You don't have to eat out of the trash. There's lots of folks in this town willing to help you," Cosmo offers. He puts his hands in his pockets and rocks back and forth, a sure sign that he's stressed.

My insides warm thinking about his big heart. "I think you'll find this community is very open. You just tell us what you need." I say kindly.

"There's no need to shoot at us," Vem adds.

I frown at her and mouth, "not now!"

The woman's hard glare travels from one of us to the next. She could be my age. Now that I have a moment to observe, I can see her face bears the signs of a hard life. She has deep set wrinkles and several age spots. Her nose is red and bulbous and her long, stringy hair has three stages of color - the bottom two from a bottle while the hairs closest to her scalp are grey. Her face is hardened and worn, but it is pretty.

A man with his back turned to the door shuffles around in the background but makes no attempt to introduce himself. "We don't want to bother anybody, and we sure don't want to have contact with people in this town. Like I says, we'll be moving on soon enough. We appreciate your letting us eat what we can. And the blankets."

She slams the door in our faces. We look at each other, puzzled.

"You could go in with your muzzleloader," Vem

suggests to Truman. "It might not scare them, but at least they'll know we mean business."

"What about just knocking again and saying we're not leaving until we get answers?" Cosmo asks. "That's why we came all the way up here. I want to know my wife can hike safely, without worrying about being shot."

"And I want to know why they have been stealing tools and why it appears they're trying to steal the identity of a dead man-my father," I say in agreement. "There's too many unanswered questions to leave now."

"Truman and I can look around back. We might come across something. You'll stay here and call if you get into trouble?"

Vem opens her mouth to respond, and Cosmo puts his hand in the air. "I know, I know. You're perfectly capable of taking care of yourselves. But just in case."

"Do you know that they were the ones that stole all the tools though, Lanie? We still have our doubts about Obie," Vem reminds me.

"What about Obie?" Cos stops, causing Truman to run into the back of him.

"Always warn your troops before you halt, Mr. Hill," Truman complains, rubbing his forehead.

"Sorry, buddy."

"I didn't have a chance to tell you but Vem has concerns that Obie had something to do with the tree coming down on us." I look at my friend apologetically. It's easier to blame it on her than it is to admit I kept something from him.

"The scrawny kid who pats his shoulders?" Cos asks in disbelief.

"We—or rather, I—" Vem gives me a sideways glance, "I think that he is trying to impress his father and set up an investigation he could solve."

"I don't think so. He wouldn't hurt a fly. Those types aren't actual physical labor types. You 'd have to prove to me he could actually swing an ax. Don't see it."

"We're still investigating, like I said. Plus, everybody has our little secrets, right, Mr. Fudge Frosties?"

He looks at Vem like a hurt puppy. "You told her? You promised you wouldn't."

Vem shrugs. "You know how she is. She's like a bloodhound when she smells deceit. Aren't you, Lanie?"

"Really? Throwing me under the bus, Vem?"

The door opens again. To my surprise, the woman has pulled her long hair into a ponytail and may have splashed some water on her face. "You can come in if you want. We don't have nothing to hide."

"If you're sure," I say, as all four of us move quickly through the door before she can change her mind. "We had a few questions we wanted to ask you."

The cabin is even messier than it was the other day. There are clothes strewn everywhere and trash, my trash, is all over the place. I'm shocked that they wouldn't at least pick up enough to walk around.

"You don't have to eat that bacon. I know it's probably bad and we've got more for you in the sack." I say, at once, and then feel bad for judging them for what they are eating. It's hard to imagine Obie Lumquest living like this, much less eating spoiled bacon when he could be with any number of relatives.

"Tastes good enough to us."

"What brings you out in these parts? If I can ask that question." Truman asks.

She smiles broadly. Too broadly. "Oh, just traveling around. We're nomads, tryna see the sights."

"Have you been up and down the coast?" I don't believe what she's saying, but I'm trying to keep the conversation going. "There are so many beautiful places. Just recently we visited the town of Charming, Oregon to celebrate our six-month anniversary." I smile at my husband and he returns my smile and blows me a kiss. "It's another lovely coastal town. They have the cutest little shops on their main street."

"No, we've had other… issues. Maybe we'll get that on the way back." She takes the bacon from the pan and puts it on a plate. There are also some slices of bread in another frying pan. She plops two fried eggs and the bacon on top of them.

"Can I get you something to drink?" she asks.

"We're fine, thanks. We just really wanted to check on you and now that we can see you're doing all right, we can come back and bring you more supplies another time," I say, hoping someone else will jump in to this conversation and help me out.

"When you say, 'going back,' where are you going, exactly?" Truman asks.

"Idaho. My friend and I had some business here on the coast, but we're just about done."

While he is speaking, I take a quick inventory of the room. There are lots of clothes lying around, but one thing catches my eye. There are women's clothes with the tags still on them, in two different sizes. "Is it just you and your partner?"

"You should stick around for a few minutes more," she insists, ignoring my question.

"Why? Cos asks suspiciously. "Is your partner someone we'd know?"

"Could be," she replies. She looks out the window and Vem and I follow suit. A thin man wearing a heavy coat and a hat low on his head scurries into the thick underbrush.

"Your–partner–appears to be leaving us. Was it something we said?"

She clicks her tongue and puts her hands on her

hips. "Thought I convinced him to stay. He's not particularly social."

"All the more reason for us to leave then," I say, walking toward the door. To my surprise, the rest of my group doesn't move.

"Didn't catch your name? My wife mentioned, but I'm Cosmo Hill." Cosmo offers a handshake to this stranger.

She blinks rapidly and pauses momentarily before putting her worn hand in his. "I'm Muriel Frost. My partner's been through some real rough patches. He don't want to socialize if he don't have to. When we met, he made me promise I'd never force him to speak to another livin' soul. I've kept my promise." She places a stray piece of hair behind her ear. "But I'm open to any kind of help you'd want to give."

Vem pushes her way in front of Cosmo. "November Bean. It sounds like your partner would benefit from my moaning studio. A good moan releases all the toxins, both mental and physical. If that doesn't work for him, we can slather him in fish guts and roll him down the hill. It works wonders for soul purification."

Muriel cocks her head to the side. "You're funny. I like that."

November furrows her brow, clearly puzzled by the comment.

Truman clears his throat. "I'll wait for you folks outside."

"Vem and I can return later in the week with groceries. Just give me a list of the things you like to eat, and we'll come back."

"You sure you can carry groceries up here?" Muriel motions to my arm. "My first husband and me lived in a camper, and we was always hurting ourselves. It's just easier to stay home. You don't have to come back if you don't want."

Muriel walks over to her purse, which is hanging on the back of a chair Cos carved our names into, and pulls out a pen. She grabs my hand and pulls it up close to her face while she writes on my palm. "This'll do. Nice of you, Mrs. Hill." Muriel slouches forward. "You should probably go now. My partner'll be angry if you're here when he comes back."

We step outside and I make eye contact with her briefly. Her eyes tell me she is hiding something. "You can call me Lanie."

She nods and steps back inside, leaving the four of us alone.

"We didn't ask her anything about the pictures!" Vem protests. "Or the fact that someone shot at us like a stag during hunting season."

"She's scared of something. Probably her partner, or Obie Lumquest. We'll need to coax her out of her shell."

Cosmo turns to Truman. "You were uncharacter-istically quiet. Cat got your tongue?"

"There is something I didn't like about this whole setup." He rests his hands in the gaps on either side of his overalls. "Her partner running off like he heard the first shot in the Battle of Bunker Hill."

"He was shy. Some people weren't born with the gift of conversation like the four of us," Cosmo replies.

Truman reaches into his pocket and pulls out a receipt. "Took the liberty of removing this."

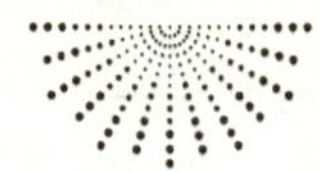

CHAPTER TWENTY-FOUR

PIPER

"Piper Moonlight Hill? You're late. It's fifteen minutes past." Obie crossed his arms and tapped himself on either shoulder.

"You said two-o'clock. I'm never late." Piper sniffed. "And I wish you would stop addressing me so formally. 'Piper' is just fine."

Obie's face was ashen. "What?" He looked down at his watch. "According to Greenwich Mean Time, which is how I set my watch, you should have arrived fifteen minutes and thirty seconds ago."

"I don't know why you'd assume it's me who's wrong," Piper retorted. She looked at her phone, which displayed an "updating" symbol. When it finished, her clock matched Obie's. "Okay, I'll give you this one," she said sheepishly.

She got into the passenger side of his two-door green sedan and waited. Obie stood outside, patting himself on the shoulders and walking in the circle twice before sitting down beside her.

"Do you have to do that before you go out on a call?"

"Yes, unfortunately. If I don't and something goes wrong, I'll know it's because I didn't complete my ritual." He started the engine and turned to look at her. "Now you know why I had to come back and work here instead of working with another department. Not everyone finds my ticks charming."

She folded her hands in her lap. "That's awful. I mean, it's not awful you have to do these things, but the fact that your co-workers would more than likely make fun of you is just… well, it's just stupid. We're all different in some way. We need to support each other."

"Thanks. Not everyone is as understanding as you, unfortunately. I've had to fight to be heard my entire life. People want to write me off as a crazy person. I'm not crazy." He smiled at her. "Delightfully odd, but not crazy."

"Of course you aren't!"

"We haven't talked about our night under the stars. I had a good time with you. To me, it was a date. As 'datey' as I get. Did you feel that way too?" Obie kept his eyes focused on the street.

"I did! It was the most romantic thing I've ever had!" done!" Piper replied enthusiastically. She giggled and impulsively covered her mouth. "Sorry. I laugh when I get excited. See? We all have our quirks."

"It's hard for me to believe that you're not more experienced than me, and–"

"Let's not talk about me anymore." There were some days Piper fought old memories she didn't want to relive. Today was one of those. "It makes me uncomfortable. Let's talk about Old Ma."

Piper relaxed and took a drink from the soda she'd brought.

Obie glared. "I usually don't allow drinks in my car. If that would spill, it would be very difficult to clean up."

She put two fingers in the air. "I promise you, Obie Lumquest, that if I spill a single drop, I'll take tomorrow off from work and detail your entire car."

He nodded slightly.

"Don't believe me?" She leaned in close to him. "Pinky swear."

"I'm not going to–"

"Pinky swear with me, Obie Lumquest, or I'll purposely spill right now!" She stuck her pinky close to his face, causing him to lean his head against the headrest.

Reluctantly, Obie stuck his pinkie up to hers and they interlocked.

"Now you have assurance that I will take care of it. That's my version of a contract." Piper smiled with satisfaction and took a long drink. "Back to Old Ma. What do you know about her?"

"Everyone at the station told me about her on my first day. She walks around town, carrying a suitcase until dark. If anyone approaches her, she yells at them. Don't think she's ever caused harm, but she sure doesn't want conversation." Obie turned on his blinker well in advance of the inter-section. "Then she goes back to her yellow house and locks the doors. No one has actually been inside, but we all know that someday, she's going to have an emergency and that place will be a nightmare."

"The poor woman. Something terrible must've happened in the Twisted Stitch Society to turn her into this kind of hermit."

"Or maybe she was just born this way." Obie turned off the car. "That's it. Old Ma's Castle."

Piper glanced out the window. A bright yellow home with aqua trim around the foiled-over windows sat alone at the end of the street. There were hundreds of tiny windmills in the bare-dirt yard, each brightly colored. There were also old dolls and rust-covered trucks sitting near the porch, as if the kids who owned them forgot they were there. Each component seemed to contradict the last.

"I have law enforcement training to deal with people like her. Is it okay if I take the lead?"

At a loss for words, Piper nodded. They walked up the steps and rang the doorbell. Eventually, the aqua-colored door opened. "What?" a sharp voice asked from the other side.

"Mrs. Watkins? It's Officer Lumquest, here with a friend. We'd like to ask you a few questions."

"I didn't steal that watermelon. I paid for it. That girl just forgot."

Obie patted his shoulders. "We're not here about a watermelon, Mrs. Watkins. We'd like to speak with you about local history. We'd like to hear what you know about The Twisted Stitch Society."

Piper poked his arm and gave him the thumbs up.

The door opened slightly further and the scent of ammonia, from too many cats and not enough litter boxes, assaulted their nostrils. "What kind of questions?" An elderly woman with thick grey hair held back by two pink barrettes appeared. Her face was weather beaten from too many hours in the sun and her eyebrows were grown out so long they curled at the ends.

Piper gulped. She now understood why this woman sparked the stories she did. "I… um… Piper Moonlight Hill. I manage the bakery. If you'd like a free scone, the next time you're downtown, just let me know."

The door opened another inch. Now visible was a living room full of boxes and a dark blue couch. "Do you want to come in?" Belle Watkins asked. "I don't have company often, so I don't bother to clean up. If it's too much for you…"

"No, we would love to come in," Piper answered, without asking Obie first. They walked through the door, and she glanced at Obie for confirmation that he was going to be all right. He nodded.

Her eyes watered as she moved through the dimly lit living room. In contrast to the startlingly bright outer shell, inside, the walls were painted a dark green. By its appearance, the house was frozen in time, sometime in the late 1980s. Two end tables, made of some type of stone with glass tops, sat on either side of the sofa. On top of each were copies of Every Day Woman magazine, April and May 1989.

"I recognize these. In one of the houses we lived in when I was a kid, they filled it with retro furniture. My parents told us if we ever touched the glass, we'd be banished to our bedrooms." She sniffed. "Not much of a threat. We spent all of our time there, anyway."

"My husband bought those for our twentieth anniversary. Last nice thing he ever did." Belle put her hands on her hips. "Can I get you something to drink? Got some sun tea I made yesterday."

Piper thought carefully. If she said no, it would seem like they were trying to insult her. "I'll take a glass," she said with little enthusiasm.

"I'm full from lunch," Obie quickly replied.

Piper frowned and shook her head.

"One thing I'll tell you kids, those ladies were all good people in the beginning." Belle pulled a jar of cloudy tea from the refrigerator and poured a glass for Piper and one for herself. She dug in the freezer, producing ice that looked as though it had passed its prime years ago, and plopped two cubes in the olive-green glass before handing it to Piper.

Piper rarely got sick, often bragging that she had lived everywhere and developed an immunity to just about every virus. Today, that theory would be tested. She put the glass to her lips and swallowed a tiny bit. "Delicious." Afterward, she noticed several cat hairs on the glass.

Obie walked carefully around the small living room, trying not to trip on the cat toys and boxes labeled, "As seen on T.V.."

"I see you've got some nice quilting projects on the wall. Piper and I spent the afternoon at the museum, leaning about different stitches. You do beautiful work."

He leaned forward, examining the stitching on a lavender and black quilt square. "It takes a real talent, I'd imagine."

Belle pulled a white sweater off the back of a

kitchen chair and threw it around her shoulders. The thick shoulder pads bulged unnaturally around her neck. "More just the ability to follow directions. That's why those women were so easily duped. They were good at doing what they were told."

"I'd like to know more about that, Belle." Piper's eyes were finally adjusting to the pungent smell of the room and quit watering. "Start from the beginning. Why did you join the quilting group?"

Belle pulled a red vinyl chair out from the kitchen table and sat down, causing a loud squeaking sound. She adjusted her long skirt, which, Piper noticed, was embroidered all along the bottom with cats and their corresponding names. From her calculation, there were nine.

"I was bored and lonely like most of the women. My husband worked long hours at the cannery. We had the largest cannery on the coast then. Through the years we've had several and in the eighties, we had a boom again. Everybody who was anybody worked at the cannery. My George didn't like it so much, but the pay was good. I sat home alone all the time, waiting for him. Our kids were old enough to take care of themselves and I had nothing else to fill my days."

"What do you think drew the other women?" Piper placed her glass on the counter, hoping Belle wouldn't notice. Her hand stuck for a minute and she tried to pull it up discreetly. When she looked up, she noticed six almond-shaped eyes observing her from atop the kitchen cupboards.

"Same as me. Just because you had kids running around doesn't mean you weren't lonely. Talking to children and talking to adults is completely different. It started out with ladies bringing their clothes to patch. Later on, that fell out of fashion, so we started making quilts. We'd make a square a week and before long, we'd have a nice quilt ready to donate to the hospital. Did that for about eighteen months and everyone enjoyed the meetings. Everyone brought a covered dish, and we made an afternoon of it." Belle's expression was serene, as if she was caught up in another time.

"That sounds nice." Piper examined the quilt closest to her on the wall. The stitching was tiny and perfect. It rivaled some of the pieces she's seen in the museum. Each little piece was intricately placed in a puzzle of triangles.

"You all got along until Scarlett came, right? Obie asked.

"Who told you about Scarlett?" Belle's face clouded. "Most folks keep that name off their lips."

"Mrs. Williams at the museum. She said she only participated for a short time because there were lots of shady things going on. Number one being that you refused to go along with their activities and were kicked out."

"Oh, that would make sense then. Did she say she quit? Don't recall her leaving before I did."

Obie and Piper exchanged knowing glances.

"I do remember that she was troubled by everything that happened. Not enough to leave, mind you, or even stick up for me. But privately she told me she didn't like the way things were going, and she wanted to quit herself. She just didn't have the courage."

"Let's go back to when Scarlett first joined. How did she interact with the others?"

"She was a fancy pants woman from the big city. From day one, she showed up with her hair all sprayed out wide and wearing more makeup than we all owned combined." Belle sniffed. "It was a time for the rest of us to let our hair down and relax. We should have seen that as a warning. She had ideas for us to make these elaborate quilts to sell. No one was really comfortable with that, so then she came back with a new idea. How about we start making quilts that mean something? Not just things that look pretty, but have hidden meaning underneath. Well, the girls were all excited about that one. The television show, Conspiracy Hill, was big at that time and they thought of themselves as being a part of a big secret."

"It sounds like it started out innocently," Piper remarked.

"No, she came to town with a plan. She sold it to

us as a way to give every woman a voice. It sounded nice. So many of us didn't have a direction in our lives." Belle stared at the ceiling as though she were trying to recall her younger self.

Obie examined the quilt on the wall that was above Belle's head. "This one is amazing, Belle. How many hours did this take you?"

"I did that in two weeks," Belle announced. "Once I sit down and start something, I can't think of anything else, day or night."

"I can appreciate that," Obie replied. "I have some strange quirks that cause me to focus on one particular thing for too long. It can be a good thing and it can also be very bad."

Belle leaned forward and examined Obie's face. "You look so similar to your father," she remarked. "He was a young man when this was all going on. I don't imagine he's got much to say about it."

Obie blushed and took a step back. "Usually folks say I favor the Petrie side. It's my brothers who take after dad. But I'm going to have a long talk with him. He needs to explain some things to me, but I'd rather right now we talk about your experiences with the Twisted Stitch Society."

It surprised Piper that Belle knew who Obie was and what was going on in the community. The way everyone gossiped about her, you'd think she hadn't socialized in years and had no grasp on reality. "We know that every woman was offered her freedom. In exchange, you had to do something for Scarlett. It's not your fault, you were her captive."

Belle tapped a gnarled knuckle on the table. "I was sucked in, that's true. But I had a choice. I wanted power no matter what the cost. I ended up losing everything."

"What was your–"

"My stitch? You want me to confess in front of the junior policeman, here?" Belle turned to a black and white cat who was sitting next to the patio door, licking his paw. She picked him up and pet him roughly. "George Junior, did you hear that? These two kids came today thinking they'd get me to confess to my crimes. They want you out on the street, starving. Isn't that something?"

Obie patted his shoulders three times. "No, Miss Watkins. I'm not here in an official capacity. Piper recently discovered some information and we're trying to track down the truth. Nobody is getting arrested. We've all got dark secrets."

Belle shook her head and stared at Piper. "I'm not going to tell you anything. This cost me my family. Scarlett made sure of that, and now you're here on her behalf. Don't lie to me." Her calm demeanor suddenly changed. "You should go now. Before I call my army."

"What army?" Piper was alarmed. Obie looked at her and shook his head forcefully.

"We want to get away from Scarlett's people. Can

you tell us how you got away?" His voice was calm and steady, like he was talking about the weather.

Belle squinted and held tightly to her cat as he struggled to get away. "She sent my husband letters from my supposed lover. He thought they were real. She forced me to send my children to her as cheap labor. They resented me after that. Scarlett ruined me. She didn't miss one single thing."

"We should go." Piper looked anxiously at Obie.

"Yes, I suppose you should go. I thought it might be nice to have company, but as usual, I was wrong. Stupid Old Ma." Tears formed in the corners of Belle's eyes. "You two g'wan now."

"I want to see you again, Belle. Could I come back? I'll bring cat food with me, along with anything else you need. Would that be alright?" Piper spoke with sincerity. She hated that she'd never known about Belle before now and wanted to help.

Belle pulled a tissue from the front of her sweater.

"You can." She blew her nose and then returned the tissue to her bra. "Just let me know ahead of time, so my army knows to stand down."

Piper and Obie moved toward the door before Piper

stopped abruptly. "Can I ask you one thing?"
Obie patted his shoulders.
"Not telling you about my stitch," Belle repeated.
"Not that. I'm wondering what happened to Scar-

lett. Mrs. Williams didn't mention it. Since there's no trace of her today, she had to leave, right?"

Belle refused to look at Obie and Piper. "In a manner of speaking, yes."

"What exactly does that mean?" Obie asked.

"The women were divided right down the middle. Half of them didn't want to continue down the path of a criminal and the other half were mesmerized by Scarlett. The seams of the club tugged from both sides until there was a big split."

"The group split in two?" Piper asked. "It's strange that Mrs. Williams never mentioned that."

"The group *would* have split in two," Belle corrected her. "If things would have continued. I watched from the sideline and I knew it wasn't going to end well. I told Elaine Lowery. She was the only one who risked expulsion to come visit me, at least for a time."

"Now you've got me curious, Belle." Piper persisted. "What happened to end the group?"

Belle cleared her throat. "Scarlett was murdered."

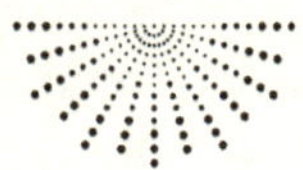

LANIE

"What is it, Truman?" Cosmo asks, gently touching his friend's back as he glances at the paper in his hand. "We should move away from her direct view. Don't want her to think we're up to something." As a group, we begin walking back to the trailhead.

"I watched out the window as her partner ran off. He was pulling his shirt on over his head. Left his coat on the back of the chair too. A feller who feels shy tells his wife, 'won't be sticking around for company,' puts on his jacket and leaves. He doesn't run like a redcoat caught in the woods."

I stop, causing a chain-reaction pile-up with

Vem, hitting Cosmo with a thud at the end of the line.

"Hey! Watch it, Bean! I'm not as spry on my feet as I used to be!" he complains.

"Sorry, guys. I was pondering what Truman said. He's right, you know. If you want to avoid conversation, you do it in a methodical manner. If you want to make sure they never see your face, you run like a scared rabbit out the back door."

"Should we ask Obie if there are any outstanding warrants in town? Or do you still think he's part of this big plot to do us in?" The corners of Cosmo's mouth turn up slightly.

"It's a legitimate concern, Cos. He has several unaccounted-for years and he may have a connection to Muriel's partner. The man we saw running into the woods fit Obie's build."

Vem puts her hands on her hips. "It all makes sense. He came back to town with an agenda–to regain his father's respect. I can't explain how he hooked up with Muriel though. We need a name or something."

Truman pulls the crumpled receipt from his pocket for the second time. "As luck would have it, she got gas two days ago with a credit card."

Vem grabs the receipt from Truman's hand and studies it. "The Lumpy Pump out on the highway! They have cameras at every pump!" She jumps up and down excitedly, like a child at Christmas. "Can we go today?"

"Of course. You can ride along with me to physical therapy and we'll go from there."

"Now just a gosh darned minute, ladies. This was my find!" Truman protests.

"We were going to finish the trim in the kitchen of the old farmhouse, remember?"

I know Cosmo is distracting him for my benefit. I grab his hand and he squeezes mine in acknowledgement.

"Duty before pleasure. We'll get it done, friend." Truman motions in mock salute. "Troops, let's head out!"

We make it back down the hill in record time, with little bickering between Cosmo and November.

"Do you want some lavender-infused lemonade? Cosmo initially turned up his nose, but now I think secretly he likes it."

"Not now, I have to change jumpsuits for the investigation!" Vem bounces off to her home without waiting for a response.

"Is she being paid to promote those things?" Cosmo snickers.

Truman, who wandered off when he was close enough to civilization to get phone service, returns. "Think I need to wait on the trim until tomorrow." He wipes his brow with the back of his hand. "Didn't want to alarm you, but Grover's been under the weather." Grover is Truman's large, black, slobbery dog who loves Cos but doesn't care for me.

"At first, I thought it was the leftover William Harrison squirrel soup, but it didn't bother me t'all. He's been lying around for two days now. Marveline looked in on him just now and he's a little peaked."

Marveline owns the Sassy Lasses Vineyard next door to Truman. She is a refined woman who, no doubt, finds urpy dogs distasteful. "Let us know if there's anything we can do, Truman."

"Do you want me to go with you, buddy? I hate to think of you there all alone if something were to happen to him." Cosmo's voice breaks as he speaks.

Truman shrugs. "It wouldn't hurt. If you're not too busy."

There are at least fifteen things on the list I made for Cosmo. After opening a second location of the bakery and my injury, there are many tasks left undone. He promised if I made him a list, he would work on them diligently until they were all accomplished. I try to convey with my eyes that the list is waiting for him.

Cosmo glances at me. "You're okay with it, right, babe?" He doesn't wait for my response. "Let me change my clothes and I'll head there with you. Should we ride together, or–"

"No!" I snap. "I don't have time to drive thirty miles and pick you up later. You can follow Truman in your own car."

Truman is taken aback. "Didn't mean to upset you, ma'am. Your husband is a concerned man who just wants to help out a friend."

"I know, Truman." My tone softens. He is a spectacular human and sometimes I forget to be grateful for his friendship. "Vem and I have many things happening today, and I meant I wouldn't have time to drive an hour. That's all I'm thinking. If you don't mind, I'm going to get changed as well for my appointment. Cos cooked steaks on the grill last night and we should have those bones in the trash, that is, if our new friends didn't find them appealing."

"Well, isn't that nice of you? No, I won't be needing those for now. You go on and get yourself changed. I'll wait here for Cosmo."

Once Cosmo and Truman leave, Vem and I head to the physical therapist. She has become more of a friend than a doctor. I tell her briefly about Muriel and she wants to contribute. "I have a surplus of canned goods in my garage, just waiting for the right donation. My husband and I sometimes sit in the garage together for a moment of peace away from the kids. We stare at those cans just about every evening."

I sigh. "I wish we had time to stare at cans."

She looks at me with concern. "Are you two having problems already? It seems like you should still be on your honeymoon." She pushes my shoulder gently and pulls my arm.

"No, we aren't having any kind of problems. We're just in life too deep and we don't have a chance to sit back and enjoy it anymore. And with our new bakery open up, it will get worse before it gets better. That's what's troubling me, I guess."

Now that I've said it out loud, I realize it really IS upsetting me. I need to find a way to tell Cosmo without hurting his feelings. All of the stress from opening a second location must be weighing heavily on him or he wouldn't be eating junk food in secret. I don't want to make that worse.

She helps me off the table. "Your arm is still weak, but that's to be expected. Do the exercises I gave you twice a day and I'll see you next week. If you want, you can stop by over the weekend and pick up the canned goods. I bought them for a school chili feed last winter and then the entire family got the stomach flu and I didn't use them."

"Thank you, Doctor."

"And Lanie? Family first. If you keep them your priority, the other things will fall into place."

I smile and express my gratitude.

Vem is waiting patiently in the waiting area, moaning softly to herself. She often does a "merciful moan" when she's in a crowd, so she doesn't disrupt them. Soft yet effective.

"Was that causing you stress?" I ask, pulling my jacket on.

"Yes, I'm not a fan of doctor's offices. They make me think of rubbing alcohol and that makes me think of finding toads in the woods when I was in the cult, and that makes me think of eating only white foods on Tuesday, and that makes me think of–"

"You said you know the owner of the Lumpy Pump?"

We walk to her car, where she pauses a moment to stare at her tangerine jumpsuit reflection. "I'm getting old, Lanie."

"What? You are the least elderly person I know. There's nothing that can stop November Bean. You're going to outlive us all."

She opens the car door for me and I sit inside. She pauses beside me, resting her arm on the top of the door. "When Cosmo and I did the bump out in the woods today, I felt a sharp pain in my back. I think I might be breaking down."

I suppress a giggle. "That's totally normal. We all have aches and pains. Just last night, Cosmo wanted me to rub his feet because they ached. It's a part of adulthood you've been able to avoid until now."

"No, I'm certain I've missed a vital component to my routine, and now I'm paying the price. I'm going to have to totally revamp my routine if I want to live another five years."

When she gets in one of these funks, there's no talking her out of them. "Let's finish what we're doing and then you can construct a new you. Is that fair?"

She nods and shuts the door, getting in the driver's side and starting the engine. "Too much baking soda," she mutters.

When we arrive at the Lumpy Pump, it is empty.

"Victor?" Vem calls.

We walk down the aisles of the convenience store and November points to an empty bag of cookies. We follow the cookie crumb trail until we see another empty bag. Around a last corner, a middle-aged man with a receding hairline is sitting on the floor. His uniform shirt with the logo for The Lumpy Pump, smeared in chocolate, is sitting beside him on the floor.

"Victor, we discussed this at your last moaning session. You said you would give up the junk and try to eat healthy."

He looks at her plaintively. "I've tried, Moan Master November. My wife refuses to change her ways. She brought home a big bag of nachos yesterday and ate them right in front of me. When I got to work today, after eating all that oatmeal and chicken breast and things that aren't natural, I couldn't help myself. One of our usual customers said he'd never come back and my boss yelled at me. I couldn't take it anymore."

Several crumbs fall from his mouth. November reaches into her large purse and pulls out a monogrammed handkerchief. She wipes his face with the letter N and then gently wipes off the front of his shirt with the B.

"We'll work on this in the next moan session. When you feel like you need to eat, just do your power moan. Once you're in control of everything, you won't need food to soothe you. And that experience will become your superpower."

He gazes up at us like he's trying to decide whether he can or will stand. November wiggles her hands insistently, refusing to move away. Eventually, he takes her hand and rises up with her help, brushing off the front of him. I notice as she's pulling him up, she winces a little.

"Victor, I want you to meet my best friend, Lanie. She and I are here on very important business. Lanie, show Victor your receipt," Vem instructs.

I pull the pump receipt from my purse and show it to him. "Do you remember this Muriel Frost coming in? Or do you have the video that we could see?"

He has a confused expression on his face, but I'm starting to think that is his normal demeanor. "Yes, we do keep that in the back. There is a timestamp on there and the pump number so it's easy to check." He walks toward a door marked, "employees only."

"You can't tell anyone that I let you in here. This

is supposed to be private but my boss made fun of me today for the 100th time, so I'm not feeling particularly loyal to him." He takes a set of keys out of his pocket and tries several until he finds the correct one for the lock. We follow him inside, where there are four cameras, one for each pump.

Victor fiddles with the equipment for a moment. "This is pump number two on the day in question. Is that your gal?" he points to the video and I can see a woman with long dark hair, wearing tight jeans and a bright red T-shirt. I can't be positive, but I do believe this is Muriel. I lean forward, trying to ascertain who is sitting in the passenger seat.

"Vem, do you think that's Obie?" I point to the screen.

She leans in close as well. "That's a woman. We've all clearly seen a man. One thing's for sure, whoever is in the front seat, doesn't want to be seen."

She replaces the pump after she gets gas and knocks on the window. The person leans forward and shakes their head. She looks as though she's arguing with them before reluctantly getting back in the car.

"I don't like this, Vem. She's in trouble. Maybe the passenger is someone her partner forced her to meet? We need to figure out how to help her without making her partner angrier in the process."

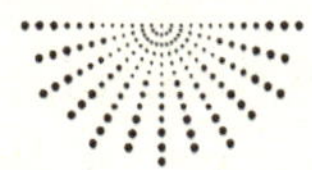

PIPER

Piper gulped. "Are you sure? I haven't seen any record of Scarlett's death."

"And you wouldn't. It was all swept under the rug. Things worked differently back then." Belle's demeanor returned to one of reason after earlier talk of her "army."

"Mrs. Watkins, you're telling me a prominent member of the community was murdered, and no one reported it? I find that hard to believe." Obie folded his arms across his chest.

Belle turned her head sharply. "You aren't old enough to understand, young man. If someone were to go missing and their family didn't report it, then no crime was committed. In Scarlett's case, her husband and daughter moved within a few days of her disappearance, telling everyone she'd gone ahead to prepare their new home. Scarlett said from day one her husband could get transferred with a moment's notice."

"All the Twisted Stitchers knew?" Piper slammed her fist on the counter, forgetting that the first time she touched it, her fingers stuck. "This was more than a women's empowerment group. It was a collection of cold-blooded killers!"

Belle shook her head. "You are looking at this all wrong. Most of those women were hardworking parents who wanted nothing more than to have their family well taken care of. We didn't have many takeout restaurants, so making dinner every night, taking care of kids and helping them with their homework was a big deal. No internet like the kids have today." She crinkled her nose like she'd just smelled something distasteful. "When we were offered a shortcut, we took it."

"I think what Miss Anders Hill is getting at, if I may be so bold," Obie touched his shoulders three times. "If I may be so bold," he repeated, "is that even when times are hard, most of us don't resort to murder."

Piper flashed Obie a quick smile. "Finn swears that his grandmother was a mild-mannered woman. He says she wouldn't hurt a fly."

"Before Scarlett came to town, that was true. She

changed after that. We all did." Belle walked over to the faucet where a silky black cat was sitting in the sink. She brought him to her face and rubbed his fur against her cheek. "Can't trust humans, but my babies would never betray me."

"What did she do, Belle?"

She was lost in conversation with her cat. Her eyes were closed. "We don't let strangers in because all they do is hurt us."

"Mrs. Watkins?" Piper walked over and touched her shoulder.

Belle spun around so quickly her startled cat jumped from her arms and on to the counter, knocking over the full glass of sun tea Belle poured for Piper. The old woman's eyes were wild as she lunged at Piper.

Piper put her arms up in "x" formation, a defensive move she'd learned from November. Obie leapt forward, shoving Belle away from Piper.

When Belle's body hit the counter, it was like a light switched on in her head. "You were asking about Elaine Lowery?" she asked calmly.

"Maybe we should go now, Piper Moonlight Hill." Obie motioned toward the door.

"I'd like to hear what happened with Elaine Lowery first." Piper nodded in encouragement. "Go on, Belle."

Obie remained between them both. "Quickly, Belle. We need to leave."

"Scarlett told everyone that they had to follow her or they were out. Every time she assigned a task that made one woman's life a little easier, she had one more ally. Elaine Lowery and her husband ran a thriving delivery business called ,"Lowery's Luxury Dairy." Their hook was that their products had a special magical taste that others didn't. No real magic, just a hook. It worked because they were the most popular dairy around."

Belle opened her refrigerator and stuck her head inside. "I've got some leftover fudge cake if you'd like a slice," her muffled voice called.

"No, but thanks. We have dinner reservations soon and don't want to spoil our appetite," Obie replied quickly.

"We do?" Piper mouthed.

Obie shrugged his shoulders.

Belle closed the door and placed a half-eaten cake on the counter. "Suit yourself." She retrieved a spoon from the drawer and began scooping bites into her mouth. "Talking about old times makes me hungry."

As I was saying," she continued between mouthfuls, "the Lowerys had a great business, until their neighbor decided he wanted to compete. He started spreading rumors that the 'magic' in their products was something real, an additive they were using to cause addiction. Didn't take but a few weeks before their business dropped to half."

"Someone's twist was to take out the neighbor?" Piper asked.

Belle swallowed and wiped her mouth on the front of her sweater. "You guessed it. The neighbor had visitors in the night. They scared him so bad he put his farm up for sale the next day. Then it was Elaine's turn to help someone else."

"What horrid task was she assigned?"

"To break into the police chief's house and steal an expensive vase. Scarlett was wealthy, but she always wanted more. This was a family heirloom she intended to sell for thousands of dollars."

"Do you have any idea what she was planning to do with the cash?"

Belle shook her head. "We didn't ask those questions. We were obedient. At least the rest of them were. By then, I'd begun questioning what it was we were doing and how long it would be before all of our twists would come from things that only benefitted her."

Obie patted his shoulders three times. "Did Elaine go through with it?"

"She tried. She broke in, well, broke is a strong word. Everybody in this town left their doors unlocked at night because, up until then, we didn't have much crime. She waited until they were at the County Fair. It was safe to assume they would be gone because ninety percent of the community attended the fair on the Friday night of the last weekend. Elaine told her husband she was going to help a friend with her quilt square and would meet him later. That was Scarlett's idea."

"Scarlett made all of the decisions for the group by that point, right?" Piper asked.

Belle nodded. "Because we all knew each other, and she'd brought a chicken and ham casserole the weekend before when his wife was feeling ill–also under Scarlett's instruction – she knew exactly where to go. The expensive vase made it into her bag without a hitch. She was halfway home when she decided she couldn't go through with it."

Belle scraped the sides of the plate with her finger, putting thick globs of frosting into her mouth. "Elaine was on her way to take it back when she saw flashing lights in front of the house. Instead of admitting what she'd done, she ditched the vase in someone's bushes. They ended up taking the fall for her."

"That must've made Scarlett furious!" "Why didn't the innocent person just say they hadn't been there?" Obie and Piper overlapped each other.

"Elaine was the first person to back out of her assignment and Scarlett wanted to make an example of her." Belle turned to Obie. "And yes, you would think the person who didn't steal the vase would have told them so. I'll never understand why he didn't."

Obie put his hands on his hips and widened his

stance. "When you say, 'victim,' what exactly do you mean? Did they turn on each other?"

"I don't have that answer for you." Belle shrugged her shoulders and looked away.

"Incredible feat for someone used to washing floors and wiping up baby spit." Obie quipped. "Just because she was a housewife doesn't mean she didn't have skills." Piper shot Obie an annoyed glance. "You don't know who possesses ninja skills they're hiding, Obie."

Obie's face turned bright red. "Didn't mean it that way, Piper Moonlight Hill. I thought she was put in a rough situation and, not being a career criminal, she didn't know how to execute the crime."

"Oh, she knew what she was doing a crime all right." Belle smiled like one of her cats who had just caught the canary.

"What happened next?"

"Piper, the poor guy taking the fall was the next-door neighbor's twenty-year-old son. He'd been going through a rough time and everyone just assumed burglary was his next step. When they confronted him, he didn't deny it. He didn't admit it either, but no one seemed concerned."

"And she didn't feel guilty about framing someone else for her crime?" Obie asked.

"Who did she frame?" Piper questioned. "Is it someone still around today?"

Belle shot her a sharp glance, but continued her

story. "Remember, these women were all under tremendous pressure. They had to perform or be ostracized and faced the consequences for their children. When Elaine failed, she was given a new assignment-to sleep with my husband and break up our marriage. This time, she succeeded. I lost everything for the crime of betraying Scarlett. Elaine was wracked with guilt afterward. When she came to me to confess what she'd done, my family was close enough to overhear. My husband felt I'd set him up and told our children so. They were furious and not one of them has spoken to me ever since."

"Did you… do the same thing with Elaine's husband as an act of revenge? We wouldn't judge you, they were impossible circumstances."

"Scarlett enjoyed playing these little games with people's lives and told me I should. Instead, I told Buzz everything. He decided he'd get his family out of town as quickly as possible. Turns out, it wasn't quick enough."

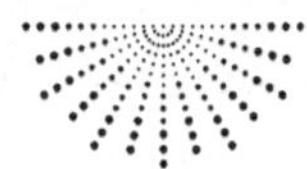

LANIE

"Piper went to visit Old Ma." I stop, trying to catch my breath for the seventh time. Sometimes I wish Vem was a little less fit; it would even the playing field. "She said the poor old lady is more or less lonely."

Vem's four-wheeler is in the shop, something about a throttle that sticks. We decided we couldn't wait to return to the cabin with supplies, so Cosmo found a device once used by Native Americans, called a travois for us to carry goods up the mountain.

It was originally a frame slung between trailing poles and pulled by a dog, horse or, occasionally, humans. The modern version has a thick belt at the waist with two light-weight metal bars attached. Those bars support a one-wheeled cart on which a heavy pack is placed. It's not an easy climb, but going slowly, we've almost made it to the cabin.

"Well, of course she isn't crazy, Lanie. No one really is. We all have our little quirks and that's what makes the world go round." Vem is hopping up and down inexplicably while I rest. "Are you about done? At the speed we're going, it may be time for my second lunch before we reach the cabin."

"I'm so sorry that I'm too slow for you. You knew that when you agreed to come up here with me." I take a large drink from my water bottle, savoring every swallow while I scan my brain for a conversation that will keep her mind off our movement. "Piper says that Obie and his father were estranged because Boysie was ashamed of his disorder. I just don't see Boysie as a person who would be ashamed of any of his children, do you?"

"No, that doesn't sound like Boysie at all. He must've been upset about something else, and Obie got it wrong. It still blows my mind that Obie would choose to live in the woods. Why would he spend so much time constructing traps?" She bounces impatiently.

"Okay, Vem. I'll bite. What kind of herbs have put you in such an electric state?" I ask with frustration.

"I'm trying to prove to myself that I'm not falling

apart. The more I move, the more confidence I have that things will stay in place."

I've talked to her nonstop about seeing a doctor for her aches and pains, but she refuses. "Let's get moving."

Vem practically skips as we move up the hill. "Back to Old Ma. She's been alone so long that she hasn't needed to get along with anyone. I can understand that. I lived out here by myself before you came and I sometimes wondered if I was losing my mind. Of course, we all know my mind would never abandon me. My body, on the other hand, is in full betrayal mode."

"The woman who used to run The Twisted Stitch Society simply disappeared. Obie can find no evidence of her existence after 1990. Isn't that strange? I mean, all of these women know about her and spoke of her, but it's like she never lived here at all."

"We are here," Vem announces. "When did you become Team Obie? I thought he was our number one suspect?"

"I'm not on Team Obie. Piper has been working with him on a project and, as long as he's helping, I don't want to alienate him. That gives us more time to investigate without anyone knowing."

Free of my cart, I continue moving toward the cabin, but I soon realize Vem isn't following. "What's wrong?"

"I'm scared, Lanie. There is something very strange about this couple. They are up here for a reason, and I don't believe it has anything to do with being down on their luck. They are hiding from someone or something. It smelled funny in there."

"What you smelled, Vem, if you recall, was the bacon we had thrown in the trash. They are going to have fresh bacon today so you'll smell lovely things, I promise you."

Reluctantly, she follows me to the front door and I knock, excited to show Muriel what we've brought. After I've knocked four times, Vem presses her head against the window. "Not sure if I see anyone. They left their dishes on the table again. Clothes still strewn around. Her partner must be a teenager."

"I hate to leave everything here on the porch. You never know what animal may take it." I look around for somewhere safe to leave the supplies. "We really don't have any options. I suppose we could wait."

"Let's go inside and leave everything there. It's not like they wouldn't expect us to help ourselves." November reaches for the door handle.

"Wait! Why would we do that? We've already seen how private they are, especially her partner. I would hate to lose their trust by traipsing through."

Vem plops down on the porch. "Okay then, we can sit here for one hour. You know I scheduled a midnight moan tonight, and I like to get myself in the right frame of mind. Some of the students drink way too much coffee before they come and I need to match their energy."

"I can't imagine you not matching their energy, Vem." I sit down beside her and rest my chin on my good hand. "I guess now would be the time we tell each other our deepest darkest secrets."

"You've never tried pizza with pineapples and your first boyfriend stole your silverware. Do you have more confessions, Lanie? Hopefully something more juicy?"

"Not that. I'm talking about whatever has been on your mind lately. You've seemed very distracted."

"It's this whole Obie thing," she replies without hesitation. "I'm worried that he was involved with those trip wires. We never actually saw them. What if he set the whole thing up just to impress his father that he could solve a case? How do we tell Boysie?"

"I guess it is confession time." I take a deep breath. "I don't think I've told you who Piper's latest love interest is."

Vem slaps her knee. "No! You've got to be kidding me! I wouldn't have placed those two together not in a million years."

"I thought so too. But the other day when she was telling me about Obie, I saw a light in her eyes just like when she first met Finn. She's falling for this guy. We're going to have to be very careful how we proceed."

"Oh, this is going to get so messy. If we don't

reveal our theory that he's conspiring with Muriel, Piper'll think you've been holding out on her."

"I tried. She wasn't too pleased." *You don't know him like I do, Mom.*

"There's something else that's worrying me too." November tucks her incredibly limber legs up underneath her. "I don't want to be the bearer of bad news, but I think that this new person working for Cosmo may have a thing for him."

"She definitely does." I chuckle. "I was in there visiting with Piper and she was all over him. Piper tells me she's always in the office with the door closed. If she's brazen enough to flirt with my husband right in front of me, I shudder to think what she does when I'm not there. As soon as things are running well at the farm house, I'm going to suggest we find someone else."

"One of my moaners recognized her. They said that she used to vacation here in the summer. Always very friendly."

"Oh really? Who? She never mentioned that." By now, I have met almost everyone in Piney Falls.

Vem shakes her head. "I think it was a widow. I didn't catch her name, just that she was a seamstress. She did the mending for everyone in town who couldn't do it for themselves."

"I wonder if she was in the quilt society?" my heart drops with a thud. "That's not good. Piper says they wreaked all sorts of havoc in town. I wonder what brought Ellie back? I'm going to look into this."

"Well, it's been enlightening, but can we finally do as I suggested and leave these things inside? I mean, we already spent more time here than I put in my schedule for today."

I hate to admit it, but Vem is right. These people are probably out in the woods, hunting for supper or picking berries or something. That could take hours. I don't want to be sitting here when it's dark because we don't have flashlights with us and I will tumble down the mountain like a heavy stone. "All right, let's go inside and leave everything just inside the door. No snooping around, agreed?"

"I will keep my snooping to a minimum. That doesn't mean I won't be smelling and trying to decipher what exactly is happening with these people. And Lanie, if you're smart, you will do the same."

As we enter the cabin, the smell of rancid bacon still lingers in the air. Our cabin is composed of two rooms. One very large room containing a bed, kitchen and kitchen table and couch and a bathroom with a soaking tub in front of an octagon-shaped window.

There are several letters sitting on the table–some opened and some sitting still in their envelopes. Twenty candles, at least that I count, line the windowsills. There is electricity in this cabin, but they must have chosen not to use it.

I glance over at the bed and see that it has a thick quilt on top, with blush colored and gray squares. I haven't seen that here before. There are two pillows plopped in the middle of the bed, even though the comforter is pulled up tightly.

The sink is full of dishes and there are flies on the syrup leftover from their breakfast the last time we came. It's not right of me to judge them. I don't know what their struggles are. I turn away.

"Hey, Lanie? Something you might want to see over here?" Vem is standing beside a small dresser. There is an open suitcase, with several pictures and some mail inside. "Vem, I thought we agreed not to snoop?"

Vem picks up one of the letters. It is addressed to my father, Gavin Anders, who died last year. There is no return address. I pick up another one, and it is addressed to my sister, who is in prison for being an accessory to murder. The handwriting on both envelopes is the same.

Ignoring my own mandate not to snoop, I rifle through the suitcase, finding pictures of me when I was a teenager. In one of them, I'm sitting on my bike, my hair in identical pigtails. That photo looks as though it was taken from the side, probably without my knowledge.

In the next photo, I'm in high school, dressed in a full-length, midnight blue gown with sequins going down the arms. My hair is piled high on my head with tiny, white flowers dotting the hair do.

"This was my junior prom!" I gasp. "I was waiting in my driveway for my date because I didn't want my mother to embarrass me. I can't believe someone was outside taking my picture! That's…that's…"

"An invasion of privacy? Why would Muriel and her partner have these photos if they hadn't already sent you that box? They weren't digging through your trash because they were hungry; they were trying to figure out what they could use against you! You see! I did smell deceit!" Vem says triumphantly.

"We need to get out of here. Take those letters and let's go before they come back. We need time to plan what we're going to do next."

I turn to leave and see one more surprise. "More of Obie's orange handkerchiefs!" I pick one up and see that it is Thursday. Underneath is a shirt I recognize from the night his father had his heart attack. Same blue Henley. Sewn across the label are the words, "Property of Obie Lumquest."

"We've got to leave, Lanie! They're coming!"

CHAPTER TWENTY-EIGHT

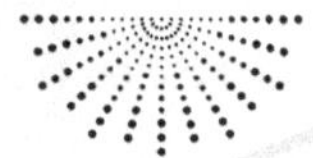

PIPER

"Are you sure you have time to visit the museum again?" Obie wiped the handle before opening Piper's door.

"I needed a break from Ellie for a few minutes. She's baking a sugar cookie today with a cinnamon-sour cream filling. Sounds gross to me, but she batted her eyes and my dad was like goo. It's disgusting."

After their conversation with Belle, they decided it would be a good idea to speak with Mrs. Williams again. They explained what they'd learned from Belle, and Mrs. Williams fidgeted uncomfortably. "My aunt wouldn't have liked this information to see the light of day."

"It's been several decades now. Wouldn't you like to get rid of the secrets? I can tell it's been haunting you." Piper leaned in close, hoping to sway her by looking desperate. "You're our last hope."

Mrs. Williams sighed. "All right. As long as no one else comes in while we're talking. Even though it's been a long time, there are people who would call me a traitor.

Obie patted his shoulders three times. "We spoke with Belle Watkins. She filled us in on the vase that was stolen from the police chief's house. We wanted to ask what happened next, to Elaine Lowery, but it was time to feed her cats and she pushed us out the door. According to your aunt's recollections, of course."

"There was an order to things. Each woman would stand up and talk about what they'd accomplished, either as a part of earning their stitch or otherwise, and then show off their quilting squares. At the very least, they tried to lift each other up. If you were behind on your square, someone else would be there to pick up the slack. It was a strange combination of activities but no one questioned it."

"What did Elaine say that day? When she didn't complete her mission?"

"Scarlett had a temper. If she was telling a story and someone disagreed, she'd yell until they felt an inch tall. We–they–learned quickly never to disagree. When Elaine stood up and said she felt wrong about stealing, it was like all the air was sucked out of the room. Scarlett walked right up to her and slapped her face. Poor woman. Scarlett, angry as a hungry badger, told Elaine she would find something else for her to do to prove herself and this time, she wouldn't be able to say no. This time it would ruin lives.

"Mrs. Williams, was Elaine Lowery the only person to defy Scarlett?" Obie asked.

Mrs. Williams cleared her throat and looked down at her desk. "After she'd humiliated Elaine, most of the ladies got together and plotted to get rid of Scarlett for good."

Piper gasped. "Is that what happened to Scarlett? The Twisted Stitch Society did her in?"

"It was a flawed plan from the start. One of the women's sons was a mechanic. The rest of the group would keep Scarlett late at the next meeting, asking about this or that while he diddled with Scarlett's car. Cutting a belt or some such thing. You can't do that in broad daylight without someone seeing."

"Who saw?" Piper asked.

"Belle Watkins. She walked right in and told Scarlett."

Piper cocked her head to the side. "Belle hated Scarlett too. Why would she try to save her?"

"To prove her loyalty. She owed Scarlett and at that point, all she had as collateral were her kids. They had to work for Scarlett to pay off her debt.

She thought this might earn her points. More than freeing her kids, she wanted to regain her reputation in the community." Mrs. Williams made no effort to hide her contempt. "Selfish excuse for a mother, wouldn't you say?"

"And did it?" Obie asked, ignoring her comment. His attention was on a painting of the two women who founded the original town of Piney Falls, which had been called Flanagan.

"No, not at all. If anything, Scarlett held her tighter. She'd whisper about Belle to everyone in power she knew, making sure they understood Belle wasn't in her right mind."

"Where does Elaine Lowery fit into all of this? She was already being punished."

"She was forced to do something really awful. Terrible. I've always felt sadness for the poor woman."

There was a lengthy silence in the room, while both Piper and Obie waited patiently to hear what Elaine had done. Mrs. Williams began fiddling with a stack of newsletters on her desk, making it obvious she didn't want to share.

"What happened to this neighbor who confessed, or rather, the one who was coerced into admitting a crime he didn't commit? Was he released when they discovered who'd really stolen it?" Piper asked.

"No. I don't know why he never told anyone the

truth. That would be something you'd need to ask him."

"We need his name in order to do that," Obie insisted. "No one has offered that piece of the puzzle yet."

Mrs. Williams squeezed her hands together. "I can't. I'd like to, but I just can't."

"You've been a great help today, Mrs. Williams. If you think of anything more, please contact us." Piper put her hand on Mrs. Williams's and placed her other hand on top. "I'm sorry for the painful memories this brings up."

Mrs. Williams took her free hand and set it on top of Piper's shoulder. "Bringing things out in the daylight accomplishes two things. It makes them les scary and sometimes it gives us fresh perspective. I hope you find the owner of that finger soon."

Obie was halfway to the door when he turned around and came back where the two women were standing. "Who was the neighbor? If he's still around, he might be willing to talk to us. You want to help us solve this, don't you? As an officer of the law, I promise you'll be fully protected if someone tries to harm you." Obie pulled out his Piney Falls Police Department leather-covered pad and produced a pen from his pocket.

"This is somewhat awkward." Mrs. Williams tugged at the collar of her blouse. "I thought you would already have that information. It was your father–Boysie."

Both Piper and Obie stood in stunned silence.

"Are you sure? Piper asked.

"Yes, I'm sure. Everyone in town knew about it, and Boysie's parents were very upset. They made apology casseroles for the police chief's family for six months. I think Gladys may have tended to their garden for two years trying to make amends."

"My dad has never said a word about this. My grandma hasn't either. In fact, no one in the family has a record of any kind," Obie said adamantly. "Other than my scrapes with the law, we're clean as a whistle."

They stood in front of Piper's car, trying to process this latest bit of information. "I'm going to ask my dad; I'm sure he can clear this up."

"Are you sure your dad is healthy enough for this kind of questioning?" Piper asked.

"I don't know, to be honest. This doesn't sound like my dad at all. He was always big on telling us when he'd made mistakes and using them as teaching moments. Why wouldn't this be his best example? It makes no sense."

"We'll figure it out." Piper reached for his hand absently, pulling back when she realized what she'd done. "Oh, sorry. I don't want to touch you and make you uncomfortable. It's just what I do."

Obie half-smiled. "When I was in college the first

time, there was a beautiful girl I fell in love with. She had these amazing dimples when she smiled. I'd just get lost in them. I wanted more than anything to ask her out, but I was afraid she'd find me strange."

"What happened?"

"It turns out she'd been wanting to go out with me too. We never even left my dorm room. Within ten minutes, she was all over me. I freaked out, pushed her off and told her to leave. That was when I agreed to see a therapist. I never wanted that to happen again." He reached for her hand. "You see? I can do this. Your hands are clean."

"I'll take that as a compliment, Obie Lumquest."

"Would you like to go out for dinner later? My treat."

"Yes, if you follow me, I'll go home and change and we could go in my car. I can't take a police cruiser because they're both in use right now, but I do have a light I can put on top of my car. If you're the type to be impressed by something like that." he winked at her.

"What you're telling me is that the Lumquests do have a wild streak? Piper asked playfully.

"Like wild animals living in the woods."

CHAPTER TWENTY-NINE

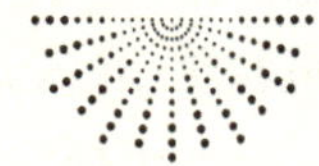

LANIE

*L*anie Anders Hill doesn't run in most any circumstance, but today I find myself in the unusual position of having to do it, anyway. My cart bumps along behind me, threatening to throw off my gait. I don't want to be shot, but of equal importance is keeping myself upright.

"Vem, slow down!" I try to yell, but there isn't enough air in my lungs to make it much more than a weak suggestion.

We finally make it to a wooded area, far from the cabin. I stop and bend over, placing my hands on my knees while I try to regain some composure.

Bumpity bump bump bump. I hear Vem's cart

coming up in front of me. "Lanie, are you going to just relax here all day like we're on a vacation?"

I look at Vem's shoes. Today she's not wearing shoes that match her the rest of her outfit as usual. They are brown and rather ugly. I've never seen her in something so lacking in flair. Her jumpsuit is navy blue and her glasses frames are bright red. "Vem, you're not in sync today."

I stand up and the realization hits me. "You aren't in sync! We came all the way out here and there was something going on with you that you didn't tell me! What's going on? Spill it!"

November is thrown off by my revelation. "I don't know what you mean, Lanie. I'm the same Bean I was yesterday." Her face is a funny blotchy color, a combination of red spots and her usual pale pallor.

"This isn't the time for games. We'll stay out here until you confess. I don't need to hurry back." My mid-woods stand-off is just as much about taking a break as it is getting to the bottom of what's happening with my best friend.

"Do you really want to stay out here until they catch us? I don't want to be roasting over an open spit tonight. I have plans."

I'd forgotten momentarily that we were in distress. "Alright. Let's keep on walking, but you need to tell me what's happening as we go."

Vem makes a wide circle with her cart and

continues moving through the tall trees, this time at a much slower pace. I wait patiently for her explanation and, when it doesn't come, I stop abruptly. "Are you dying?"

"No, I'm not dying. But I did see a doctor. He thinks I might have arthritis in my back."

I'm startled when the tears begin to flow. November does not express emotion in that manner. It comes in howls and moans, but never tears. Immediately, with my cart close behind, I take her in my arms.

"Vem, I'm sure this comes as a shock, especially when you've always been so active. You know there are things you can do to manage it though, right?"

"It's just that…I'm not supposed to be … human. Everyone looks up to me because of my physical prowess. Now they'll decide I'm just… ordinary."

I pat her back with my good arm. "People love you because you are one-of-a-kind. Being so physically fit is just one aspect of the incredible you."

She wipes her face on my shirt and pulls back. "Do you really think so?"

"I KNOW so. November Bean will not be defeated by a little thing like arthritis. Heck, you may come up with some wonderful remedy and the world will revere the woman who discovered the cure!"

After she's dried her tears, we continue our trek down the mountain. It is much more difficult to pull an empty cart down a steep hill than it was going up. It wants to steer me off the side of the mountain.

"I've decided that there's nothing more we can do. We brought supplies for Ellie and her mystery man, and I think, now, we'll just have to be patient and wait for them to move on. We've given them supplies and a roof over their heads. That's all we can do."

Sometimes being lost in the trees gives me the best overview of the whole picture. "You know what else? We never looked at the date on that mail. It could have been old. Maybe I left it there and forgot about it. And they found the pictures there and mailed them to me to be nice. I've been looking at this all wrong."

Vem stops again. "There is one more thing bothering me." She is oblivious to my words, but sometimes that's best.

"Is this regarding Piper? Or is one of your moaning students giving you a hard time? Cos said the other night he heard you arguing with one of them. I didn't want to bring it up, but–"

"It was a student. Cosmo Hill is a snoop. I'm surprised he didn't tell you who it was, because he knew them."

"What?"

"Yes, Mr. Snoop was listening to an argument I was having with his awful new employee, Ellie. She saw my flyers and decided to try a moan out for herself. At least, that's what she said she was doing. We were three-quarters done with class and I was explaining the woeful moan, the one that starts with a low chin and ends in a joyful face to the moon."

"That's my favorite," I muse. "Very empowering as far as moans go."

"She certainly didn't think so. I opened one eye to make sure everyone was doing it right, and Ellie was off her mat. She was heading right for your place!"

"Are you sure she wasn't looking for the bathroom?"

Vem sighs, clearly irritated with me. "I have a sign, Lanie. Truman made one that says, 'moan at will. Tap three times if it means something serious.' It's a nice big sign you'd have to be dense to miss."

"Sorry, I forgot about that. You got up and followed her. What happened next?"

"She was trotting herself towards your driveway. I grabbed her arm and pulled her back, just before she reached your property. 'Hold on there, miss. You can't run out on a moan class!' That's what I said in my most professional voice."

The hairs on my arm rise. "There is something wrong with her. I knew it from the first day I met her."

"This Ellie-person, well, she smiled like a cat who just finished the biggest mouse. 'Oh, Mrs. Bean," November's voice is high and nasally. "I didn't mean to offend you. I was interested in your neighborhood. I might want to move here someday. Isn't the house over there for sale?"

"Where Cos and I used to live? Why was she at our new place? I'm really confused."

"That's what I said." Vem pushes her shoulders back and her chin up. 'Oh. Mrs. Bean, I must've been confused. I like to know all the neighbors before I move into a neighborhood.' I knew she was up to no good right then and there. No one skips a moan class for something that frivolous."

"Exactly where does she think she's moving? Didn't you already find renters for our old place?"

"I told her there wasn't anything around here to suit her needs. She still didn't budge, so I picked her up and threw her over my shoulder. I hauled her over to her car and told her to leave and never come back. I've never had to remove a student before."

"This will cause such turmoil at the bakery. Especially when they don't have time to train another new employee. I'm torn. Maybe I should wait to tell Cos until they've finished the new place and things are calmer?"

Vem clenches her fists and pinches her face. "If it were me—"

"There are employment laws, Vem. We have to be careful. I've been so consumed with Obie and Muriel that I haven't been paying attention to other things."

When we reach the bottom, Vem and I take turns helping each other out of our travois: she undoes my

belt and I undo hers. It's nice to be free of the cart
and stretch our backs a little. I follow her lead as she
stretches to one side and then the other.

"Are we going to call Gladys and ask her to find
this Ellie person on the dark web?"

"No," I shake my head. "I've been thinking all the
way back. Maybe we can take care of two problems
at once. I'll go see Obie tomorrow. If he's not honest
with me, I'm going to make it clear I'm not comfortable with him dating my daughter. I'll see what he
knows about Ellie too."

Vem shuts her eyes. "I don't like this."

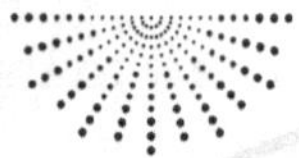

CHAPTER THIRTY

PIPER

She brought the wineglass to her lips and glanced around the room. Chez Falls, the newest upscale restaurant in Piney Falls, was noticeably empty. Despite the low occupancy, they were seated at the smallest table in the mauve-colored room and their knees were touching. Piper worried their close proximity would bother Obie, but he didn't seem any more out-of-sorts than usual.

Obie observed her and tapped his finger on the table. "You're relieved there's no one to see you with the freak?"

"What?" She set her glass down and wiped her lip print from the rim. "You've got to quit assuming things about me. I'm not like the people you went to school with. I've had a hard life too, so I know what it's like to be ostracized."

Obie patted his shoulders three times and blushed. "I'm sorry. It's an automatic response, Piper Moonlight Hill. You've been nothing but kind." He touched her hand lightly and then pulled it back when she noticed. "I'm new to this world of dating. I make a lot of mistakes."

"Me too, Obie. Normal life is something I've tried hard to embrace. I finally came to the conclusion that 'normal' has many definitions."

"I guess you and I have more in common than I realized." He smiled broadly and leaned forward as if he were about to kiss her, but then changed his mind.

He grabbed his menu and then dropped it quickly. "Not sanitary. Why wouldn't they wipe these down?" He reached into his pocket, pulling out a packaged wipe.

"Here, have mine. It's sparkly clean." She exchanged menus with him before he could protest. "What did your dad say when you asked him about the vase?"

Obie shook his head. "Denied it, flat out. I called his bluff and said I would look it up in the police records and he said, 'go ahead, son. There's nothing there. He was right. Mrs. Williams must've been confused, or worse yet, she was playing us." He stared out the large window at the people scurrying home from their activities.

"I've been struggling to understand why Boysie didn't accept you. He's one of the nicest men I've ever met," Piper's eye were wide and she felt frustrated he wouldn't meet her gaze.

"My family just didn't function well after my Aunt Carlene disappeared. I'm sure you've heard the story."

Piper nodded. Obie's aunt was a part of the same cult her parents were and disconnected from the rest of her family for years.

. "She was a real rock," Obie continued "When she joined the Fallen Branch cult, we didn't know where she was. We were all convinced she was going to walk through the door. Every Christmas they bought her presents and every Easter she had a place at the table. It's hard to function normally when you're living every day on the edge of your seat. I was an added concern they didn't need."

"But still, her disappearance should have made them treasure you even more." Piper insisted.

"I wanted to be the hero, the person who found her. In my young mind, once I brought her back, the family would be able to ignore my strange habits." Obie took a deep breath in, then let it out slowly. "There was a picture of Aunt Carlene in middle school that sat on Grandma Gladys's piano. At least once a week, I rode my bike around town looking for anyone who resembled the picture. A couple of times I thought I saw her, but when I approached these women to ask if they were my aunt, they acted like I was a freak." Obie nodded and touched his nose three times.

"I'm so sorry. That must have been difficult for all of you."

Their eyes met, and Piper felt deeply attached to this practical stranger. She looked away quickly.

"Most of all, it was hard on Grandma Gladys. She talked about Carlene every day when I was growing up to keep her alive in our home. Dad made a point of telling us that Grandma was going through something terrible. I think they bonded over that. You've probably figured out that those two are as close as a mother and son. Well, some mothers."

"I've noticed." Piper grinned.

"It was very confusing for a kid," Obie continued. "I saw how much they were all hurting and I needed constant reassurance that it wouldn't happen to me. But they were grieving and nobody had time for that kind of attention." He patted his shoulders three times.

"That's when I started hugging myself. Giving myself these hugs made me feel safe and loved. The longer it continued, the more it started becoming a habit that I couldn't break. I'd hug myself like my mom or grandma did when I was little, just to reassure myself that I was loved. Three pats for safety and protection." Mentioning it out loud triggered the act, and Obie patted himself before continuing.

"I've gotten most of my ticks under control, like washing my hands obsessively and brushing my teeth 30 to 40 times a day. Just a handful left.."

Piper felt an ache inside for Obie. She'd been alone as a child, too. "It didn't help when Carlene came home? I know it doesn't solve everything, but it didn't make your OCD better?"

"It was an established pattern for me. And by the time she returned, I'd already left the family. It made it worse, in a way. I suppose I should tell you why I ran away from my family."

"You don't have to tell me anything, Obie. We all have our demons. It's okay if yours are different from mine."

"No, I think you should know about this. When I was in high school, my OCD was at its worst. My parents only communicated by yelling. I skipped classes to wash my hands or pat myself or whatever it was I needed to do that month. it seemed to change frequently. My parents didn't really understand, even though they were trying. My dad told all of us boys he wanted another cop in the family, but the way he looked at me, I knew he didn't mean the one with the strange habits. It crushed me. I spent long hours hiding in the bathroom."

Piper glanced across the room, where a large family had just been seated. The kids were poking each other and joking around. Normal activities that she and Obie would not have been able to do for different reasons. "What changed you? If you don't mind me asking. "

"Our family was miserable and I viewed myself as one of the problems. If I took myself out of the equation, they could go on without Carlene. I know it doesn't make sense. That's when Obie Lumquest, bathroom hider, went off and joined the circus."

She looked up in shock. "You're kidding, right?"

"Nope. I traveled the country with the Flayme Brothers circus. It's the perfect gig for people who feel disconnected from the world. In a way, it was exactly what I needed. They didn't care what I did or why I did it. They just accepted me for who I was."

"Spaghetti Carbonara?"

Piper raised her finger, and the server set a steaming plate in front of her.

"Roasted half-chicken with a separate plate of vegetables?"

"I had that." Obie stared at the plate with dismay. "Do you have a clean cloth I might use to wipe the edges? The vegetable plate touched the chicken when you set it down."

"I'll be back in a minute." The server pursed her lips and returned to the kitchen.

"I'm trying to picture your circus act," Piper commented. "Wasn't it dirty? Did you train animals?

Perform acrobatics? I give up. What circus activity is on your resume?" She smiled shyly.

Obie placed his dry, cracked palms in front of her. "I took tickets. I wore gloves and an industrial mask, so that I was safe from all of the dirt and germs. It was an easy job. I like things neat and in their place, and this troupe was disorganized by nature. I saved them hours every time they moved to a new location."

As Obie spoke, Piper tried picturing him bundled from head to toe. The only thing visible would be his beautiful, expressive eyes. "What brought you back to Piney Falls?"

"Here is a clean cloth for you, sir. My brother has OCD too, so I can tell you we just opened a package today. You're the first one to use it."

"Thank you so much," Obie replied, before patting his shoulders three times. He returned to his conversation with Piper while wiping the rim of his plates. "My mom called and told me they found Aunt Carlene. She had been living out on a farm outside of town."

"Naybor Manor. Yes, I know all about that. I bet you were thrilled!"

Obie shook his head. "All of those years, I thought I was going to be the one to bring her back into the family. I was going to be the one to make my grandmother's eyes light up and be the hero. Instead,

I ran away, and she came home without me or my assistance. They didn't need me at all."

"It was all just circumstance," Piper insisted. "You'd done everything you could."

He picked up his wine glass and held it up toward the light, wiping his finger smudges with his napkin.

"My mind doesn't always work the way it should, though, remember? I went through a deep depression trying to figure out how to change the story so I could still be a person they admired. Then it hit me: I could make my dad's dream come true and be the son who entered the family business. Law enforcement."

"That's a huge sacrifice unless it's something you really wanted for yourself."

"Not really. If I could save another family from going through what ours did with Carlene, it would give me a sense of accomplishment."

"Well, I still think that was noble of you." She reached out to pat his shoulder and then thought better of it.

"I need to explain that, too. I struggle with new people, women in particular."

"How is that working as a police officer? You meet new people every day!"

"In the context of my job, I don't have problems. In my mind, they are safe and distant because I don't have feelings for them. They are part of my work. Things like holding hands on a meaningful level are a real challenge. It may seem small, but it's a mountain for me. You're the first person I've let into my protected circle. I guess you could say I'm smitten. That's what Grandma would say, and it's current, right?" He half-smiled at her.

Piper absorbed his words. "What you're saying is that you like me? You're a hard man to understand, Obie. Finnegan was my first boyfriend and he explained everything before it happened. 'Now, Ms. Moonlight," She lowered her voice and put her chin against her chest. "I shall take your hand and bring it perilously close to my lips." She giggled, but noticed when she raised her eyes that Obie's expression was stoic. "We had a nice time together under the stars, but then you've kind of sent me mixed messages ever since." Her pulse quickened. "If it bothers you, you don't have to worry. We're friends and I wouldn't force you to–"

Obie took her face in his hands and kissed her quickly. When he finished, he patted his shoulders three times and returned his hands to their place, clasped together on the table. "That was what I wanted to do, but I should have asked you first. I don't always get it right. Impulse control is my challenge. As a police officer, it's an especially large challenge."

She stared at him, unsure of the mixture of hormones swirling through her body. When she and Finn kissed for the first time, it was sweet and simple. It felt uncomplicated. This was something she didn't understand. "It was fine. It was good. Fine and good."

"Officer Lumquest?"

They looked up, both relieved for a break from their intense discussion.

"You've been asking around town about Scarlett? I may be able to help."

Piper recognized the man's face. "You're the soy milk decaf latte and Chagal Chocolate scone, right?"

Obie raised his eyebrows.

"Chagal is a planet. It's our theme, but sometimes I think Dad gets way out there when he chooses names." Piper quickly explained.

"Yeah, that's me. I was having coffee with the boys yesterday and heard you talking about Old Ma. You were asking Doris what she knew. I'm on the reunion committee for my class at Piney Falls High and I know her son, Teddy–he was in my class. He lives in Tellum. I could even get you the address, if you'd like."

Obie nodded solemnly. "We'd appreciate that."

The man looked around nervously. "Can I ask why you want to find him?"

"We met Old Ma, I mean Belle, the other day. She's a little odd, but she's so devastated that her children aren't in her life. I'd like to convince her son to go see his mother." Piper sounded more hopeful than she felt.

"I know you're hoping for a happy ending here, Piper Moonlight Hill, but that's not always possible." Obie cut his chicken into small pieces before placing one in his mouth.

"For sure. But wouldn't it be spectacular if it was? A happy ending engineered by you and me. Not like Carlene, but just as important to another family."

Obie blushed. "Thanks for being understanding about that."

"Officer Lumquest is right."

They both looked up, forgetting momentarily that they weren't alone.

"Her son is abrasive and rude. At the last reunion, we kicked him out by nine o'clock, but the guy refused to leave. He sat outside harassing all the women who walked by."

"Thank you for telling us, sir."

"Your next latte and scone are on me!" Piper called after him as he walked back to his table.

"I don't tell many people about Carlene. It's easier to let them make assumptions than it is to explain why I'm the way I am. It's like swimming uphill. You're a special person for understanding that."

Piper reached across the table and kissed Obie impulsively. "Turnabout is fair play," she said, wiping her lipstick from his face with her slightly soiled napkin.

A large bank of windows faced the main street of Piney Falls, where the street lights reflected off the wet concrete. Tonight, someone happened to be walking by as Piper and Obie shared a kiss. She paused, cupping her hands around her eyes as she peered inside"I've waited my entire life to see you happy, son."

CHAPTER THIRTY-ONE

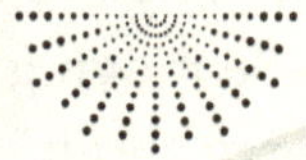

LANIE

decide it's best to visit Obie first thing in the morning, before he gets busy with police duties. When I arrive at the station, there is one other person waiting to see him, the owner of Pat's Pawn Shop. She is yelling at the officer working the front desk.

"I've told you people again and again that someone is stealing our trash. Nobody will listen. I'm new to this community and we should have been told ahead of time that this is how you operate!"

"You're having problems with someone stealing your trash?" I move in between Pat and the desk, hoping to calm her. "I think I can help you."

"This isn't any of your business," she replies curtly.

"We had people digging through our garbage as well. They live out in a cabin outside of town and we've discovered they are completely harmless. They are just trying to find enough to eat to survive, and I think they'll probably be moving along soon. There's nothing for you to worry about." I smile at her, hoping she will appreciate the advice.

"Look, lady. You don't know me. You have no idea what it's like when these vagrants come and steal our things. I don't want them knowing my business. If you know who they are, tell them I'm going to have my shotgun ready the next time they come around. It's not going to end well for them."

Obie appears outside his father's office. "Is there something I can help you with?"

She tells her story again, this time embellishing by adding that she's afraid for her life.

Obie pats his shoulders three times. "There is no reason to shoot at someone for taking something you already discarded."

"I was just telling this lady that we know who the people are and they're completely harmless." I study Obie's face intently, waiting for a reaction, but there is none.

Obie says nothing as the woman fumes and spits out expletives. When she understands she won't get a reaction, her angry words stop.

She turns to walk away, but comes back with her finger aimed at his chest. "You're nothing like your father. As soon as he's well, I'm coming back with a petition for your removal!"

Instead of exploding, he nods his head and crosses his arms. As she storms off, he smiles engagingly at me. "Don't worry about her. I'm discovering everyone in this town gets a little emotional over trash." He motions for me to follow him into his office and, when I enter, I'm surprised to see we're not alone.

A dark-haired woman about my age is seated beside the desk. When she sees me, she rises and smiles. Her cheeks are plump and pink and her eyes twinkle invitingly.

"I'm Beverly Lumquest." She announces. "Aren't you the cutest thing? You remind me of that movie star from the 1940s."

"Tulip Sloan. I get that a lot." First meetings are never the time to discuss my complicated connection to my grandmother. "I'm Lanie Anders-Hill. You must be Obie's mother! I've heard so much about you from your mom and from Boysie!"

She stands and hugs me tightly. "I'm Beverly. I've heard about you too, Lanie. All good things."

Vem taught me that a hug can have many meanings. Sometimes a person is insincere and their hug is light. Sometimes, the person is truly happy to see you and their hug is one in which you don't want to let go. Beverly's hug is that strong.

"What a surprise! Obie, your mother is gorgeous."

His eyes dart around the room. "Sit down, Lanie. Tell me what's bothering you."

"I don't want to interrupt your time with your mother."

Beverly places her arm on my good one. "I surprised everyone, my son included. He was in the middle of a date with a cute girl and I just happened to be passing by and saw them through the window last night. It really threw my poor boy for a loop."

Obie's face is a combination of pain and discomfort. "Mom is just here briefly. If you need her to step into the hallway, she can."

"Oh, no." Now I feel silly. My problems with Ellie are small compared to Obie's. "You haven't seen your mother in years. It's more important that you two catch up. I'm glad to see you're not letting past hurts keep you apart. You must have so many things to discuss, from your time in the circus to your return to Piney Falls."

Obie's eyes dart back and forth quickly.

"I'm somewhat of an empath," Beverly says, closing her eyes. "You're concerned about a… woman. You view her as a threat to your marriage–no–you view her as a threat to your safety." She opens her eyes and looks at me with concern. "You're worried she might harm you?"

"Yes–I," I stutter. There are so many thoughts swirling around my head, the least of which is Ellie.

"Someone is threatening you?" Obie asks with concern. "Who is it?"

"It's nothing like that. The woman Cosmo hired to work in the bakery was snooping around our place." I stand and put my purse over my arm. "I really should go and give you some time with your mother."

"Come back if you feel it's serious," Obie says.

I want him to stop me and tell me he'll help, like his father would. Instead, he and his mother are in a strange stand-off that is consuming all of his energy.

As I walk out the door, Beverly grabs my hand. "That woman is dangerous. Please be careful."

CHAPTER THIRTY-TWO

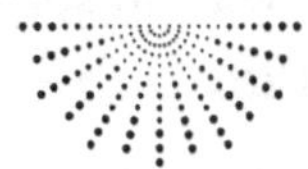

*P*iper knocked on his door for the third time. "Obie? We were planning to meet Old Ma's son, Theodore, this morning. I hope you're okay in there?"

She was trying to decide if it would be an overre-action to call the policeman on duty when the door opened. The disheveled mess in front of her was not the Obie Lumquest she'd come to know.

"Obie? I was worried about you. Did you forget to set your alarm?"

His hair was uncombed and his rumpled, green-checkered pajamas looked as though they'd been on for at least a day.

"I can't go with you today," he answered, touching the corners of his mouth.

"Why? Did it upset you when your mother

showed up? I can't imagine how that felt. We were having a nice dinner and then–"

Piper's expression went from light and happy to morose. "Is this about your mom showing up in the middle of dinner? You never said any more after she barged in."

Obie stared hard, his shoulders cinched up around his ears. "She never said she was coming and I don't like surprises."

"I sense there's more."

"My parents were always fighting about 'what to do with Obie' and 'how to help Obie.' They'd spent so long with that as their only common ground that, when I left, they had nothing to say to each other." He paused. "I should have said that slower, so you could write it down to tell your mother."

"Why would you say that?" Piper asked, her cheeks burning. "That's really insulting."

"Lanie was in my office yesterday. She mentioned things I thought were private. You promised you wouldn't tell anyone, Piper Moonlight Hill."

"I didn't just gossip to anyone. I never had a mother I could talk to, so now most everything comes out. It wasn't meant to hurt you."

As tears formed in her eyes, Obie looked away and patted himself three times. "You convinced me you were different, but I should have known you were like all the rest." He turned away from her.

"You'd better get going. Theodore spends his afternoons in the bar and you don't want to miss him." Obie shut the door abruptly, leaving her alone on the porch.

She didn't expect the emptiness to hit so suddenly. They'd only just met, after all. She sat down on the porch and tried to push away the negative words in her head. *You're dumb. You'll never have anyone because you aren't good enough. Piper Moonlight Hill deserves to be alone for the rest of her life.* The therapist she'd been seeing said to go for a walk and clear her head when the bad thoughts creeped in. As she rose, she heard the door open again.

Obie's hair was combed and he was dressed for the day. "Only in the interest of finishing what we've started," he stated, straightening his collar.

She hated that he could see she'd been crying. Wiping her tears on her sleeve, she nodded. "Your car or mine?"

"I'd feel more comfortable taking two cars, but since neither of us has been to this location before, it's probably best to ride together." He hit the unlock button for his car and got in. "Are you coming?" he asked through the closed window.

Reluctantly, she got up and joined him for the silent ride to the home of Theodore Watkins.

* * *

THE TWO-STORY BRICK house was surrounded by neatly manicured flower gardens and newly planted trees. Piper shaded her eyes and stared up at the second-floor windows, which were covered in foil. "I don't like this, Obie. People who want to keep everything out usually hide something dark inside. His mother had foiled-over windows, and we barely made it out of there alive."

Obie patted his shoulders three times. "Don't worry, Piper Moonlight Hill. You're with an officer of the law. Theodore Hopkins won't try anything. And if he does, I'm ready."

"I'm not afraid, Obie. He's just an average guy, not one I'd trust to kiss me," she retorted.

Obie got out of the car and slammed the door with Piper following suit.

They walked up to the front door as the three-car garage door opened. A hot pink bicycle with a blonde-haired rider burst out of the garage and came to a screeching halt in front of them. "Who are you?" Her small head cocked to the side. "You don't look like my friend."

Without waiting for a reply, the little girl turned her bike around and rolled down the driveway. When she reached the sidewalk, she paused once more to view the strangers before continuing down the block.

"She looks like Belle. Did you see that nose?

Exactly like Belle. I can't wait for her to meet her granddaughter!"

"Don't get too excited. We might not–"

The front door flew open and a blonde woman wearing a Beer Time is All the Time t-shirt almost ran over the top of them. "Sadie! Get back here!" she screeched. "You know the rules! Stay in the driveway unless you're with an adult!" She slapped her thighs. "That damn kid. She'll be the death of me." She turned around and stared at Piper and Obie. "Who are you? We don't want to buy anything today, or ever."

"Officer Obie Lumquest, Piney Falls Police. Not here on official business, but Miss Moonlight Hill and I would like to ask Theodore some questions."

Her eyes traveled up and down his body, and up once more. "You're a cop? Don't look like you could win a fight with the other guy blindfolded."

"We're trying to clear up some Piney Falls historical issues and we'd like to talk to your husband if he's around." Piper used her bakery manager smile.

"Teddy ain't my husband. He's my boyfriend. He's not the type for commitment. If you'll go down the block and bring Sadie back, I'll get him for you. I'll warn you, she won't come without a fight."

She disappeared inside the house and shut the door. Piper and Obie stared at each other awkwardly, both still reeling from their earlier conversation. "I guess I'll go then," Obie finally offered.

He walked for two blocks before discovering the girl, her bike lying on a neighbor's lawn while she pulled flowers from a large plantar and put them in her hair. "Sadie? Your mom sent me to get you. It's time to come home now."

She shook her head vigorously. "You're a stranger."

"That's right, I am. That's why I'm not picking you up and putting you under my arm. You're going to come by yourself. You shouldn't be on other people's property. You're a stranger to them too."

"Nuh uh. These are the James. I've been here lots of times." She made no effort to return to her bike.

"I'm sure they don't want you pulling their pretty flowers out of the pot." Obie thought back to his police academy training. He knew how to deal with stubborn and intoxicated adults. A little girl was nothing. "I'm a police officer, Sadie. If you don't come with me, you'll be in trouble."

She sat down on the porch, making herself at home. "So? I don't care."

Obie patted himself three times and stomped his feet.

"Why'd you do that?" Sadie asked.

"It's just part of who I am." He thought for a minute and smiled. "You know when you get upset and get on your bike? To make sure your mom knows you're mad? That's kind of the same thing. I have things I do to make me feel like I'm in charge."

She looked at him curiously. "You don't have a bike?"

He rubbed the back of his neck and chuckled. "I do, but that's not what makes me feel safe. This," he patted himself again, "is what makes me feel safe."

Sadie got up and walked closer to Obie. "I like that," she said. She poked his leg as she rocked back and forth. "If I tell you something, do you promise not to tell my mom or dad?"

"As an officer of the law, I promise."

When they returned to Sadie's driveway, Piper was standing beside a younger-looking, male version of Belle. His pear-shaped build was exactly like his mother's and his hair was parted on the same side. "Obie, this is Teddy. He was just explaining to me why Belle isn't welcome here." Piper shaded her eyes as she viewed Obie and the young girl, who was now hugging his leg.

Sirens wailed in the distance, disturbing the quiet of suburban street.

"Belle ain't no mother of mine. She let Scarlett torture me and my sister. She told Scarlett every one of our deepest secrets. Back then, secrets. I still wet the bed and Scarlett told her kid. I was always teased after that. School was hell until our dad took us and we left town. Belle didn't care."

"Do you know what happened to Scarlett?" Piper asked, without emotion. "Is she still around?"

Teddy scratched his large belly. "You heard about the pregnancy? Her daughter got pregnant by a cop." He eyed Obie. "Can't ever trust 'em."

Piper clasped her hand over her mouth, stifling her shock. She pretended to cough, so it wouldn't seem suspicious.

Obie patted his shoulders and stomped his foot. "We heard it was a big scandal. When Scarlett found out, she must've been furious. Did she threaten to kill him?"

Piper stared at Obie admiringly. He had no idea Scarlett's daughter was pregnant. She'd seen Boysie do this with a suspect before and get exactly the information he needed. Obie was a chip off the old block.

"Him and every other man in town." Teddy stuck his hands in the pockets of his low-hanging shorts. "When that woman was mad, she made sure everybody knew. She threatened to kill all of them."

"Who was the cop? Do you remember his name?" Obie asked.

"I dunno. Rob or Bob. It was a long time ago and I was nine when it all happened. Not sure why you'd come all the way to Tellum to ask me. All of their secrets, including that one, are buried in a box behind the old library."

Piper and Obie exchanged glances.

"Why do you hate your mother so much?" Piper interjected. "We spoke with her this week and she told us she misses you and your sister. She was trying to keep you safe, as far as I can tell."

"She always put on a good show," Teddy snickered. "Do they still call her Old Ma? Does she talk to herself and paint her house wild colors? Crazy old woman. Did she mention how she offered up me and my sister to Scarlett to get herself out of the group? She told Scarlett she didn't want to do her dirty work, but her kids would."

Piper and Obie exchanged stunned glances.

"Now you do what Auntie Scarlett says," Teddy continued in a creepy sing-song voice. "We owe her a debt and you can do her chores until it's paid. My sister Tia and me, we were scared of what we'd walk into every day. Sometimes it was just doing laundry, but other days, she was bonkers. One time she told us we were to clean out her refrigerator. We started takin' the dishes out and she said, 'you're gonna eat every last one of those containers.' We both got sick on the way home. But that wasn't as bad as the day we had to cut off a finger." Teddy's voice faltered.

"YOU cut off the finger?" Obie asked, incredulous. "It was in a box along with some letters."

Teddy pulled his t-shirt to his nose and wiped it. "You know then. About all of her dark secrets."

"We'd like your version of events, though," Piper interrupted.

"You're gonna arrest me? Is that what you're saying?" He looked at Obie.

"Just fact finding today. I'm not here officially."

"What was the debt your mom talked about?"

"It was how Scarlett punished those who didn't obey. Poor Tia looked the other way while I went to serve up Scarlett's punishment. Instead of playing with toys, our own mother forced us into that life. Scarlett paid us a dollar that day, just like all the others."

The sirens were close enough now that Piper looked around to see if someone's house was on fire. Three police cars came barreling down the street and screeched to a halt in front of Teddy's place.

"What's going on?" Teddy asked.

"I promised I wouldn't be arresting you today because I don't have jurisdiction outside of Piney Falls, but I didn't say anything about the Tellum police. Sadie told me how you afford this fancy house. You bring criminals into your home where a small child lives. Sadie should be eating cookies and playing with dolls. Every kid deserves to feel normal…His voice trailed off.

Three police officers approached them, one instructing Teddy to put his hands on his head. "You screwed me over!" he snarled.

"You did it to yourself!" Obie yelled while patting his shoulders. "The girlfriend is inside, as are the drugs. Sadie says her room is full of cocaine."

Another police officer bent down to Sadie's side. "Would you like to ride in a police car? I'll let you run the lights and siren!"

CHAPTER THIRTY-THREE

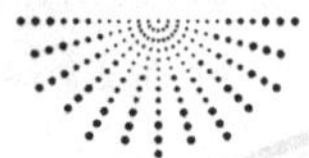

LANIE

"You're looking good, Boysie." He is propped up in the living room, watching a sports channel with a bowl of dry popcorn on his lap. Not a normal position for Boysie Lumquest. Nor is his attire regular Boysie-wear. He's wearing grey sweats with several food stains on them and a blue t-shirt with Petrie Family Reunion 2017 written across the top in red.

I sit down on the couch closest to him, setting a card and a black coffee from the bakery on the table beside him.

His eyes are glazed over as if he's been planted in the same position for so long he's melted in place.

The television blares a replay of a basketball game that happened two years ago.

"Could we turn that down and talk shop for a minute?" I don't wait for his response, reaching for the remote control to shut off the television..

He is suddenly aroused from his coma, and takes a drink. "Why'd you bring me black coffee?" He grumbles. "Hate that stuff. Might as well drink motor oil."

"I'm worried about you, Boysie. Gladys says you hardly move from this spot. Your doctor wanted you out exercising so you could return to work. Isn't that what you want? Beverly is concerned too." She is leaning in the doorway, wiping her hands on a kitchen towel, and nods vigorously.

"My boy's taken over. I hear glowing reviews from everyone. They don't miss me. Guess I'll just sit here until I rot. Nobody will notice." He turns his head away from me and stuffs a handful of popcorn into his mouth.

"About that. I wanted to talk to you about Obie." I'll have to tread carefully. "Do you think he's going to stay on when you come back?"

Boysie puts his popcorn bowl on the stand and squints his eyes suspiciously. "Why would you ask that? Of course he's gonna stay on. He's family."

"Well," I swallow hard. "Vem and I are concerned that he might be trying to show you he's competent and making some poor choices. You could understand how a boy would want to impress his father." I hold my breath, not sure how he will react.

Boysie's face tightens. "You're worried that Obie is going too far? Has he offended someone? Did he leave a task undone? Doesn't sound like my boy."

I decide to go a different route. "I've had problems with someone snooping around our place. Obie isn't concerned because he's working on an old murder case, and—"

"What old murder case? This is the first I've heard of it."

"One involving a sewing group from the nineties. They called themselves The Twisted Stitch Society. He and Piper have been trying to track down the woman who ran the group, and they found information she may have been murdered."

Boysie sits up straight and looks me in the eye for the first time today. "Why would the boy keep that from me? I need to read the file and see what's been done. I'll go in first thing tomorrow morning."

"I'm glad you're enthused about that, Boysie, but there is also a more pressing issue. There's a new woman working at the bakery who has an abnormal attachment to—"

I can't tell him she's all over my husband. He'll think I'm a jealous wife and discount my concerns. "She's been acting suspiciously. November thinks she tried to sneak into our home while she was supposed to be doing a moaning class."

Boysie raises his eyebrows. "Can you blame her? Never understood that moaning nonsense."

"Be that as it may, it wouldn't hurt to see if she's keeping something from Cos. I'd hate for her to cause problems at the bakery when Cos and Piper are working so hard to get the second location open."

"What's her name?"

"Ellie Fine. Cos doesn't know anything about this, so I'd like to keep it quiet for now. He's got so much to worry about that he doesn't need one more–"

"My mother-in-law may have belonged to that sewing group at one time. Did you ask her?"

I sigh. I'm getting nowhere. "Gladys doesn't sew. She's made that perfectly clear. She likes to watch other people sew, but it makes her blood sizzle when she thinks about making those tiny stitches. We've had this conversation many times."

"You should still talk to her. She knew everyone. Still does. She'll be able to tell you what happened to the missing woman. You scurry along now. I've got to pick up my uniform from the dry cleaner and get myself ready for work tomorrow! Can't keep a good cop down!"

I stand and reach for my purse. "I'll show myself out. Just remember, Ellie Fine. Check her out, please!" He doesn't respond.

Beverly grabs my arm as I'm about to touch the

door knob. "Boysie knows more than he's telling you."

"What?" Now that I can examine her face, she looks identical to Gladys. Same long nose, same downturned mouth.

"Those Twisted Stitchers made his life hell, " she whispers. Her breath smells like shortbread cookies.

"Bevvie? More popcorn please!" Boysie calls from the living room.

"Coming!" she responds before turning to me once more. "It would kill Boysie if he knew this was all being dredged up again."

"Why? Boysie's never had a problem confiding in me." I'm hurt that she thinks I'm an outsider. In her time away, Boysie has become connected to more people in the community.

Beverly shakes her head. "Goodbye, Lanie. Nice seeing you again!" Her voice is pronounced for Boysie's benefit, but she's opened the door with her other hand and is actively pushing me out.

The very last thing I wanted to do today was see Gladys. She will tell everyone in town what I'm doing regarding this investigation with Ellie Fine. There is nothing worse than Gladys giving away the story before the truth is known.

As I walk into the county records building, I can hear Gladys's device playing Polka Beatz. It is her new favorite album, and she listens to it daily. She's been trying to teach herself to polka, and it is the only album that she thinks has the right rhythm.

"Get down, get around, swing your partner off the ground." Some strangely hip-sounding polka caller is telling Gladys to do things I'm certain someone her age should not even consider. Gladys is in her own world, doing contortions of her own making as she raises her hands in the air and swings them around her head.

"I'm so glad you're having a good time. Just don't try to convince anyone this is actually a polka," I say when I get close enough that I know I'm not going to scare her.

She rips the headphones off her head and spins around. "Good gravy, toots. You know this is usually my nap time. What brings you in?"

"I have some things I need to ask you about, Gladys, and I need your explicit promise that this will not go any further than this room." As I'm saying it, the absurdity of my request hits my ears. There is no stopping the Gladys Gossip Train.

"Well, you know you don't have to worry about me, toots. I don't tell anybody anything less than they're asking me. What is it? You got some kind of problem at home? Marital issues? I thought there might be some coming soon. I've been suspicious of all that lovey-dovey nonsense. You're using that to cover up a deep issue, aren't you?"

"Not today, Gladys. I just had an interesting conversation with your daughter, Beverly."

Her face widens into a grin. "Isn't it something that she finally came back? Poor Boysie's been missing her something fierce. Glad there's someone else to do the cooking."

"I'm happy for him. But she said something strange when I left."

"Oh?"

"I was asking about a sewing group. Boysie said he'd never heard of it, and Beverly said Boysie's got some secrets regarding the group. Were you ever involved with them?"

Gladys looks up at the ceiling and thinks for a minute. "Doesn't ring a bell. You know I don't do the sewing. I've been known to knit a cap or two."

"That's what I thought. I told Boysie you knew nothing about the Twisted Stitch Society."

"The Twisted Stitch Society?" She leans forward so far, I'm afraid she'll fall off her chair. "You should have said that in the first place! Of course I knew about them. Everyone did. They were a nasty group of women who went around after dark, destroying things for their own wellbeing. There were rumors that the police were in on it, too. They would tell them who to target next and the women would do it and no one was ever caught."

"My daughter has been looking into them. She found some information when she was remodeling the house and it relates to these women and some crimes they may have committed. Do you know anything about Scarlett?"

"Well, let's see. She came here from Texas, I believe. Really had her nose high in the air, expecting everybody to follow her rules. I can remember my kids were in afterschool activities, and all of a sudden, she was the gatekeeper. If I didn't agree to join her group, my offspring wouldn't be allowed to participate any longer. Hmph. The nerve!" She crosses her arms over her chest. "It bothered me so much that I started my own scout troop for my sons and didn't include anybody else in town."

"That's what my daughter has been saying. Beyond that, do you know what happened to her? What ended the group?"

"Now that is an entirely different matter, isn't it, toots? Those nasty women got what they deserved. Each of their crimes came back to them in their own way. You know Old Ma, who lives on the edge of town? She's all by herself now. And Elaine Lowery and her husband were ostracized and nobody bought their dairy products. They ended up moving because they couldn't make a living."

"And Scarlett moved also? Her husband got a job somewhere else?"

"I never heard what happened to Scarlett. I can tell you this: there was a big scandal at the school.

She was involved with all the teachers, you know, because she told them what to do and who got the best grades. It was ridiculous. The policemen even came to her house for dinner every week. One of them was a young guy fresh out of the academy, like my Obie. He was sweet on her daughter. Before you know it, her daughter ended up pregnant. Oh, the scandal. The daughter was sent away to give birth and never returned. Not long after that, Scarlett's house was for sale. The Twisted Stitch Society just ended. Life went on in Piney Falls like nothing had ever happened. I can't even remember the last time somebody brought that up."

"Gladys, I wish I could say this surprises me, but it doesn't. I'm glad you weren't a part of this group. Your daughter, Beverly, convinced me they were somehow involved with Boysie."

Gladys bites her lip and taps her fingers on the desk. "Boysie's sworn me to secrecy on this one. Wish I could say more, but it's out of my hands."

It's so unusual for Gladys to keep anything to herself that I sit in stunned silence.

"You caught me off guard, toots. Thought you'd be here askin' about that trollop at the bakery. Tongues are wagging all over town."

I bite the inside of my mouth, giving a straight face my all. Whatever I say now will be repeated, word-for-word. "She's a hard worker, I hear."

Gladys leans in again, this time wrapping her

knuckles on my forehead. "Are you in there, toots? This one's spending her days trying to steal your man. Doesn't that burn your bonnet?"

"I trust Cos," I reply calmly.

"Well, I wouldn't." She leans back, causing her chair to squeak dramatically. When enough time has passed, she moves on. "Have you figured out who lives out in that cabin? Are they gonna come into town and strangle me in my sleep?"

My face burns as I remember how many of Obie's shirts we found. "Vem and I are working on it."

I look at the clock and realize I need to get to the bakery. "Gladys, before I go, please tell me about Boysie. I want to know how he was involved with the Twisted Stitchers?"

"I'M HERE to see my husband." The less I say directly to Ellie, the better.

Today she is wearing a tight-see-through pink shirt. Piper has already told her the bakery logo t-shirt is required for employees, but she says it itches.

"I'll go and check if he's available, Mrs. Hill. Would you like a coffee while you wait? You can sit down at the table and I'll bring it over after I have a little chat with your handsome man." She winks and turns away from me.

Maybe it's just the way she presents herself: she's probably completely harmless. If Piper hadn't put thoughts in my head about her chasing after Cosmo, I wouldn't be so upset, would I? There is the matter of her trying to snoop around our place, too.

"Oh, Ellie? Before you get Cos, I was wondering if you were planning to buy a home in the area. Do you have plans to stick around?"

She turns around so quickly her long hair whips into the pastry case. *Health code violation.*

"Settling down doesn't suit me."

She puts her hand on her hip and leans her head to the side in a pose I've seen in far too many online photos. "I could be persuaded to stay, though, by a certain ruggedly handsome guy." *Wink, wink.*

If I take the high road now, I won't regret it later. "If you don't want to repack clothes you haven't worn in a while," *Anything workplace-appropriate.* "I'm collecting clothing for a couple who have recently come to town. A little down on their luck, unfortunately."

"I remember. Cosmo was telling me all about them yesterday while we shared a beer."

Now I'm angry. "I'll go get my husband. You stay here and find yourself a hair tie for that mop." I stomp past her and back to Cosmo's office. I raise my fist to knock on the door, but then realize this calls for the element of surprise. In my irrational mind, he's hiding in here with three women, taking turns kissing their necks and alternately offering to wash their dishes.

He looks up from his paperwork as I storm in, his beautiful eyes peering over his black-rimmed half-glasses. "I wasn't expecting you! Do you need a ride home? That's a nice way to take my mind off out-of-control construction costs." He stands and comes around the desk, taking me in his arms.

As we kiss, my steely resolve melts into a puddle on the floor. I nuzzle his neck. "You're here by yourself."

He pulls away and frowns. "Who would I be here with? Didn't know paying bills required an audience." Cosmo cocks his head to the side. "Is there something you want to ask?"

"Yes, Cos, I would like to know why you would share a beer with an employee. It's terribly unprofessional and–"

"Stop right there." He holds up his hand in protest. "You're taking this out of context. I was having a beer at the end of an exceptionally hard day. We had not one, but two kids vomit all over the pastry case, meaning we lost an entire day's profit as well as having to take the darn thing apart and clean it. Ellie stayed late to clean it, so I offered her a beer as a thank you. That's it."

"She makes it sound as though you two were on the floor in the throes of passion as you drank," I snicker. "Gladys says everyone around town has noticed how she flirts with you." I hate myself when I say it out loud. I'm not usually childish and jealous.

"You sound just like our daughter. It's sad that you two would be parroting Gladys." He rolls his eyes. "Believe me, I understand your reservations. There's something off with her, but right now, I don't have other options. I need the help and she's the only one who's come in with experience. Piper's been taking more time off when I need her the most."

"Vem says Ellie was snooping around our place in the middle of a moaning class. She's got a bad scent."

"I'll talk to her about her–scent–when things slow down. I don't want her getting upset right now when Piper doesn't have time to pick up the slack." He nuzzles my neck again before pulling away. "I'm glad you came by, though. There's something I need to show you." He motions for me to sit in the chair across from his.

There is an unwanted knock at the door, and I inexplicably glare at my husband before opening it. "Just thought you'd want your coffee, Mrs. Hill. A mocha with extra whip, right?" Ellie sits a frothy, overflowing mug in front of me.

"Yes, that's great, thanks." I shake my head. I've had a standing order of a latte, half foam ever since I moved to town. "Oh, Ellie, I just wanted to thank you for all that you do for my husband and our business. We're grateful you're here." My face may just fall off if I strain any further to show her how happy I am.

She pulls her fingers through her long hair, causing several strays to float down to my pant leg. "Well, your husband makes it easy. He's such a nice guy. I'd love having someone like him to come home to at the end of the day. You're a lucky lady!" She winks at Cosmo and closes the door.

"Do you see? She's trying to upset me."

Cosmo shrugs. "I told you I'd talk to her later. Right now, I need to show you something." He reaches into his top drawer and pulls out a folded piece of paper before sliding it over to my side of the desk.

When I unfold it, there is fancy, curly handwriting. "Did someone from the 1700s send this?"

"Just read it, Lanie."

"Dear Mr. and Mrs. Hill, thank you for the items you shared. We are grateful for your help and for not judging us. We'd like you and your friends to come for dinner on Thursday at six p.m. My partner and I want to show our thanks. Don't need to bring anything. Muriel." I look at Cos with surprise. "She's inviting us for dinner? Do you think her mysterious partner will make an appearance?"

"All the more reason to go." Cos smiles his million-dollar smile, the one that still makes me weak in the knees. "It will be too late for Truman to drive home afterward though. Do you mind if I ask him to spend the night?"

"A sleepover? Ahh, you boys. Do you want to set up a tent in the yard so you can tell ghost stories?"

"You know Truman's old bones couldn't handle that."

"How did this note arrive? Did she send it by raven?" I'm only half-joking. "Or her mysterious partner delivered it and nobody knew."

"Ellie said it was sitting on the counter after the noon rush. She had no idea who left it. Piper is right, I need to install some security cameras."

"Oh, one more thing before I go. I heard today that the Twisted Stitch Society buried a box behind the community center on Pine Street. Have you heard anything about it?"

Cosmo shakes his head. "Truman has a metal detector. If he's coming to our mystery dinner, I'll just ask him to come into town early so he can look for you."

We stand and hug one last time. "Sorry, I didn't trust you. I don't know what got into me."

He kisses the top of my head. "Rather have you jealous than willing to let another woman come in and slobber all over my beer bottle. I'll see you at home."

I leave quickly, hoping I won't run into Ellie again.

CHAPTER THIRTY-FOUR

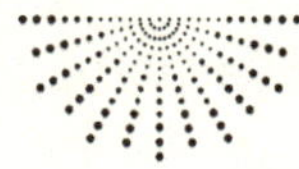

LANIE

It's a brisk sixty-two degrees in my car.
Vem insisted the blast of cold air would
help her sore back. "It's four-fifteen, Lanie. Truman's
not coming," she says as she leans her back closer to
the air conditioner.

"He's probably run into some traffic. We've had
an uptick of tourists lately. That can really clog up a
two-lane highway."

Secretly, I wonder if she's right. He's not fond of
treading on property that he doesn't own or Cosmo
hasn't given him express permission to excavate.
Finally, I hear his old red pickup chugging around
the corner.

He gets out and grabs the metal pole from the

back and his ear phones. "Afternoon, ladies," he says.

"You're late, Truman. I've got a Moans for Mamas class in thirty minutes and then I'll change for our hiking and dinner venture." Vem puts her hands on her trim hips and shakes her head. "No sense of time, this one."

Truman ignores her and places his headphones over his ears. He lowers the circular device to just above the grass and begins moving slowly.

"I've got a shovel in the trunk," I whisper to Vem. "If you'll distract Truman, I'll dig this up. He'll be upset that we're digging on public lands."

"Got it!" she says out loud.

"Shh!"

We watch for several minutes before he pulls off his headphones. "Got something right here, Lanie!" he announces proudly. "Could be money or some-body's watch, though. Don't get your hopes up."

I nudge Vem.

"Truman, I'm having car troubles. My air condi-tioner makes a Weerrrrp, Whellop sound when I turn it on."

He places a marker where he picked up the noise. "Just light digging, Lanie. We're in a public space," he reminds me. "Now what kind of sound does your air conditioner usually make?" He and November walk over to her car and I quietly retrieve the shovel.

Ten minutes pass, and I'm ready to give up when I hit something solid. I bend down and dig the rest of the way with my hands until I'm able to make out the shape of a metal container. Quickly, I bring it up and replace the dirt and grass I dug, tamping them down with my feet. If we can keep Truman away from this spot, he'll never know. This isn't a place he normally visits when in town.

I can hear Vem telling her tale to Truman. "The radiator sometimes goes fftttaw. Is that normal?"

The box and the shovel are safely in my trunk. I wipe my brow and re-apply my lipstick before joining them. "You were right, Truman. Just an old watch. I've seen a million of them. It's not worth a penny."

"I could keep looking if you want? We've got a little while before our dinner, don't we?" he asks earnestly.

"Oh, that's alright. Cosmo wanted me to show you the guest room and where to put your things. He'll be home soon and you two will have plenty to discuss."

"Suit yourself."

I mouth, "Thank you!" to Vem.

CHAPTER THIRTY-FIVE

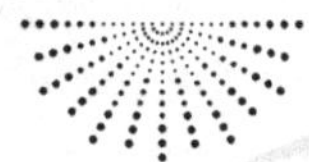

PIPER

"**I** got a call from the Tellum police chief. He said that Teddy wants to tell us something." Obie said matter-of-factly. He wiped the bakery counter with a spare orange cloth from his pocket before carefully placing the cloth in a plastic bag and tucking it into his coat pocket.

"Is this some sort of trick?" Piper's eyes narrowed. "I've seen this in police dramas and once they get the people back into the jail cell, the perp tries to murder them."

She'd been trying to come up with a way to tell Finn to back off. Between that conversation and the one she wanted to have with Obie, she didn't have much space left in her brain for anything else.

"You will be completely safe, I promise, Piper Moonlight Hill. And you don't have to go with me if you don't want. I'm informing you because we were researching the Twisted Stitch Society together."

The way Obie spoke was as if he were telling his elderly neighbor to leash her dog. *I'm informing you that Peaches pooped on our begonias.* "The farmhouse is almost finished, so I'm slammed with work. But I want to see this through. Even if I mean nothing to you now."

She was surprised when a look of pain crossed his face.

"I'll be going then." He turned to walk away.

"Wait!" she called in a louder voice than she'd planned. "I suppose it's too much to ask that he had a change of heart about his mother. At some point, we're going to have to tell Belle that her son is a drug dealer.. It would soften the blow if we could add that he forgave her."

"I'll leave that to you, Piper. I'm not good at the emotional stuff. I was planning to leave here about three. Will that work for you?"

"I'll meet you at the police station. I need to do something first."

This time, she watched until he got into his car. Her mind went to wonderful places when she thought about their evening together, how she'd felt at ease even as he'd picked cracker crumbs off her shirt. But he wasn't meant for her. Maybe she was better off alone. "My therapist will charge me extra this week," she lamented.

There was a loud noise coming from Cosmo's office. Thinking her father was in trouble, she ran for the back of the store.

Ellie stood, propped on one leg leaning against the doorframe. Piper could hear laughing and easy conversation. When Ellie disappeared into the office, Piper immediately followed.

What she saw infuriated her.

"You're such a good storyteller, Cosmo. The county fair sounds like a real hoot. I bet you've got a thousand more." Ellie was standing beside the desk, rubbing Cosmo's arm.

Piper stormed over to them and slapped Ellie's hand away. Cosmo looked up at his daughter with surprise.

"Keep your hands to yourself! Did you read our employee handbook? You're not to touch other people in the workplace unless they are in physical danger. Does my Dad look like he's in danger?"

"We have an employee handbook? First, I'm hearing about it," Cosmo called as Piper stomped off.

To get her mind off the uncomfortable situation, Piper began unpacking a supply box in the storage area. It wasn't long before she smelled Ellie's cheap perfume. "What?" she snapped, without looking up.

"Your daddy and I were just shooting the breeze between customers. I think you're making too much out of this. With all of your secret errands, I'm the only one around to keep the place running. You really should be thanking me instead of treating me like dirt."

Piper could not believe what she was hearing. "You are not saving anything, Ellie. You are just here as a placeholder. We did just fine before you came and will do just fine after."

Ellie seemed caught off guard. "I…I came here to find my back story. You know how some people have family lore passed through generations? Well, in my family, it's like my parents were Adam and Eve." She looked away. "I begged my parents to tell me where they came from and they refused. It wasn't until last year that I found out they lived in Piney Falls once. I wanted to find out more." Her voice wavered. "I didn't get this job to be judged. Just to have some spending money while I found my kin." She sniffed and wiped tears from her cheek.

It was the last thing Piper expected. "I wish you would have been straight with me from the beginning. I know all about searching for my roots."

She set a box of powdered sugar on the shelf and wiped her hands on her pants. "Maybe you don't understand how it looks when you're so friendly with my dad. But that's no reason to yell at you." She'd been looking at Ellie as the enemy when she should have shown compassion. "When I was new to town, people judged me without asking for my story.

I'm sorry, I did the exact same thing to you. Who were your family members, Ellie? You've never mentioned anyone before."

"My father was a policeman when he lived here—his name is Chester Fine. My mom was quite a bit younger and her parents weren't too happy. Her name is Margarite."

The hairs on the back of Piper's neck stood up. "Was your grandmother's name Scarlett?"

"Yes, how did you know?" Ellie's eyes widened. "Are you related to them?"

"I know a little about Scarlett and her sewing club. But I think there's someone who could tell you more."

She stood up and walked to Cosmo's office, pulling Ellie behind her. "Dad? I'd like to take Ellie with me this afternoon. It's pretty slow here today and Doris said she could come in too close if we needed her. Would that be okay?"

Cosmo, who had buried himself in bookwork to get away from the ongoing drama, popped his head out and glanced from his daughter's face to his employee's, trying to get a read on the situation. "If you're planning to drop her body outside of town somewhere, I'm afraid that's been done and the cops will be on to you before you make it back for supper."

Piper shook her head. "You don't have to worry.

She wants some answers and I'm going to see that she gets them."

Obie was surprised when she showed up with an extra person that afternoon. "This is Ellie. She wants to ask Teddy some questions about her grandmother… Scarlett." She paused, waiting for that to sink in.

"Scarlett is your grandmother?" He raised one eyebrow. "We've been trying to track down information on her whereabouts."

Piper opened the door to the police cruiser, hiding her delight. "Would you mind riding in back, Ellie?"

"Will do," she replied cheerfully, sliding into the seat and pulling the door shut behind her.

When they'd begun their journey, Piper turned to Obie. "Ellie doesn't know what happened to her grandmother either."

"When I'm worried about something, which is most of the time, I can't sleep." Obie patted one shoulder three times. "Our conversation the other day is weighing heavily on my mind and now I'll never get a night's rest. You hurt me deeply. I want to be with you, but I can't trust you."

"Is it the right time to discuss this?" She blushed, pointing her thumb at the backseat.

Ellie leaned up between the metal rungs separating them. "Well, that's just the sweetest thing ever. I know your daddy is really excited about you finding someone. He told me that when we talked in his office yesterday."

Piper turned around and glared. "This is one of the reasons why it's so hard to like you, Ellie. Sometimes you say things that are really irritating. There is no reason you should be sitting in his office shooting the breeze. All conversations with my dad should be of a professional nature. Got it?"

Ellie frowned. "Just pretend like I'm not here, okay? I'll stay back here and keep to myself until we arrive."

Piper turned back to Obie. "I never betrayed you. It was a casual conversation with my mom. That's all I want to say, while there are an extra pair of ears in the back."

"I'm still deep in my OCD. I've made progress, but chances are, it's always going to be a problem. I'm sensitive about it, and I have to be able to trust that whatever I confess will stay between us."

"My dad had OCD. He went to a therapist, and he's doing so much better, "Ellie interjected. "He's always struggled, though. I wish he'd talk to his kids about it."

"Pretending you aren't there!" Piper reminded her. "My dream all through my childhood was to have a mother I shared everything with. When Lanie and Cos adopted me, I vowed we would never have any secrets between us. Can you understand that? It wasn't about hurting you."

"You didn't tell her the truth the night we were on our date; she thought you were working late at the new bakery. Why is that different?"

"You guys went on a date? I can't believe I missed that!" Ellie remarked.

"Quiet!" Piper and Obie shouted in unison.

They pulled up in front of the Tellum police station and Obie stopped the car. He adjusted the mirror so that Ellie's face was visible. "I just want to explain that you're visiting a violent criminal. Don't expect to get all the answers you're looking for, Ellie Fine."

"I know that. When Piper explained what you were doing, I was grateful to be included."

Piper bit her lip, trying to remember to be kind. As they walked into the police station, she grabbed Ellie's arm. "You wait in the lobby for a few minutes while we get what we need. I'll come get you when it's your turn."

Piper and Obie were escorted to the interrogation room, where Teddy was already seated. Obie wiped the door knob with his orange Friday handkerchief and then the chair before he sat down.

Teddy's disheveled appearance was a stark contrast from the day before. Instead of wearing his T-shirt and shorts that were too short for his large body, he was wearing an orange prison jumpsuit. His hair was messy, and he looked like he hadn't slept.

"Thanks to the two of you, I'm stuck here," he grumbled. "Don't have enough money for bail and my girlfriend's in the wind. Said she didn't want anything to do with me. Who knows what will happen to the poor kid?"

Obie leaned back in his chair and patted his shoulders three times. "Since yesterday, I received some interesting news about you, Teddy. You have several children that you've abandoned. You owe thousands of dollars in child support. I don't imagine they would be too happy to find out you had another child and chose to pay for her care." He tapped his foot rapidly. "Although, your idea of care leaves something to be desired. And as far as your girlfriend goes, I heard she was arrested this morning. So you don't have to worry about her running off. She's going to be right here beside you."

Teddy rapped his knuckles on the table. "Never got along with those women. It was better for them if I wasn't around. I suppose you're wondering why I asked you to come here."

Piper resisted the urge to explain it was his choice to be in this situation.

"Gotta get this off my chest. I wasn't totally honest with you when we talked the other day. I hadn't thought about that time for years."

He took a deep breath and folded his hands together. "We went to Scarlett's house every day after school. In the beginning, we did chores. We got her laundry, washed her car, that kind of thing. We worked our butts off till six o'clock every night. I already told you about the occasional torture, like eating her spoiled food. She'd tell us we were one day closer to paying off our mother's debt. Never saw any proof of that," he scoffed. "One day, Scarlett says, 'If you want to work off your debt to me quicker, you'll have to do something permanent. Something that will always make me grateful." He ran his fingers through his hair. "Sheesh. Didn't think it'd be this hard."

"What happened next, Teddy?" Obie asked calmly.

"She found out her daughter was pregnant by a cop and she wanted us to get rid of him. Two little kids. She gave us a special knife and the key to his house. We were supposed to kill him when he came home from work. Only we chickened out."

There was a heavy feeling in the room. Piper watched Obie carefully, worried this news might push him over the edge. The expression on his face never changed.

"Tia and me were so scared. She had this idea that we could make it look like we killed the cop without actually doing it."

Teddy folded his hands in front of him. He has an almost gleeful glint in his eye. "Most days we were starving. Belle didn't feed us much because she was sure we were eating well at Scarlett's place. She didn't believe us when we said we ate her rotted food after doing all of that physical labor.. One day Tia says, 'watch this.' She tripped this goofy kid and then sat on him and reached into his pocket and pulled out five dollars. It was so easy. Pretty soon, he was so scared, he'd empty his pockets as soon as he saw us coming. He was gonna be our mark."

"What do you mean by 'mark.' Did you kill the poor kid?" Obie continued writing in his notebook as if he were writing a grocery list.

"No, we only need one body part to prove to Scarlett we'd done the deed."

"So you cut off this poor kid's finger," Piper said dully.

Teddy shrugged. "We didn't see any choice. We gave it to Scarlett and told her it came from the cop. It didn't make sense from an adult perspective, but, like I said, we were kids who panicked while trying to find our way out of a horrible situation. It was Belle's fault we were there. If she hadn't–"

"Whose finger was it, exactly?" Obie asked, shifting uncomfortably in his chair.

Teddy smiled wickedly. "Frankie Lowery."

CHAPTER THIRTY-SIX

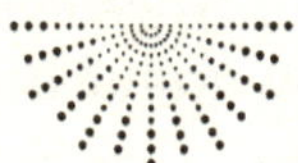

LANIE

We're almost at the cabin and I can't shake the feeling that walking in the dark won't be the only concern this evening. Cosmo packed his backpack with headlamps to wear as well as flashlights, rescue flares and extra food.

There are tiki torches I recognize from November's last luau moan surrounding a fire pit. Muriel and her partner fashioned benches out of two logs, one on either side of the fire.

"Well, isn't that nice," Vem remarks. "It looks like a set from 'Hacked in Two,' the slasher movie I watched last week."

"Hoping they aren't planning to roast a few

locals," Cosmo quips. "I've got my knives in the bag though in case they start something funny."

"You two," I say, exasperated. "Let's keep an open mind!"

Muriel greets us dressed in a bright red blouse and long, colorful skirt that makes her positively glow. As she gets closer, I recognize it from one of the bags of clothing we donated. Two long braids hang on either side of her head and she is wearing bright red lipstick.

"Glad you folks could make it. I wasn't sure you'd come."

It's almost like she's an entirely different person. Not the distrustful woman who slammed the door shut when we first encountered her. When she reaches me, she pulls me in for a hug. One more surprise.

"Sit. My friend will be out soon. He's gotta collect himself first."

Cosmo looks around, no doubt thrown by Vem's comment. "We don't want to put you folks out. If he's not up for visitors, we can come back another day."

"Oh no! That's not it at all. You'll understand everything in time. But for now, just enjoy the fire. I'll get some wine."

"What kind of wine would you folks be having? I'm a little particular as far as my drinks go. I'm a presidential sort of drinker, and don't like anything foreign." Truman sits down on a bench and wipes his hand on his dark blue overalls.

"Sassy Lasses. It's their special blend for this year, Naybor's Labor?"

There are so many questions swirling around in my head. When and how did they get to the winery? How did they know about it? Now is not the time to ask. "I would love a glass. I've tried some, and it was my favorite blend."

She disappears inside and returns momentarily with five mismatched mugs. One of them says Piney Falls Salmon Packers on the front. I know this is an old baseball team that used to play here in the summer. That mug has to be at least 25 years old. The one she hands me is purple and has a smiley face on the front.

We sip our wine quietly while staring into the fire. Muriel watches the door expectantly, but no one comes out. I'm trying to envision the look on Boysie's face when confronted with the news that his son is behind our traumatic event.

It's unusual for Vem to go this long without some sort of remark and for once, I need her to intervene. "Is there something that you need to say?" I prod.

"Well, now that you mention it, Lanie, there is something I've been wondering about."

I hold my breath, hoping she doesn't bring up anything that might cause problems, such as the fact that they are able to afford wine but not basics like food and clothing.

"Muriel, did you make your shoes?"

I looked down at her feet and she's wearing some moccasins that are a familiar fabric. They are made from the pink-flowered jeans that I put in the bag for her.

"Yes, I did. There was an old sewing machine at the antique store that they gave me because they were out of space. I've been sewing all sorts of things since then." She smiles shyly. "I used to be a seamstress."

"You've been in town quite a bit," I remark. Things aren't adding up.

"Will there be eating involved soon? I was kind of hoping we would eat something and then jump into saving the world." Cosmo's stomach has been protesting its current empty state for the last half hour. I tried to get him to eat something from his backpack, but he refused, saying it was for emergencies only. If we wait much longer, he'll be more dangerous than any animal out here in the woods.

"Oh, I forgot. I made these appetizers out of the crackers and some cheese that you gave me. Hold on." She disappears once more into the cabin.

"Isn't it nice that she's making us appetizers,

Cos?" I say, trying to make everyone, including myself, feel a little better.

"Yes, Lanie, it is." He puts his hands on his knees and leans forward, looking around once more. "Something is off. Can't quite put my finger on it."

"She didn't speak like this the last time we were here," I whisper. "It's like she's got an entirely different personality."

Muriel returns with a plateful of crackers topped with cubes of cheese and passes them to each of us.

"As I was saying, my partner wanted me to talk to you before he arrived. He ain't used to being around people, and I'm supposed to make sure everything is fine. That's why we… well, we…" She looks at the ground. "We had to dig through your trash to make sure you were on the up and up, so we knew if we could trust you or not."

"All you had to do was ask," Vem says. "My life is an open book. If we have an hour or four, I could tell you everything. You want to know about the toilet paper, king? That might take longer."

"I was actually talking to Mrs. Hill. Her sister is a cold-blooded murderer, and we wanted to make sure she wasn't having no contact with her."

I'm in shock. "How do you know about my sister? She is in prison after stalking both me and my father. Why would I want contact with my stalker?"

"Well, we heard she didn't work alone." Muriel

blinks rapidly. "Don't trust anyone. Life's taught me that."

"I can assure you, anyone involved with that woman is either dead or in prison," I snap. "My father died before we were able to reunite, thanks to her. I'll never forgive her for that."

I haven't thought about this for so many months. Now that it's back in the open, it's like pulling a band aid off a healing wound. It hurts.

We sit in an awkward silence, listening to the snap and pop of the fire.

"When might the actual meal be served?" Truman asks finally. "An old man can't go too long without food."

I turn to Muriel, ignoring Truman. "The other day when we dropped off your supplies, we noticed that you had some photos of me. I'm very uncomfortable with that. My family history is one I don't care to relive. If you're going to continue to live here, I must demand that you respect my privacy."

I glance at Cos, hoping he will catch my "it's time to leave" vibe. Instead, he nods.

"No, ma'am, that's not what we're doing."

"I sense you would like to know the history of the area? I've been developing a historical moan class. I'll be making a compilation of historical facts that I'll speak over music that I compose before each moan. I've already begun the research." Vem stands up and winks at me. She leads Muriel away from the rest of our group so we can talk.

"Ten points to November." I throw my hands up with exasperation." I've been trying to get your attention to tell you that I'm really uncomfortable with all of this."

"We haven't eaten yet! Don't you want to see how this plays out? She seems harmless. Strangely into you, but harmless," Truman proclaims.

I grab Cosmo's backpack and open the large pocket. There are four energy bars that I toss toward Truman. "This isn't something from a movie; this is real life. I never had a chance to spend time with my father as an adult. He came all the way out here to meet me and died before we could have any kind of relationship. It was extremely painful and still is when it's brought up like this. I'm ready to leave."

"I'd like to hear what her partner has to say, Lanie." Truman puts half a bar in his mouth. "Got all sorts of question marks in my head."

"Cosmo?" I look at my husband, hoping he will back me up.

"As soon as November gets back. We don't want to leave her here. Or maybe we do."

This has gone on long enough. I march up the stairs to the cabin door. "Yoo-hoo? Mr. Partner? Or should I say, Obie? It's time for you to show yourself. I'm tired of your games. Come out here now and explain yourself, or we're leaving."

I turn around and storm back to the campfire. "One day, the shoe will be on the other foot. You'll be in a situation you don't like and you'll want to leave, and I'll just sit there like a bump, completely unaware of your pain."

Cosmo and Truman drink from their wine mugs uncomfortably. Cosmo hates it when we have disagreements in front of his friend, so he does everything he can to avoid them. He hands his mug to Truman and stands, so that he can put his hands in his pockets and rock back and forth. It is his way of saying he is stressed.

"We're out of crackers and cheese," Truman announces.

Vem and Muriel rejoin us, as Muriel taps her finger uncomfortably on her opposite arm. "I'll keep that in mind when I decide to do your moaning thing."

I take the mug of wine and down it in one gulp. This may make my trip down the mountain challenging, but at this point, I don't care. "Muriel, it's clear you put a lot of work into this evening. I'm sorry, but you've really upset me. I'm heading back, with or without my family." It's going to be scary walking down the mountain by myself, but I've made my stand and I can't back down now.

The door to the cabin opens and I can hear footsteps behind me. Judging by the look on Truman's face, I'm afraid to turn around. Just as Vem thought, it's a serial killer moment.

There is a tap on my back. "Obie, you'll need to start from the beginning." When I turn, I drop the mug on the ground and it shatters into several pieces. The face illuminated by the fire is a familiar one, but it's not Obie. "Are you real?"

CHAPTER THIRTY-SEVEN

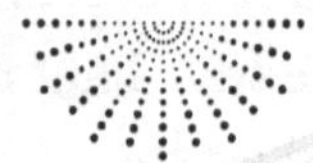

PIPER

Teddy leaned back in his chair and stuck his tongue in his cheek in mock serious-ness, though the glint in his eye told a different story.

"It took Scarlett about a minute to realize the finger we'd given her wasn't from a cop. 'nice try, kids, but it's too small,' she said her in syrupy voice." Teddy shook his head.

"When we failed, she asked the cop to meet her out in the woods and demanded that I come with her. Actually, she wanted me sister to come but I told her to go home and I'd take her place. I was brave back then."

He paused, as if he expected props for his "heroic" actions. When none came, he continued.

"As we were driving over, she said she wouldn't allow anyone to disrespect her. That was why she started the Twisted Stitch Society, to make sure she was always feared and respected."

"You were a kid, Teddy. That must've been scary." Piper said softly. She'd learned from her time with her biological mother's disturbed friends that making them feel comfortable always led to more information.

Teddy nodded. "When we got to the pull off, she told me to wait in the car, that he was meeting her at the clearing just off the road. 'When I whistle, Theodore,' that's what she called me—pretentious bat. 'When I whistle, you'll come running with the shovel and hit him hard from behind. You won't quite kill him.' She wanted me to watch as she choked his last breaths from his body. She said that's how she learned to kill, by watching the old lady who gave her sewing lessons. One day she showed up, and the woman hit her husband over the head with a shovel."

"She watched a murder as a child?" Obie asked. "That explains a lot."

"Mmhm," Teddy agreed. "She wasn't gone five minutes before I heard arguing. There was one gunshot and another, but no whistling. Part of me wanted to run home. But I'll admit, I was also curious." He grinned as if he were telling a funny story at a family reunion. "I got out of the car with the shovel and ran and that's when I saw them."

"Scarlett and the cop?"

"The cop was there all right. He looked up at me, surprised there was someone else in the woods. He confessed right away. Said that she came at him and he shot her in self-defense. Instead of burying a cop that day, I helped him bury my tormentor. After we finished, we ran her car into the river. He took me back to town and said he was leaving and, if I ever told anyone what happened, he'd come back and bury me right beside her."

"You're saying my father killed my grandmother?" Ellie appeared in the doorway.

"Didn't I ask you to wait until I said it was time?" Piper snapped. "Honestly, Ellie, you are frustrating!"

"Scarlett was your grandmother? You're that cop's daughter? Well, I'll be!" Teddy crossed his legs and pushed away from the table. "Now that you've said it, I can see the resemblance."

"What do you know about my grandmother? I don't believe my dad killed him. He's a wonderful man."

"Did I say the cop shot Scarlett? Guess I left out one important piece of the story."

Piper despised him. He was the one imprisoned, yet they were his captive audience as he doled out small bits of his story. "I'm on a tight schedule, so whatever you've got to say, make it quick." She glared hard, unafraid of his bravado.

Teddy cleared his throat. "There's more to the story, like I was saying. The cop told me he'd shot Scarlett, but that isn't what happened. Standing behind him was Scarlett's daughter, Margarite. We'd smoked some weed together before when her mom wasn't home, so I knew her well enough to understand how much she hated that woman."

"Just because she hated her, doesn't mean she killed her!" Piper yelled.

Obie jumped at the sharp sound of her voice, but said nothing.

"Margarite had a glint in her eye," Teddy continued. "It took me a minute, but I understood. I pointed at the cop and said, 'you didn't kill nobody. Margarite did it before you got here. It was her arguing with her mom and, when you heard the shots, you came running, just like me. When you saw what happened, you told Margarite you'd take the fall."

"Are you telling me that my parents were complicit in a murder and no one knew? That's ludicrous," Ellie scoffed.

"Just about everyone in town feared or hated your grandmother. Not the least her own daughter. She resented being dragged from town to town every time your grandmother ticked off the wrong people."

"I just want to make sure I'm understanding all of this." Obie took out his Piney Falls Police Department notebook and pen, along with an orange cloth to wipe them both. "You worked for Scarlett to pay off your mother, Belle's debt. Scarlett asked you to kill the cop who got her daughter pregnant and instead, you cut off someone's finger. Do I have that right so far?"

Teddy nodded.

"Whose finger did they cut off?" Ellie asked.

"Frankie Lowery. Elaine and Buster's oldest grandkid." Piper interjected. "I will tell you the whole story on the way back to Piney Falls."

"Why would you do that to a kid? That's messed up." Ellie made no attempt to move further into the room.

"Because your grandmother didn't give me any choice. I didn't have the kind of experience it took to take out a cop." He smiled slyly. "Back then."

"Poor Frankie aside, I'm wondering how this all went unnoticed. Nobody reported Scarlett as missing? Her family just went on with their lives?" Obie patted himself on the shoulders three times.

"I still had a conscience back then." Teddy put his feet up on the table, exhibiting a level of comfort no one else was feeling. "I hightailed it straight to her husband after it all went down. To my surprise, he told me to keep it to myself and nothing would happen. He even gave me a hundred bucks. Next day, he was in the wind."

"You're telling me that my grandfather would just move away without ever reporting his wife missing? Wouldn't there be someone in the family who questioned where Scarlett was?" Ellie asked with skepticism.

"Yeah, my mom said there was another daughter who was away at boarding school." Piper added.

"All I can tell you is he left town, and we went about our business like nothing had happened. Guess it worked out okay, cause here you are." He pointed at Ellie.

"Some of this isn't making sense, Teddy. Did you tell your parents? Or anyone?" Obie continued writing as he spoke.

"I did tell one person. A thirty-year-old neighbor who still lived with his mother. I knew it wouldn't go any further." Teddy glanced from Obie's face to Piper's, the corners of his mouth slightly upturned. "You'd think he would have done something about it once he became the chief of police though."

Obie's mouth fell open. He stood and patted himself three times on the shoulders and then spun around twice. "No. Not my dad."

"He was sitting on the porch that day as I walked by. Guess I must've looked like death, because he said he could tell I needed a friend. That's when I told him everything."

"My dad would have arrested you. Now I know you're lying."

"Boysie said he'd already had a run-in with Scarlett. He thought his brother stole a fancy vase to impress his girlfriend. He worshipped the ground that guy walked on. After I saw what happened in the woods, I walked all over town, trying to get my head right. I saw him and sang like a canary."

"That sounds like your dad, Obie. He would want to help," Piper said comfortingly. She touched Obie's sleeve, and he took a step back.

"Kinda bothered me all these years. I guess you could say that's why I'm such a mess. Never thought I'd feel good about being arrested, but getting that off my chest is freeing.. Makes sense doesn't it?"

"No, none of this makes sense." Obie said, pacing back and forth behind the visitor chairs. "Boysie Lumquest is the most law-abiding person I've ever known. There is no way he knew about a murder and didn't say anything. At the very least, he would have gone and uncovered her body and made sure she had a proper burial."

Piper shook her head in stern disapproval. "How do we know you're telling the truth now, Teddy? You were evasive yesterday."

"Why would I lie to you? I already tried telling my attorney, and he cut me off and said I was full of it. No use storing blackmail information if I can't use it."

"If you think you my dad will cave to threats, you don't know him very well!"

Teddy shrugged his shoulders. "That's all I have to say. I'm ready to go back to my cell. Can you go tell the officer to take me?"

Ellie opened the door and called for the officer to come in. When Teddy was gone, she wiped her eyes with the back of her hand and crossed her arms over her chest. "I'd like to bury my grandmother with my grandfather. Oh, and I'd like to go somewhere for a coffee. There's something you both need to hear."

CHAPTER THIRTY-EIGHT

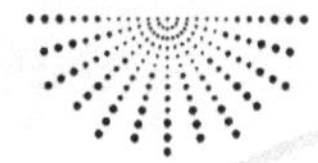

LANIE

"*I* don't know who you are or why you think this is funny, but this needs to stop now. I'm shaking so hard I can barely get the words out. "My father died of a heart attack at a rest stop in Idaho." I point at his face without actually studying it. "You're an imposter. You had surgery, or maybe the reason you took so long to come out this evening was because you were putting on prosthetics and makeup. Well, I'm not falling for it." I glance at my husband and my best friend, hoping to find support in their faces. Instead, they are deeper in shock than I am.

The stranger smiles and I can see a crooked tooth on the bottom, just like my dad's. He'd always been self-conscious of that imperfection. "Lanie, don't you recognize me? I've been waiting for this moment for so long."

He looks away for a minute, lost in another time. It gives me a moment to sneak a glance. The same square face and dry, cracked lips that I remember. His full beard and wrinkled forehead make him appear much older.

He tries to grab my hand, but I shake him off. "Fairy tales belong in the trash. All they do is set a girl up for failure. Besides, if you were really my father, you would have shown up long ago, when Berit went to prison. Instead, we've been playing this game of cat and mouse for months now. That's not what a father does." My chest feels tight, like it won't ever let in air again. "Although, the more I think about it, that is exactly what MY father does."

Vem moves in behind him and sniffs his collar. "It's him Lanie. It's the same scent from the other day." She moves around to face him, standing so close I'm worried he might shove her away. "What's your game, Mister? Why would you pretend to be dead just to hurt my Lanie?"

"I spent too long afraid of Berit. She was her mother's daughter, through and through and eventually it came back to haunt us both." He sighs deeply and edges away from Vem. She moves with him, not allowing any distance between them. "You have to understand my frame of mind. She'd been chasing me for years. If I found a new hobby, she was there, watching. If I went out for dinner, she found out where I was and what I was eating. It was frightening. I realized I had to stage my own death in order to break free." He runs his hand through his thick beard. "Ridiculous as it sounds, I thought if I came across the country to see you, she wouldn't follow me. She had a life, a husband and a job."

I think back to my confrontation with my sister. Berit admitted her marriage was over and she was fired from her job. All because she was obsessed with her-our-father.

"After I faked my death, I fell into a pit of despair. I was paranoid that she was hiding somewhere, waiting to make her next move, and I fell apart. If it weren't for this beautiful woman…" He takes Muriel's hand and they gaze lovingly into each other's eyes. "I'd probably still be there."

Vem is standing awkwardly close, making the three of them a strange silhouette.

Gavin kisses Muriel on the cheek and continues, "She saved my life in more ways than one. She helped me to give up gambling and learn to live with very little. I hid my true identity from her for months. I was still too afraid of Berit, and maybe of admitting my part in her upbringing. But she was willing to support me in any way she could. Slowly, I found myself. A different me."

Muriel is not the type of person my father has

courted in the past. She isn't well-spoken, or wicked smart. "And why is that, Muriel?" I ask suspiciously. "A normal person wouldn't agree to go on the run like this and live out of people's trash. Walk me through that."

Instead of training my eyes on the perpetrators, I turn instead to my husband and click my tongue in disapproval. He hasn't come to my defense as I'd hoped.

Wisely sensing an eruption of emotion from me, he jumps into the conversation. "This doesn't really make sense, sir. You have to know by now that your other daughter is in prison . She's not going anywhere. Why would you participate in this silly game hiding in the woods when you could just enter town like normal people do and come by for a scone?"

Gavin shakes his head emphatically. "You don't know my daughter. She's been manipulative her entire life. She brought about her mother's death and was determined to cause mine. I just didn't want to take that chance."

"Gavin still screams in his sleep every night. He's terrified she'll come back," Muriel adds.

"I've been able to watch your life, Lanie. From a distance, I can admire your smile and enjoy your laugh and the love you share with your husband and daughter. It warms my heart to know that all the mistakes your mother and I made haven't left their mark on you."

I'm so angry, I'm shaking. My teeth are chattering, something I haven't done since the beauty pageant in tenth grade when I had to give a speech about saving the world. I stood, silent while the spotlight glared in my face and people spoke in hushed tones "The idea of you watching me in the shadows is incredibly disturbing. And Gavin–if that really is your name– you have no idea how your actions twisted my life. If it wasn't for the love of my family and friends, and I don't mean those who share my name, but those here in Piney Falls, I wouldn't be standing."

Truman ventures over to Muriel, hands resting on either side of his overalls. "Ma'am, I'm pretty hungry right now. As much as this drama has got me thinking about things, I'd really like to get the vittles on the table."

There is a moment of silence, where I contemplate the absurdity of all of this. Flies circle my head and crickets chirp in the woods as though the most earth-shattering news hadn't just been uttered. I can hear someone's stomach growling; it's not just Truman's.

"I'll make up some plates and bring them out," Muriel says, walking towards the cabin before pausing to direct her words at me. "I just want you to know, Lanie, I love your dad more than anything.

He's a great man and, if you don't see that, well, I feel sorry for you."

Truman follows her as she opens the screen door and walks into the cabin. "Have you heard of Purely Presidential Barbecue sauce? I find it's the best one around."

Her words do nothing for my current state. "Why are you here now, Dad? What is it you want for me, or from any of us?"

Gavin sits down on a bench and motions for me to sit beside him. I shake my head firmly. "I'll stand here, thank you," I say.

"I need to moan. I missed my early evening moan and my head is clouded now," Vem announces. We all look at her, surprised.

"Don't go too far, Vem," I caution. "There are critters out this time of night."

"It'll be fine, Lanie," she replies with confidence. "If I accidentally seea big one, I'll give you the signal."

"What's that? You have many. The Moan for Misery?"

"No, I'll scream."

As she walks off into the woods, Cosmo takes a deep breath. "I think it would help Lanie if you would just start from the beginning, where you are supposed to be dead at a rest stop and someone got your body and ashes and that was that. Only it wasn't that." Cosmo sits down next to Gavin.

Gavin puts one leg over the other and folds his hands on top of his knee. "As I mentioned earlier, I wanted to see Lanie and make things right. I came out here to the West Coast because I thought I was dying. I had been struggling with cancer for some time and it had its grip on me. In my mind, things would have a happy movie ending. As was always the problem, your sister found out, and she wanted to make sure that you were experiencing the pain that she was. I can tell you that there was no pain worse than what she inflicted on those around her. Berit's mother was alone and bitter in her last few years because her daughter was always trying to find a way to hurt her."

"I'm not going to be upset that her mother, who ruined your marriage to my mother, was hurt. She deserved everything she got."

"You are partially right about that. But I'm just as much as at fault. And that's why, when I knew she was on my trail, I had to leave Piney Falls in a hurry. My dream of owning a home here was gone." He strokes his bearded chin the way I remember him doing every time my mother had an episode. I never understood if that was his coping mechanism, or if he was really dissecting the crazy things coming out of her mouth.

"My whole life has been a misstep in one way or another and it all came to a head," he continues. "I was sitting in a coffee shop in Idaho Falls, thinking about how I should end it when Muriel showed up." He smiles a broad smile I recognize. It is mine.

Cosmo looks at him suspiciously. "I'm new to the parenting thing, but if you want to be with your daughter, I'm fairly certain this isn't the way."

"You're right, Mr. Hill. At that time, I was desperate to accomplish my dreams before my life was over. Muriel helped there, too. She found some herbs that put my cancer in remission. I didn't believe it until I saw the x-rays myself. The doctor was astounded."

"Muriel is as devious as you are. We're clear on that now," I say with irritation. "What was her plan for the theatrical end of Gavin Anders?"

Gavin clears his throat. "To fake my own death. She had friends working for the state who had done it before. I gave them $3,000, and they took care of everything–the morgue, the paperwork, even a nice urn filled with an unclaimed soul's ashes. That was all the money I had left. Muriel promised we would be fine. She sold her trailer and agreed to come on this adventure." He stares longingly at the cabin. "I've never met anyone like her."

"I still don't understand why you had to live in secret. And did you set the trap that caused my injury?"

" Those traps were to alert us of strangers approaching, that's all. They were Muriel's idea. I had to make sure you weren't–like her."

"Like her? Are you kidding me?"

"Lanie, don't–" Cosmo tries to caution me.

"You think the crazy came from your side, then? Is that what you're saying?" I scream.

"MWWWAHHHH!"

"What's that?" Gavin jumps up. "Who did you tell we were here?"

CHAPTER THIRTY-NINE

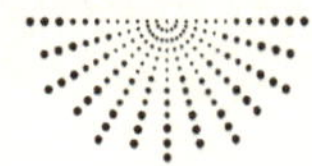

PIPER

A girl with torn jeans and a side ponytail made an impressive bubble with her gum. It popped, and she sucked it back into her mouth without incident. "Somebody had a latte with four shots? That's a lot of shots, man."

"Piper raised her hand. "That's me." She glared at the girl with disgust. No boss worth his salt would allow her to chew gum while she was working.

"And the mocha with extra whipped cream?"

"That was me," Ellie said, grabbing the drink from her hand.

"Plain coffee, nothing added?" The girl looked at the group, clearly irritated.

"That's mine, thank you," Obie replied. "So, Ellie, enlighten us."

Ellie crossed her muscular legs and took a long sip of her drink. She had a thick layer of foam on her upper lip, but Piper didn't bother telling her.

"I grew up with a loving family. My dad worked security and my mom was a secretary. They never complained about anything. I noticed on weekends that my friends would go and do things with their relatives, their cousins, aunts, uncles and especially grandparents. I asked them several times where my grandparents were and they were always evasive. You know how, when you're a kid and people don't give you the right answer, it makes you want it all the more?"

Piper thought back to her strange childhood. Her parents were always on the run and when she asked why, they would give her excuses that didn't make any sense. "I do understand that, Ellie. My childhood was beyond bizarre. You went searching for your grandparents, and what did you find?"

"My aunt was the only person who understood what I was going through. She'd been on her own since she was fifteen. When her father died, she cleaned out his house and found a letter from a relative. She wouldn't tell me the contents." She ran her fingers through her long hair, causing Piper to shake her head.

"Is something wrong, Piper Moonlight Hill?" Obie asked.

"Huh? No, I just want her to get on with the story." Weeks of frustration with Ellie were bubbling up to the surface, even though she tried to stuff them back inside.

"I can wrap it up for you real fast. The letter was signed C.H. I knew my family had unexplained ties to Piney Falls, so I wanted to check things out myself. The end." She gave Piper a cold stare and ran her fingers through her hair again, slower this time.

"Well, that's definitely not my dad. He doesn't write letters unless he's contacting a supplier and they always end in four-letter words, definitely not C.H." Piper said dismissively. "More importantly, you came to town thinking my dad is your relative, so you're all over him like flies on honey?"

Ellie cheeks turned red. "I'm a friendly gal. I can't help it. If my relative isn't Cosmo, then who is it?"

"I have some thoughts on that," Obie said. "But we need to talk to my dad first, or rather, I should talk to him alone. Could we meet up later and discuss all of this? At least Ellie and I can meet, if you're busy, Piper Moonlight Hill."

"My parents are out for the evening, so we can meet at their place. I can even make dinner. Would that work?"

* * *

THE THREE OF them were finishing Piper's expertly prepared meal of steaks, mashed cauliflower puree and crisp green salad with homemade dressing when the doorbell rang. Piper jumped up and answered it, surprised to see Boysie dressed in street attire. "Boysie! Can I get you a steak?"

"My doctor probably wouldn't care for that right now. Wouldn't mind a coffee though." He sniffed the air. "And whatever goodie you baked, I'd like in a bowl with some ice cream."

He stepped in and nodded to his son. His eyes traveled up and down Ellie, Piper noticed with dismay. She thought he was a better man than that.

Piper put coffee on and cut up chunks of pound cake, slathered with whipped cream and berries. She made a bowl of plain berries for Boysie, much to his dismay.

"You can't just sneak a little whipped cream on top?" he complained.

She put a dollop of whipped cream in his bowl. "Don't come to me when you have your next heart attack."

They all settled into the living room and Boysie cleared his throat. "You know how broken up I was when your Aunt Carlene went missing? There was a reason for that, besides the obvious." He crossed his legs and leaned his body to the side.

"You were even more upset than Grandma Gladys was about her own daughter."

Boysie nodded. "The reason for that was that I had an older brother who disappeared, too. He was the star of the family. Got the best grades and played a mean forward on the Piney Falls High basketball team. He was offered a full scholarship to Portland State, but he turned it down. Said he wanted to be a cop instead."

Obie stood up and began pacing frantically. He patted his shoulders and stopped behind his father. "I've had an uncle all of this time that you never told me about? I thought we didn't keep secrets, Dad!"

For a moment, Piper saw Boysie as a young man—with the same face as Obie's in a different shade.

"Take some deep breaths, son." He waited patiently for Obie to calm himself before continuing. "Cornelius Haven Lumquest was his name. I idolized him and Beverly agreed we should name our second born after him. Even took the rap for him when I thought he'd stolen from our neighbors because I couldn't stand to see the hurt on my mother's face."

"Why would you think he stole something? He's a Lumquest. We don't do that."

Boysie smiled, revealing a dark berry skin between his top two teeth. "No, we don't. Cornie had a girlfriend from a dangerous family. He'd done things for her mother and I thought this was one more."

"Scarlett." Piper's jaw dropped. "We know all

about the Twisted Stitch Society."

"When he and Margarite disappeared, I thought it was because someone else in the department found out that he'd been looking the other way when it came to Scarlett. Me, personally–I thought it was because of the stolen vase."

"Dad, he left because his girlfriend , killed Scarlett and he helped bury her. He didn't have a choice. Some of us leave because we don't see a way to survive as members of the perfect Lumquest clan."

Boysie's face twisted in pain. Piper wanted to hug him, but resisted the urge.

"Son, I looked up to my brother and would've done anything for my him. When we were kids, he stole expensive jewelry from our aunt. I told him it was wrong and I was going to get him in trouble." Boysie sighed. "He took my chin in his hand and said,'Boysie, you aren't gonna do that today. Do you want to know why?' I tried shaking my head, but he held me tight. 'It's because we all have a responsibility to this family. Mine is to be a cop just like dad wants. I need nice things my job doesn't give me, and that's where your job comes in. Your job is to keep this secret so Dad's heart doesn't break. Do you see how important that is?'"

"You lied?" Obie asked, patting his shoulders.

"I didn't see that I had a choice. Just like you, I thought I was doing the right thing for our family. When an expensive vase went missing from the police chief's home, I thought Cornie took it, so I confessed right away. To save his job and my dad's heart. Does that sound perfect to you?"

"Elaine Lowery stole that vase! She couldn't go through with it, so she left it in the bushes!" Piper insisted.

"Well, I'll be." Boysie shook his head. "I guess that makes sense." He turned to Obie. "Son, your mother and I always accepted you. We didn't care that you were different."

"Not to my face, but you told other people around town how embarrassed you were. That's why mom left–it was the stress of dealing with me." Obie was in full panic mode, his arms flailing above his head.

"You don't have the facts straight. Your mother left because we didn't see eye-to-eye. She wanted us to move away from Piney Falls and I'm attached to your grandmother and just couldn't do it."

Obie wiped tears from his eyes. "Really? Why would you move?"

Boysie cleared his throat. "You were gone and your siblings were long grown. She thought a change of scenery would help our marriage. I didn't want to leave your grandmother. She was my biggest supporter when my brother disappeared and we've been close ever since. Your mother's never understood."

Now Piper wanted to hug them both. Instead, she

got up and put more coffee on.

"We were devasted when you left, son," Boysie continued. "And sure, that put some strain on us, but the straw that broke the camel's back was your mother's idea to leave this town."

"Aren't we supposed to be talking about me?" Ellie asked impatiently. "Before this conversation veered off, you said my father, Chester Fine, is actually your brother, Cornelius Lumquest? Why wouldn't he tell me?" Her voice quivered.

"Probably ashamed he couldn't live up to the Lumquest family name."

"C. H. from her letter is my long-lost Uncle Cornie?" Obie blew his nose and immediately went to the kitchen where Piper was standing and washed his hands. "Why would Scarlett's husband have a letter from him?"

"Cornie was always the peacekeeper. I'm guessing he wanted to mend things between Margarite and her father." Boysie studied Ellie. "I see the resemblance now. You've got the Lumquest forehead."

Ellie touched her forehead absently.

"Are you going to arrest your brother? For the murder of Scarlett?" Piper asked.

Boysie took a big bite of whipped cream. "Ooh, doggy. That's the best. Haven't had something that delightful to the tastebuds in months. I guess what they say is true – absence does make the heart grow fonder."

"Dad, you just dropped a bombshell. Put the bowl down and explain!" Obie patted his shoulders three times and circled around his father's chair.

"No need to get yourself worked up there, son. I've got more pressing matters." Boysie set the bowl on the end table beside him and patted his stomach. "Tasty. Now on to some unpleasantness, right Ellie?"

"I was making a plan–" Ellie stuttered.

"You made a plan, all right." Boysie smiled and stuck his finger in the bowl, scooping the last bite of whipped cream into his mouth. "Don't suppose you'd give me just a touch more?"

"No, I won't." Piper replied firmly. "What's going on here?"

"Your mom and Auntie Vem dug up a box buried by the Twisted Stitchers. It contained some confessions of crimes, including a real interesting one where a young couple murdered someone and buried her out in the woods. There was something else inside. Do you want to tell them, Ellie?"

Ellie frowned. "I think your dad has something against me. I'd really like to go back to town now."

"Tell us, Boysie," Piper insisted.

"There were confessions from all the Twisted Stitchers. Every single crime committed at Scarlett's behest. Whoever found that information would be able to blackmail those families for lots of money, isn't that right, Ellie?"

"How would Ellie know that, Dad? She didn't

uncover the box, Piper's mom did."

Piper stood. "You already knew about your brother before you got here, Boysie. You called him and he told you about his daughter, Ellie."

"A super sleuth, just like your mother!" Boysie shook his finger in the air. "Son, she's the one for you."

Both Obie and Piper turned red.

"Didn't take long to track him down once I knew where to look. He and his wife–Ellie 's mother, –put their confessions in the box before they left town and re-buried it."

"My mother wasn't there! You're lying!" Ellie sputtered.

"Teddy told us that very thing today, Ellie. Gosh, we're not stupid." Piper snapped.

"Margarite was there all right," Boysie continued. "She told you all about it and then told you where the box was buried. According to your father."

"Why didn't she unbury it, Dad? And what did it matter to her, if their secrets were buried forever?"

"I didn't want anyone knowing about my mom and dad." Ellie's voice changes abruptly, dropping an octave. "You can understand that, can't you? I just needed to find the exact location where they were buried. It was the last time they used their real names–Margarite and Cornelius Lumquest. And yes, those other confessions were going to make me very rich."

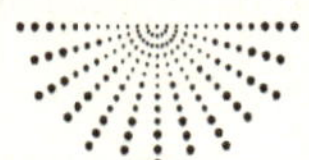

CHAPTER FORTY

Muriel barrels out of the cabin with a crazed look in her eyes and a rifle in her hands. It would appear she's practiced this more than once. "Where? Gavvy, tell me where to shoot!"

Cosmo walks over to Muriel and pushes the barrel of the gun toward the ground. "Nobody is getting shot today. That's just November doing what she does best."

"Awwoo!"

"See? That's November Bean. Believe it or not, it's one of the least crazy things in her repertoire."

Gavin Anders takes Muriel in his arms and holds her comfortingly. "We're fine, dear. Our friends came in peace."

It's all making sense now. "Obie didn't saw that branch. You did. For all of your fake sincerity, you could have killed me. My arm will never be the same!" The familiar sense of betrayal gnaws at me once more. Every time I think I'm done feeling hurt about the abandonment, something happens to bring it back. "Cos, let's find Vem and get out of here. I have nothing left to say to Gavin Anders." I wipe the tears from the corners of my eyes and stare into the crackling fire. "My father died long ago, when he left me alone with a woman who wasn't capable of caring for me."

Cosmo takes me in his arms and pushes my head to his chest. I'm a sucker for the familiar scents of his cologne and clean shirt, and I burst into tears. "Why did he have to come back?"

"Let it all out, babe. We'll get through this." He smooths my hair and kisses the top of my head.

When I've finally composed myself, Cosmo turns his attention to my father and his girlfriend. "We've been generous because we thought you were down on your luck. But that generosity has run its course. You'll need to clear out by Monday. That's more than fair."

Gavin ignores Cosmo and tries to get my attention. "Lanie, if you would only let me explain. I wanted to find out about you. You're right, I was a coward for leaving you with your mother. I should have stood up to my second wife and made you a part of the family." Gavin Anders has tears in his eyes, too. It occurs to me that I've never actually seen him cry. "Digging through your trash was the only way I could find out about you without risking my safety.

"I've never heard of that method of communication," Cosmo snickers and then turns to me. "I'll go inside and get Truman. You go find November Bean. It's time we got out of here."

"I'm with you, Cos. But I do have one more question for Muriel. Why would you follow a man you barely know and live in someone else's cabin? What's in this for you?"

Instead of answering, Muriel looks tentatively at Gavin.

"You don't have to ask permission, Muriel. You have your own voice." I move so that my body is between Muriel and Gavin. "I deserve some answers before we leave. I've been nothing but kind to you."

Muriel nods slowly. "I talked your daddy into this trip. I'm a free spirit myself. Ever since my parents abandoned me at boarding school, I've been on my own. I move around from one place to the next and Gavin just happened to catch me in Idaho. Told him I was ready for a change. That's when he laid out the whole story, about you and your sister Berit."

"That doesn't make any–"

"You may want to rethink that answer, ma'am." Truman appears carrying a familiar cardboard box.

"I didn't bring any pastries today," Cosmo says. "Where did that come from?"

"There's something written on the top." Truman

removes his readers from his pocket and clears his throat:

"Thanks for coming, Auntie. I'll be out to visit soon. E."

We've hiked all the way to the top of the mountain and it's the end of the day, when I'm typically at my worst. I haven't eaten in hours. All of those things combined add to my confusion. "Who is that? Do you know someone in town?"

"It's Ellie. My new employee." Cosmo sticks his hands in his pockets and kicks the dirt with his boot; his signature move when he's uncomfortable.

"I'll be a pink-butted baboon!" Vem exclaims, her translucent skin glowing in the firelight like an otherworldly spirit. "That little vixen was playing you all along?"

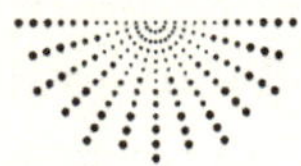

CHAPTER FORTY-ONE

PIPER

"*B*oysie, you're telling us that Ellie already knew she was related to you? How?"

"I didn't," Ellie protests. "I thought C.H. was Cosmo Hill. That's why I got a job at the bakery." She smiled sweetly. "Men are always putty in my hands."

"I'd believe you if you hadn't just admitted you came for the confessions." Boysie pulled an envelope from his pocket and opened it.

"It's all here. Your dad, my brother, Cornelius, says Scarlett met him in the woods to talk to him about Margarite's pregnancy. They had to meet somewhere private, so none of the Twisted Stitchers would get wind of it." Boysie held back tears. "Cornelius sensed evil. Like a true Lumquest, he wanted to protect your mother, even if it meant Scarlett was going to kill him."

"Why was my pregnant mother there?" Ellie's demeanor transformed. She was no longer the flirty young woman from minutes earlier. "I don't believe any of this."

"Oh, it's true. Cornie described his surprise when a screaming Scarlett suddenly fell into his chest. Your mother shot her in the back of the head. She was smiling, even." Boysie opened the letter and put on his classes before reading out loud.

"After the events of today, I felt I had to confess before leaving town, about Scarlett's unfortunate death. Margarite wouldn't have killed her if she wasn't pushed to her limits. We gave Scarlett a dignified burial, more than she deserved. From this day forward, I'll be known as Chester Fine. Margarite refuses to let her mother take one more thing, so she's keeping her first name. These secrets will stay buried so we can start our lives over." Boysie pulled his glasses off and looked up at Ellie. "What I can't figure out is, why did you need that letter now?"

"If I tell you, I need something in return."

"Police don't make deals, Ellie Fine." Obie hiked up his pants and patted his shoulders. "Are we going to issue a warrant for Chester–Cornie's–arrest, Dad?"

Boysie put his hand in the air. "Not yet, Son. What is it you want, Ellie?"

"Well, first I'll need a bargaining chip." Ellie lunged forward, grabbing Piper by the hair.

Piper screamed out, struggling in vain to get away from her attacker.

"My aunt and I planned to come back to Piney Falls to run a con. I wanted to get my parents' confessions so they could live in peace. My Aunt Muriel has spent her life running cons. When Gavin Anders showed up, the whole thing just fell into place. I would find out where the box was buried and she and Gavin would dig through trash, finding what she needed to steal bank and credit card information."

"You don't have to do this, Ellie." Obie pleaded. "We can work things out. Let Piper go and Dad and I will help you."

Ellie chuckled. "You, my little cousin and my uncle have the family tell. The twitchy eyebrow. I can tell you're lying. I'm leaving and she's coming with me. If you come after my parents, she's going to end up like Scarlett."

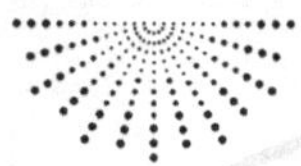

LANIE

"You got supplies from your niece. You were never in desperate need of anything. And why did you eat out of our garbage?" I ask, incredulous. "Ellie Fine is here to—scam—us? But why? Gavin? Do you want to tell me exactly what's going on?"

Gavin opens his mouth to reply, but Muriel responds first. "I grew up in boarding school, so I never really knew my sister, Margarite. My father called the boarding school and left a message when Scarlett died. He didn't bother coming to tell me himself." Ellie shakes her head. " I was chosen for the lead in the school musical. *Tessa* was about a woman who lived her life on the run, pretending to be whoever it took to survive. When they told me I had to go home, I ran away. I never got the chance to play Tessa, but I've been playing her game ever since. Method acting, they call it."

"How did you and your niece find each other?" Truman asks.

"I was on social media. One day, a message pops up from an Ellie Fine, saying she's my niece. I looked at her face and I saw my sister. She told me all about my sister's life. The two of us worked together for over a year, trying to figure out how to find the Twisted Stitch Society box my mom told me about when my dad wasn't around. She wanted me to find it and remove their confessions. She's always worried they would be caught. She just couldn't remember quite where it was buried. Mom seems to have blocked out most of her memories of this town."

"I'm sorry, Lanie, I–"

"I'm not finished!" Muriel snaps.

Gavin's face is twisted in pain, but he says nothing.

"It was an ordinary day in the bakery when Gavin Anders showed up, looking for a donut and a shoulder to cry on." Muriel touches Gavin's hair. "He was beside himself, talking about this daughter he wanted to get to know in Piney Falls."

"That was your 'in'? You could have just stayed in

a motel and behaved in a civilized manner. Or maybe even come to my door." I glance at one face and then the other. "This whole charade is a lot of wasted energy."

"Not really." Muriel walks up the steps and opens the box beside the door, which used to contain our fishing lures. She returns to us with a gun in her hand. "I'm good at the con, like I mentioned. The first time, I played a poor girl, down on her luck, who had just given up her baby for adoption. That bought me a year as a maid for a rich family. My cons just got more sophisticated after that." Muriel smiles with satisfaction. Gavin, on the other hand, is ashen.

"What could you possibly gain from this?" Cosmo asks.

"Gavin wanted to know everything about you. I instructed him to dig through your trash, as well as several other places in town, so it looked random. As a result, I have bank account numbers and identification for ten different people. It will keep me flush with cash till the next con." She glances over at Gavin, whose mouth is hanging open. "Did you really think I'd attach myself to a loser like you?"

"Where are they?" I move quickly to her porch. "In your phone? In a suitcase? There's more of us than there are of you. We'll search this place from top to bottom until we find what you stole."

"No need, Lanie." Vem has reappeared from her

moan, and she's carrying a large bag filled with papers. "I was doing a moan for clarity and when I was doing the big finish—you know the one where I raise my hands dramatically and call for any moose in the area––and I hit a branch. This thing fell from the tree and hit me in the head.. Talk about luck!"

Muriel dips her head and charges, like a bull. Watching Muriel, who is street savvy, tussle with Vem, who knows every self-defense move in the book, is quite the sight.

"Aren't you going to stop them?" I ask Cosmo half-heartedly. He's just as engaged as I am.

"I should, shouldn't I?"

Just as he moves to break them apart, Vem does her signature, "Rodeo Rump," and puts Muriel on her back, sitting astride her.

"Ow! Okay, I give!"

Muriel puts her hands out like she's an airplane and Vem lifts an object high over her head. "The Veminator Two!" She wields a pink hairbrush dotted with nails like a sword from battle.

"Vem! Don't hurt her. We want her in perfect condition when Boysie takes her to jail." The thought of that makes me warm inside. For the first time tonight, I feel good.

"We don't have service here," Cosmo whispers. "You and Vem should go down the mountain and Truman and I can watch the prisoners."

Gavin is standing motionless. It's hard to picture my father as a con man. "No, Vem and I will stay. Once she trusses Muriel like a Thanksgiving turkey, we'll be perfectly safe."

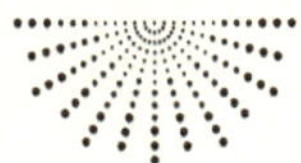

CHAPTER FORTY-THREE

PIPER

"Where do you think you're taking me?" Piper asked, her head twisted in an uncomfortable manner. She could see Obie and Boysie watching helplessly from the porch.

"Come after me and she's dead!" Ellie called back. "Somewhere they can't hear your screams, sweet Piper."

She pulled Piper's hair so that her head was firmly ensconced in the crook of her arm.

"What makes you think I'll scream? There's no one in the woods to hear me, so what's the point?"

Ellie came to an abrupt halt, causing Piper to lose her balance. Ellie quickly pulled her up to her feet by her head. "You're going to make this difficult, aren't you? I knew from my first day in the bakery that you'd be trouble. All I wanted was to clear my parents' names. Is that such a bad thing?"

They moved deeper into the woods, tripping over fallen branches and twigs until they reached a camp. Ellie shoved Piper into a makeshift shelter, where Piper saw familiar decorations her mother threw away months ago. "You took these? Why?"

"To build my little home. Isn't it cute?" She took some rope that Piper also recognized from her parents' garage and tied it around her hands and feet.

"You've been living out here the whole time? How is it my parents never saw you?"

"I was careful. My aunt is a survivalist, and she taught me how to remain unseen. It's so peaceful."

Piper scanned her surroundings for anything she might use as a weapon.

"I know what you're thinking." Ellie smiled. "I'm older and stronger, and there's no way you're getting out of here, so don't try it. I only need you until my aunt messages me that she's got the letter and we're leaving."

"Why do you hate me so much?" Piper rubbed her hands together behind her back, trying to make space between her hands and the material binding them.

" You and your stupid family; always acting like

you're in a sappy movie or something. You've never had to walk around feeling ashamed, like I did."

"This is all about–jealousy?" Piper was stunned.

When my aunt calls, I can bury you in the woods if I feel like it. You think you're so cute. You and your dad."

"What makes you so angry? If you're trying to protect your parents, they must've loved you!"

"They've lived their lives in a state of apology. Never able to look anyone in the eye, and we kids learned shame from them. I couldn't figure out why. One day, I got curious and started digging through their safe. That's when I saw a picture of them together in Piney Falls. I did some research, so that when I confronted them, they couldn't lie. I have two younger brothers and they would be devastated to learn my parents were murderers. I knew I had to get rid of the evidence."

"Why did you work at the bakery, then? Why not just find the box and leave?"

Ellie flipped her hair behind her shoulder. "I didn't know where it was and I was hoping you and daddy dearest would lead me to it."

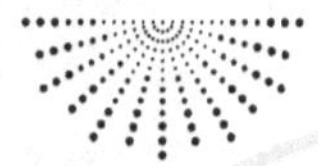

CHAPTER FORTY-FOUR

LANIE

"Get off of me!" Muriel screeches. "You're hurting me!"

I can see Vem from the window of the cabin, as she sits astride the criminal. She looks as if she's captured her first wild animal. It's kind of charming.

"Not until Cosmo and Truman return with Boysie. I can sit here all night. Awooo!" She howls at the moon in joyful November Bean release.

Since she's got Muriel safely secured, I continue my task—searching for anything else they might have plundered from Piney Falls' residents. I bend down to look under the bed and find Cosmo's missing tools.

"Lanie!" Vem yells. A quick peek out the window has me suppressing laughter. Vem is riding Muriel like a wild stallion. Muriel is doing her best to rid herself of the jump-suited wonder, but she's no match for my incredibly fit friend.

"I'll bring some zip ties. You've had your fun," I call out the door.

"Lanie?" Gavin's voice breaks. Cosmo tied him to a chair in the cabin before he left. It's given me time to search for other things they've plundered.

"I'm sorry I abandoned you. I planned for us to enjoy this time in our lives together."

I walk out the door, refusing to engage with him.

"That's why I bought the old farm house–to have a place for my family to gather!" he calls after me.

Until just now, I hadn't thought about that. With Gavin miraculously alive, the farm house would be his. After all the work remodeling and setting up our new business, that should open in days, the whole thing could come crashing down.

Before delivering the zip ties to Vem, I bend down to Muriel's eye level. "Just tell me one thing. How are you involved with Obie Lumquest?"

"The cop? He's been out here a few times. The first was before you came around. He dropped a fluorescent cloth right up there on the porch. I went through his trash and found a few more. I told Gavin they offered us leverage if we needed it."

I hand the zip ties to Vem and think while she

tresses Muriel with ease. "Vem, what if he wants to reclaim the farm house? We've put so much work into it."

Vem rubs her hands together as though she's just finished a dirty chore. "Tell him what you want. This is your chance, Lanie."

She's right. This is my chance. Working myself to death in Chicago and pushing Cosmo away; challenging every memory of my mother and fighting the urge to treat men as something other than human. These things happened because of Gavin Anders. It's all led me to this moment. I take a deep breath to center myself and, to my surprise, I let out a howl. I have no idea where this came from-maybe it's the years of watching November release her demons, or maybe it was something that was always inside me and today is the day I can let it out. I've never felt more powerful.

Vem is jolted from her peace. Her eyes widen and she puts a hand on either side of her mouth. She joins me and we howl together. "Awooo!"

"Lanie? What's going on out there? Are there wild animals?" Gavin calls worriedly.

"I need to confront him once and for all. He was a dark shadow for most of my life and now he needs to be exposed to the light."

"Do it, Lanie," Vem encourages. "I'll be waiting."

I hold my head up high and push my shoulders back. I've never felt so sure of myself before. Gavin blinks rapidly as I position my body in front of him, blocking any view of Muriel or Vem.

"Do you remember when I'd sit beside your bed at night? Telling you stories about the Princess named Lanie? I'd spend my lunch hours writing those."

I don't want him thinking this meant anything to me, so I don't respond.

"I…I'm sorry about the tools," he continues. "It was Muriel's idea to steal them. After your accident in the woods, she wanted me to construct something more elaborate. I cut myself taking down the old traps. I'm sorry I bled all over your garage."

"There are some things I need to say to you. When you ran out and left me with my mentally ill mother, I blamed her for all the misery in my life. She didn't know how to raise a daughter and left me to do it on my own. That made me resent her while I idolized you."

I take a deep breath, slowing my words down so my brain can keep up.

"I've come to realize that the Gavin Anders who read bedside stories was just a blip in my life. He had no comprehension of what it took to care for a daughter. And sadly, you didn't learn from your mistakes. Berit is a mess, that's true, but in part that's because you abandoned her too. You threw her away just like you did me and in her mental state, it just made things worse."

I move around behind Gavin, where a kitchen knife sits in the sink. Cosmo bought a new, pearl-handled set before we got married, so I wouldn't feel like we were living like cavemen every time we stayed here. I touch the fancy handle and realize I've never had a chance to use them.

"I didn't know how to deal with your mother, that's true. Her illness scared me. When it happened again with my second wife, I thought there was something wrong with me. I thought they would both be better off without me."

"You ran away, Gavin. It wasn't about making anyone's life better but yours."

I can see the top of his head is balding. I missed out on all of that life he lived as a handsome young man with a full head of hair. The anger begins bubbling up inside me.

"I came back though! I came back twice because I love you! Doesn't that mean anything?"

"My mother used to say, 'whiners aren't winners, Lanie.' Every time she made me perform as Tulip Sloan, I wasn't allowed to complain. And now, Gavin, your complaints are going to be the end of you."

"What does that mean? I wish you'd face me."

"Tell me that you are a stupid man who is attracted to mentally ill women who need real help. Tell me that you ruin everything you touch. Say it, Gavin." I'm strangely calm. I know what I'm going to do and the fact that my husband will most likely never speak to me again doesn't matter.

"I… I hadn't thought of it that way. It makes sense, though. I should have seen through Muriel's tricks. If you'll forgive me, we can build a life together. We'll enjoy holidays around the table and share stories. Think about it." He hops a little in his chair, trying in vain to turn it around. On this hardwood floor, nothing moves that easily.

"You assume having a father is still something I want. We haven't even addressed the fact that you set up trip wires and caused my injury." My fingers curl around the handle and squeeze.

"That was Muriel's idea. She wanted to make sure no one snuck up on us when we weren't prepared. She's a survivalist."

My face is twisted in contempt and I think about how easy this will be. My jaw loosens and I smile.

"She and her aunt planned everything out behind my back—you heard Muriel. It was all a con to her. I swear, the only thing I wanted was to be your father again. I came back, Lanie."

Something in me snaps. I move behind him once more and grab the knife.

"Lanie! No!"

CHAPTER FORTY-FIVE

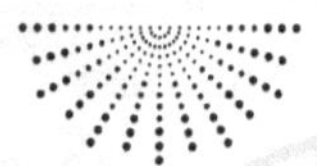

PIPER

*P*iper stretched her neck as far as it would
comfortably move so she could read
Ellie's phone. Ten-thirteen. It had been over an hour
they'd been waiting for a phone call.

"My hands are falling asleep. Do you suppose you
could loosen this?" She squirmed, over-emphasizing
her discomfort.

Ellie had just returned from another patrol of the
area. "If I'm going to kill you, what's the point of
having functioning hands?"

"You might need help taking the tent down. If
you're a true survivalist, you don't leave a trace of
yourself in the woods."

"I'm not the survivalist," Ellie huffed. "My aunt

had this great idea. She thought the less people who knew about me, the better. She and that rube, Gavin, got to spend their nights cozy by the fire."

Piper nodded in mock agreement, still shocked over the revelation that Gavin Anders was alive. "My dad really likes you," she stuttered. "He thinks you're… like another daughter."

Ellie frowned and then immediately smiled. "My dad has always been so proud of me. 'Ellie-bean is going to law school. I'm sure of it.' I couldn't bear to let him down and hid it from him for six months when I flunked out my senior year. I carried that guilt for years, and then when I found out he'd covered up a murder, it made me mad he thought he could judge me."

"I'm sorry he made you feel bad. My first parents–"

"Though he never actually said anything to me. He told me he loved me, whether I went to law school or became a gardener." She stared at Piper. "That wasn't his disappointment at all. It was mine. Thanks for helping me to realize that." Ellie chuckled. "You've come in handy in more ways than one, Piper."

Piper had a realization of her own. Her father would love her, no matter what. The unreasonable expectations came from her head, and from Booger, herself doubt, not Cosmo. She hoped she'd have a chance to tell him that.

"What is your plan, Ellie? I'm dead weight. If you're wanting to disappear, you won't want me with you."

"Exactly. You're just my assurance that we can leave. My aunt is getting rid of your parents as we speak. As soon as my uncle hands over the letters, this tent will make a great place to die, won't it?" She chuckled. "Poor widdle Piper, dying alone in the woods."

"Piper! Are you out here?" a familiar voice called.

"I'm here, Dad!" she screamed at the top of her lungs. "In the tent!"

Ellie stuffed a shirt into her mouth and quickly taped over the top of it. "Don't be stupid! You think I don't know how to use this gun? My dad taught me. He said you never knew who was going to come after you. I'm an excellent shot."

She sat back on her haunches for a minute. "I'm going to go see who your father brought with him. As you've learned from working with me, I've got zero patience. If I come back and you've moved even an inch, I'll finish you off now."

As soon as Ellie was gone, Piper scanned the tent for something to at least cut the tape around her legs. She kicked a pile of magazines with her feet and saw that underneath them was a pocket knife.

Booger always found a way into her mind, especially at times like these: *Your life is over and you never had the chance to prove yourself to your parents. Now you'll die as a disappointment.*

She imagined him as a short weaselly man with a pointed chin who, all of a sudden, didn't seem so powerful. "You're wrong, Booger. I'm much more. Just watch."

She was grateful for the stretching classes she'd taken with November Bean. She was easily able to maneuver the knife between her feet and up to her body. After twisting several times, she was able to grab it. She had just begun sawing through the tape when Ellie returned.

Ellie looked at magazines and frowned. "Why'd you go and make a mess?" She stacked them up, pounding one on top of the next. "It's a whole gaggle of idiots out there. Your parents, November and Gavin are all scouring the woods."

When the magazines were neatened to her liking, Ellie yanked on Piper's arm, forcing her to the standing position. "C'mon. We're going to make this as dramatic as possible. You're kind of a drama queen, so this is the way you'd want to go out, right?"

Piper pushed the knife into the sleeve of her shirt and pressed her palms together, willing the tape to stay in place until she was in a good position to pull it apart.

She hopped beside Ellie until they reached a spot with fewer trees. The moon was shining down on them in its full splendor, and Piper could hear the sounds of the angry ocean. It wasn't so different from the night she and Obie spent at the look out.

"You hoo! Hill family! I've got your precious cargo! All you have to do is bring me those letters and you can have her back!" She grinned at Piper. "I didn't say you'd be in one piece," she whispered.

Cosmo, November and Lanie appeared, faces drawn and worried. "Piper, hon, are you okay?" Lanie asked.

"Of course she is!" Ellie said. "You have the letters, right? I want them all. Those are my terms."

"Boysie has them and he's searching in another part of the woods. I've messaged him and he'll be here soon. Let's just talk for a few minutes, first," Cosmo soothed.

Ellie looked at her watch. "I'll give him…five minutes. That seems fair, doesn't it?" She looked up with a sudden realization. "Hey, why are you all alive? And not laying in pieces at the cabin?"

"They were no match for the fearsome foursome." November puffed out her chest. "Lanie and I were babysitting your aunt and Gavin while Cosmo and Truman went to get Boysie. He was otherwise occupied, so we all came down together in Truman's truck. Not quite what you planned, eh?"

"Ellie, just let her go. We'll walk away and let you run," Gavin pleaded. "I'm not even mad."

"Gavin, you're really simple-minded. You never questioned anything we said. Do you know why you went through your money so quickly? Every time you fell asleep, we took bills from your backpack."

Ellie took two steps backward and raised the gun. "I'm going to show you how we do things in the Fine family." She locked eyes with Gavin.

"No, please don't, Ellie!" Lanie begged, her arms outstretched.

Ellie fired two shots as Gavin shoved Lanie out of the way. They struck him in the arm and back and he fell to the ground.

She turned the gun toward Cosmo, but at that moment, November hurled the Veminator ll at Ellie's head, causing her to lose her balance and fall backward.

Truman reached her just as she was about to tumble into the brush-covered pit Cosmo dug months ago. He grabbed the gun from her hand and then stepped back quickly, allowing her to fall.

Piper was able to free one hand and push herself away from Ellie in one quick movement. She teetered on the edge, but Cosmo was able to catch her before she fell in.

Lanie, who had removed her shirt to bandage Gavin's wounds, rushed over to check on her daughter. "Are you okay? What is this thing?" She peered over the edge and then shined her flashlight in the pit, just to make sure she wasn't seeing things. "Is that–junk food?"

CHAPTER FORTY-SIX

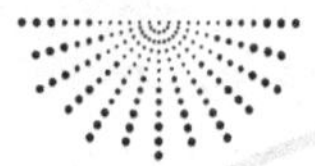

LANIE

The events of last night play on a loop in my head: Muriel's confession, Gavin's wounds and finding out Cosmo has been stashing junk food in the forest. It's all so absurd and yet so normal for the Anders Hill family.

I've been so stressed about the remodel...and I almost lost you, Lanie. I didn't know how to deal with it. Buying unhealthy snacks and storing them in the woods seemed harmless.

It DID save your daughter's life, Cos, so I can't be too angry. I just wish you'd've talked to me. You and Piper have been so stressed about this remodel.

As I push the button for the third floor of Piney Falls General Hospital, I rehearse the words I'm going to say. "Dad, I'm sorry. If Cosmo wouldn't have shown up, I don't know what would have happened." *No, I can't tell him that I contemplated ending his life.* "Dad, I see now that you were struggling with your demons, just like we all do. I forgive you. I think we can move forward. Slowly."

When the doors open, I'm relieved to see his room is closest to the nurse's station, in case I need to make a quick getaway. *Shame on me.*

I clear my throat and adjust my new lavender top before shifting the bouquet of dahlias to one arm so I can open the door. "Dad, I hope you slept…"

The bed is empty.

"Where is he?" I turn around and yell. "What happened? Did Gavin die?" I sink to the ground, unprepared for these emotions. They are more than I can take after all we've been through.

"Mrs. Anders-Hill? I recognize you. How's the arm?" A kindly nurse helps me to my feet.

"What happened to my dad?" Those words feel at the same time foreign and comfortable.

"Mr. Anders checked himself out this morning, against medical advice. He left a note for you. Can I get you some water while I find it?"

"No, thank you." I shake my head.'

When she returns, I realize my teeth are chattering, just like last night. *Be brave, Lanie.*

I wait for her to walk away, just in case I can't handle what comes next:

Dear Lanie,

I really made a mess of things this time. Something you said resonated with me. "You don't know how to have a normal relationship, Gavin." You were right. I attract people who are broken, but I don't leave them better than I found them.

Darling daughter, you aren't broken. Therefore, I have no idea how to be your father or even a friend. For the first time in your life, I'm going to be your parent and do what's best. The farmhouse is yours and I'm sure you and your family will be wildly successful. I'll send you a card at Christmas.

All my best,
Gavin Anders
(Dad)

CHAPTER FORTY-SEVEN

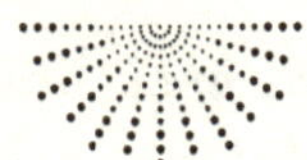

Two months later

"Cosmic Bakes is charming!" A reporter from Astoria, Oregon, exclaims as she wanders around the first floor of the old farmhouse. "I can see why it took longer than expected to complete." She pulls out a newly carved wooden chair and sits at the table. "You mentioned on the phone that you encountered unexpected obstacles. Can you tell me about a few?"

A kidnapping. An unexpected relative. A box of confessions.

"It's more about my dad and I overextending ourselves. We both took a step back and realized there is more to life than deadlines. Our family pushed the opening to work on some personal issues and we don't regret it."

You'll like my therapist, Dad, I promise. He won't judge you for building a candy pit in the forest.

"I read the article my colleague wrote about the Twisted Stitch Society. Whatever happened to the Lowery family? Didn't you find a family member's finger right here?"

Piper smiled. She'd told this story enough times that it didn't bother her any more. "Elaine and Buzz Lowery moved away when they both realized they'd been manipulated by Scarlett Peters. They wanted to give their marriage a chance, so they didn't leave a trace of themselves. They were already estranged from their children, so they didn't tell them where they were going. Their nephew, Frankie–"

"The poor guy who lost his finger, right?"

"Right. He lost his finger, also because of what Scarlett put in motion. When they moved, Elaine thought Frankie would inherit the farmhouse, so she left a note for him hidden in the wall. Instead, shortly after they moved, Frankie died in a car accident. She and Buzz had planned for Frankie to inherit everything when they died, and their kids weren't speaking to them, so they left the farmhouse to their two remaining grandchildren, Faythe and Finnegan."

"What a remarkable story!" She took a sip of her coffee. "Mm! This is delicious! Do you think you'll have a lot of people driving out here for a coffee?"

Piper shook her head. "Not necessarily. We

wanted to give people an option though, in case they are here picking up a commercial order and would like to sit for a few minutes before driving back to town. Our family friend, Truman, carved all the chairs. He supervised the remodel as well."

She glanced over her shoulder anxiously. " I'll have someone bring you a piece of my special recipe chocolate cake. I've got to check on something."

The smell of refinished wood hung in the air. It was just twenty-four hours ago that Cosmo and Truman put the finishing touches on the woodwork.

She made her way through the slew of local dignitaries and those who were just curious about a new business and opened the screen door and walked out to the graveled driveway, where multiple cars were parked. Just not the one she was looking for.

Piper folded her arms over her chest and walked back up to the porch, where she had a good view and smell of the cows grazing in the neighboring field.

She thought back to the evening Finnegan sat on her porch, weeping as she told him about his cousin. She wished she could take that pain away.

Getting to this point was harder than she'd expected, but what in her life had been easy? She felt hands on her shoulders and spun around.

"What?" she snapped.

Cosmo Hill, dressed in his best navy blue Henley shirt and brand new jeans, grinned at his daughter.

"That's not the response a father expects when he sees his daughter."

"Dad, I'm sorry. Too many unexpected shoulder taps." She hugged him around his shrinking waist. "Getting rid of your secret stash has done amazing things for you!"

Cosmo smiled. "I know who you're watching for. Don't get your hopes up. You can't change a person, no matter how hard you try."

"I know. I just thought—"

"That reporter has had two pieces of cake and wants to ask you more questions about the new location before she, 'dies in a luxurious sugar coma,'" one of the newly hired employees announced. "Her words, not mine."

"Is Mom on the way? She said twenty minutes."

Cosmo gestured to the driveway. "Just pulling in now." He waved and blew a kiss at his wife before turning to open the door. "Don't keep the reporter waiting long. We don't need bad press today."

Lanie got out of the car and opened the door for her passenger. An elderly woman, wearing a long skirt with embroidered cats along the bottom, got out and smoothed her hair.

Piper waved and jumped off the steps gleefully. "Belle! I'm so glad you came!" She kissed her mother quickly and hugged Belle Watkins.

"Wasn't sure I'd be welcome. Most folks don't care for old Belle. Now that everyone knows my son is a monster, that's even more reason to hate me."

"Not in my business," Piper replied firmly. "Come on in and have some cake. I have a surprise for you that will be arriving soon. Oh, and Mom?" she turned to Lanie. "There's a reporter here. You're better at dealing with that kind of thing. Could you speak with her?"

Lanie nodded. "Sure, hon." She kissed her daughter's forehead and ruffled her dark hair. "I'm so proud of you. It doesn't hurt to say that a million times, does it?"

"Of course not, thanks, Mom!" Piper took Belle's hand and guided her up the steps.

"Oh, it smells just the way I remember Todd Jones's Bakery did when I was a child. Has anyone mentioned that?" Belle asked as she sits down in a rocking chair with a thud. "Todd's Tarts. It was the best bakery on the coast."

Piper was just about to encourage Belle to go inside when the sound of a police siren caused them to turn back to the road.

Obie Lumquest smiled and waved as he pulled into the gravel driveway. There was someone else in the front seat, too.

"I think that's for you!" Lanie said enthusiastically. "Belle, why don't you and I sit down on the porch for a few minutes while Piper takes care of some business."

"Will there still be cake?" Belle asked hesitantly. "We could just go inside and wait for them."

"I won't be long, Belle." Piper walked slowly to the cruiser. When she got to Obie's door, he opened it and stood smoothing his official navy police shirt.

"I wasn't sure you'd come," Piper said softly. "I mean, we had it all worked out, but I thought maybe you'd change your mind because you didn't want to see me."

Obie raised his one eyebrow. "Why would you think that? We had a disagreement, but people who care about each other move past those things, just like I told you on the phone. I came to realize it was more about my mom. She and I had a good talk before she left this morning and–"

"Oh," Piper's face fell. "I thought she'd stay with your dad. I'm sorry for him."

"She's coming back. She just went to pack up her things. It's all good."

"Obie Lumquest!" Piper punched his arm playfully. "You scared me! I'm so glad your family will be together. That's so important."

"I'd like it if we could resume our relationship, too–if you're open to that idea. Now that everything is back to normal, there's nothing standing in our way."

She turned away from him and kicked the gravel. "Nothing stays normal here for long, Obie." Piper sighed. "If you could somehow learn to be a little spontaneous and roll with the punches, then…"

Obie grabbed her arm and pulled her close, bringing his face to hers. She put her hands on either side of his face and held tightly while they kissed.

"Ew! That's gross!" A blonde head appeared on Obie's side of the car. "I wanna do the siren again!" Sadie jumped out, her blonde curls bouncing.

"On the way home, I promise I'll let you do the siren one more time. You remember Piper Moonlight Hill?" Obie playfully tussled her hair. "We've got a surprise for you up on the porch."

Sadie hesitated for a moment before running toward the midnight blue porch.

"This was a great idea, Piper. You're a special person." Obie rubbed her back.

"Look at you, being spontaneous!" she teased. "I can't wait to see what happens next."

The girl bounced up the steps and stopped when she reached Lanie. "Who are you?"

"My name is Lanie."

"My foster mom's name is Duh-lanie." She wrinkled her face. "Are you my new foster mom?"

"Oh, no. I'm just a friend. But this lady with the pretty skirt is your grandma, Belle."

Belle looked at Piper with uncertainty. "I don't deserve anything good," she said, her voice breaking. "I made horrible mistakes."

"Scarlett put you in an impossible situation."

Piper replied. "And now, you can start making things right." She nodded toward the child.

Belle's bottom lip quivered as she pulled her shoulders back. A moment later, she bent down, smiling broadly, and opened her arms. "Can you give your grandma a hug?"

The little girl didn't hesitate. She melted into her grandmother's arms. Belle began to cry and in turn, so did Lanie.

Cosmo stepped out onto the porch and, upon seeing the sight, came over to hold his wife. She stood, and they wrapped their arms around each other. He kissed the top of her head and didn't bother wiping the tear from his eye.

If you enjoyed this book, please consider leaving a review. Authors rely on readers to let others know the book is worthy of their time. Thank you for your help!

Review The Twisted Stitch Society Now

Sign up on my website to be the first to hear about new releases!

http://www.joannkeder.com

Find me on social media!
Author Facebook Page

"What do you mean, he's missing?" Gemini Reed glanced at her husband, Leo, and then at the woman behind the imposing admissions desk of Charming General Hospital.

"Just what I said, ma'am. Unfortunately he's out for now, but we've been told he'll return soon." She looked down at her paperwork, refusing to meet Gemini's harsh gaze.

Gemini pushed her silver-gray hair behind one ear. "Let me get this straight. We sold our home in Fassetville – the one we built together with our own two hands–"

"Four," Leo corrected her. "Your hands and mine."

She made a shoving gesture to quiet her husband, and reached into her oversized turquoise bag where she kept all of their paperwork. She pulled out a pile of papers and slammed them on the desk, making an unintentional whacking sound. Everyone in the busy lobby stopped what they were doing for a second, startled by the noise.

A short, dark-haired man wearing a navy blue jacket walked up to the desk. "Is there a problem here?" He scratched the upper part of his chest, over a name tag that read, "Gary J., Maintenance."

"Yes, I'd say there is a problem," Gemini sputtered. "My husband and I are here so that he can take part in the drug trial for Atomycin. We gave up our lives and our retirement dreams. And this woman tells me that Dr. Wilson thinks it's the time for a holiday? Cheese and Biscuits. I'm flabbergasted." She placed one hand at her throat, trying to control her anger and not upset Leo in his fragile state.

Gary J. put his hands on his small hips. "I'll grant you it's strange he would leave abruptly, but we can't really tell you anything further. They're investigatin'." He seemed to miss the receptionist shaking her head back and forth violently.

"Investigating? Did something happen to him? Is he dead?" Gemini leaned over the desk. "I have experience in investigation. I could offer my services."

Leo pulled himself up shakily from his wheelchair to a standing position. He was still just as handsome as the day they married--steely blue eyes and a movie star face that reminded her of 1960s actor, James Dean. Just a little thinner these days.

"Gem, what you did for the law firm is hardly the same. I'm sure there is a logical reason for his absence."

Upon turning and seeing Leo out of his wheelchair, Gemini moved quickly to assist him back to the sitting position. When she finished, she stared harshly at the receptionist. "It's just that we spoke with him three days ago. He said this miracle drug – Atomycin – was going to cure Leo's cancer. He promised to meet us at check in; said that he was excited we were coming, Ms.–" Gemini squinted to read the nametag. "Ms. B.?"

The tiny woman pushed her thick glasses up her nose. "It's a security thing the board president thought would be wise. None of us have our last names on our name tags." The thirty-something brunette hesitated. "But you can call me Beverly." She put one hand to the side of her mouth and whispered, "Beverly Buttons."

Gemini reached her hand across the desk. "Nice to meet you, Beverly." She smiled broadly, her perfect white teeth gleaming. Her silver hair was still thick and full and her bright blue eyes glistened. She always prided herself on being told she looked like actress, Rita Hayworth. If Rita and James Dean owned a hardware store, of course. They always chuckled about that.Her silver hair was still thick and full and her bright blue eyes glistened.

Gary J. cleared his throat. "Strangest thing.

Yesterday, he didn't show up for work. They called all three of his phones, his golfing buddies and his next-door neighbor. Nobody'd seen him since the evening before. The police are trying to figure out exactly what happened. He never fed his dogs or opened his refrigerator. Got one of them fancy ones that's like a computer. I've been telling the wife we should invest–"

"Should we go back home and just continue as we had been?" Gemini asked Leo. "You haven't gotten worse this month." Despite his obvious decline, each day she told him how robust he looked.

"We came this far. I don't want to turn around," Leo replied firmly. "You said they are continuing the trial, even without Dr. Wilson?"

"Yes, sir. We're continuing everything with Dr. Natchez at the helm. He's well-regarded here at Charming General. This is Doctor Wilson's second drug trial and he has everything set up to go smoothly. Doctor Natchez has been a part of every detail."

"Doctor Wilson likes his vacation time," Gary J. added. "Always heading somewhere interesting. Wish I had that kind of money. You know the type– they don't have a clue how the rest of the world lives."

Gemini Reed put her hand on her forehead and glanced around the spacious lobby of Charming General Hospital, where large plants filled every corner, complimenting the multi-colored floral-print carpet. Everyone was going about their business as if something terrible hadn't just happened within their midst.

Read Oceanberry Blues Now